Praise for Catherine Arnold's pr...

'Nice surprises and shocks in and out of the courtroom'
The Sunday Times

'Lawyer Catherine Arnold's first novel is cleverly put together'

Sunday Telegraph

'A winner ... sharply drawn characters, clever plotting, super suspense and fine writing. Karen Perry-Mondori is that rare species of lawyer you can love'

Nelson DeMille

'Attorney-turned-author Arnold clearly knows what elements are necessary for a good thriller'

Publishers Weekly

'A fast-paced, slickly told story, with a heroine who manages to stay a step ahead of the opposition inside and outside the court'

Sunday Telegraph

Class Action

Catherine Arnold

CORONET BOOKS
Hodder & Stoughton

First published in Great Britain in 2000
by Hodder and Stoughton
First published in paperback in 2000
by Hodder and Stoughton
A division of Hodder Headline

A Coronet Paperback

10 9 8 7 6 5 4 3 2 1

ISBN 0 340 75165 7

Printed and bound in Great Britain by
Mackays of Chatham PLC, Chatham Kent

Hodder and Stoughton
A division of Hodder Headline
338 Euston Road
London NW1 3BH

For KDG,
Who, after all these years, is still a class act

PROLOGUE

Gerald Brock was going to die.

As the doctor leaned over the narrow bed and shone a light into Brock's eyes, a monstrous, almost fluid belch filled the crowded corner of the emergency room of County Hospital in St. Petersburg, Florida. Even the experienced doctor gagged and backed away.

He turned to the nurse. "Get me a mask, will you?"

The rumpled Social Security card the doctor found in the man's otherwise empty wallet identified the patient as Gerald Brock. Brock looked like what he was—a homeless alcoholic. His clothes, filthy and worn, reeked of cheap wine, urine, and vomit. His scabby face was unshaven, his puffy eyes red and teary. Spittle dribbled from one corner of his mouth. He was in a great deal of pain.

"Am I gonna die?" Brock mumbled, semi-awake now.

"You'll be fine, Mr. Brock," the doctor, adjusting his mask, assured him. "Just relax."

"Where am I?"

"You're in a hospital. We'll take good care of you."

"It hurts like hell, dammit."

"Try to relax. This will go much easier if you let me do my job."

Brock grunted. The doctor motioned to the nurse, who picked up a clipboard and pencil.

"How old are you, sir?" she asked.

"What?" He seemed not to hear her.

"I asked how old you are," she said loudly.

"Ahh . . . sixty-three, I think. Maybe sixty-two. I ain't exactly sure."

"Do you have a history of medical problems?"

The man looked at her blankly.

"We're trying to ascertain your problem," she explained, almost yelling now. "You can help by telling us if you have any medical conditions we should know about. Diabetes, heart or respiratory problems—do you have any of these?"

Brock shook his head and groaned. "I never been sick before. Goddamn, it hurts."

"Have you ever been in a hospital before?"

"I jus' told you. I ain't ever been sick."

The doctor and nurse exchanged doubtful glances.

"Do you have insurance? A Medicaid card?" the nurse persisted.

Brock sighed. "Can't afford no insurance."

"You don't have to afford Medicaid, sir, you just have to register. Have you registered?"

"Hell, no. Don't want no truck with the goddamn government."

The nurse scribbled a note. "Where do you live?"

Brock groaned again. "Jesus, screw the questions. Can't you stop this pain?"

"You'll be fine," the doctor said. "As soon as the examination is complete, I'll give you something for the pain. You were found in an alley, so do us a favor and answer the questions, okay? The more we know, the better we'll be able to treat you."

Brock relaxed a bit. The doctor seemed friendly enough, his voice soothing rather than demanding.

"I need the name of your next of kin," the nurse said.

Brock belched again. "Damn, you ask a lot of questions. I got nobody, hear? I live on the street. I never asked to come here. And if I die, there ain't nobody you need call. I got nobody."

The doctor motioned the nurse away.

"Just be quiet now." The doctor checked Brock's ears, then gently palpated his abdomen. Brock screamed with pain.

The doctor stepped away and conferred with the nurse. "What do you have?" he whispered.

She consulted a sheet on her clipboard. "Elevated blood pressure. One-eighty over ninety-nine. Pulse is ninety."

"What did the initial tests show?"

She checked a computer printout. "Blood and urine tests indicate liver and kidney damage. Alcohol reading is point-one-five. We wanted you to see him before doing other tests."

She handed her clipboard to the doctor.

"Looks like he's suffering from pancreatitis as well. Did you talk to the paramedics?"

"They know him. Said he's been hanging around Central Avenue for years, but he was never sick enough before to be brought in."

"Do the police have a sheet on him?"

"Nothing serious. Urinating in public, that sort of thing. He's just a homeless drunk, nonviolent, never in any real trouble."

The doctor scratched his chin. "So, what do you think?"

"It's your decision, Doctor."

3

The doctor returned to Brock. "You said you have no next of kin. Are you sure? No family at all?"

Brock winced, then shook his head. "My daddy died twenty years ago. My mama ten years before that."

"No brothers or sisters?"

"Nope."

"No wife?"

"Wife died a long time ago. Never had no kids. What's the matter with me? Am I going to die?"

"We're going to do some more tests," the doctor said impatiently. "The hospital is jammed today. I may have to transfer you to another facility. Do you have a problem with us taking you somewhere else?"

The fear in Brock's eyes intensified. "You're gonna dump me back on the street, ain't cha? I heard about people like you. You're gonna let me die 'cause I ain't got no insurance. Cocksucker!"

The doctor ignored the epithet, smiled, and patted Brock's shoulder. "No, I promise. It's just that the other facility is less busy than we are. You'll be in very good hands."

Brock groaned again. "Why do I have to go anywhere? Why can't you stop this pain?"

"The nurse will give you something in a moment, but we need to do more tests so we can treat you long-term. You don't want this pain recurring, do you?"

"I just want it to stop."

The doctor sighed. "I need your permission to make the transfer. If you don't cooperate, you might have the same pain tomorrow. Is that what you want?"

Brock simply stared at the doctor.

"Fine. You'll sign the papers and we'll transfer you. You'll get another ride in an ambulance, okay?"

Consumed by pain, Brock surrendered. "I don't care

where the hell I am, just so they stop this goddamn torture. You think I'll be needin' an operation?"

The doctor smiled. "I doubt it."

The doctor ushered the nurse out of earshot. "He'll be all right for a few hours. Give him fifty milligrams of Demerol, i.m., and start an IV. Have him sign the consent forms, then call Dr. Iverson and let him know what we're doing."

The nurse hesitated. "Shouldn't we verify his lack of next of kin? He might be lying."

The doctor shook his head. "That's Iverson's department, not ours. That's why he gets the big bucks and we feed on the crumbs. Get Brock ready for transfer. He's a perfect candidate." His eyes narrowed. "You got a problem with that?"

She met the cold glare of his eyes, then slowly shook her head.

"Good," he said. "Let's get it done."

The nurse nodded, then moved down the hall to the nurses' station and picked up the phone.

ONE

Six months later

Defense Attorney Karen Perry-Mondori threaded her
Beemer through midday traffic over the Bayside Bridge
onto Center Street, a road she'd driven so many times
she could almost travel it blindfolded. Work-bound
traffic, cars and recreational vehicles of Northern visitors, escaping to Florida for its sunshine and beaches,
clogged the six-lane expressway and slowed progress
to a crawl.

After turning right into the Pinellas County Jail com-
pound, she showed her Florida Bar card to the gate attendant, then searched for a parking space in the
crowded lot of the complex.

The day wasn't half over, and she was already exhausted. The cumulative stress of the past eighteen
months—her brother's death, preparation in a circus
atmosphere for a major civil suit, and her nephews'
murder trial—had taken its toll on her usual feisty
spirit. The worst part was being treated like an invalid
by everyone from Carl, her physician husband, to Liz
Walsh, her secretary.

"I have just the ticket to perk you up," Liz had an-

CLASS ACTION

nounced when Karen arrived for work that morning at Hewitt, Sinclair, Smith & Perry-Mondori, one of the larger law firms in the Tampa–St. Petersburg area.

"I know you mean well," Karen had countered firmly, "but, please, no more offers of megavitamins or energy cocktails. I'll be fine, just as soon as I have a good case to sink my teeth into."

Liz regarded her with a mother-hen look. "How about an easy, low-profile murder defense to take your mind off other things?"

Karen's interest stirred. "Felony murder?"

"Don't get excited," Liz said. "It's very straight-forward. One homeless bum beat another to death in a St. Petersburg alley."

"I gather it's a pro bono case?"

Liz nodded.

"Did Brander put you up to this?" Brander Hewitt, senior partner in the firm and Karen's mentor, was another who had hovered over her with suffocating concern the past few weeks.

"Not Brander." Liz consulted her notes. "Herman Gaylord, the accused, asked for you specifically."

Now, as Karen signed in with the busy desk sergeant behind the bulletproof glass, she wondered why Herman Gaylord had requested her and how a derelict had known her name. As if preparing for a competition, she brushed her shoulder-length brown hair off her forehead, straightened her well-cut dress in moss green linen that matched her eyes and enhanced her five-foot-two frame, and marched through the sally port.

After traversing two long hallways, she entered a small four-by-six room with a thick metal table bolted to the wall and floor. She tossed her attaché case on the table, took a seat on one of the two round metal stools, also bolted to the floor, and waited.

After a few minutes, Herman Gaylord, alias "The Professor," according to the police report in her briefcase, was brought into the room. His nickname was well earned. In spite of the dark blue prison clothes issued to major felony prisoners, the elderly man carried himself as if dressed in gray flannel and tweed. Intelligent blue eyes, unclouded and perceptive, shone behind gold-rimmed glasses. Contrary to the slovenly and sickly derelict she had expected, The Professor exhibited almost compulsive neatness and apparent good health. His thick white hair had been meticulously combed, his lean face scrubbed until his cheeks glowed pink, and his fingernails were clipped and clean. He maintained his dignified carriage as he sat on the round stool opposite her.

"I'm gratified, Ms. Perry-Mondori, at your swift response to my request." His cultured, educated tones matched his appearance.

"How did you get my name?"

"I read the newspapers. You've been mentioned frequently over the past months. Naturally, because of your outstanding reputation, you were my first choice."

"You were arraigned this morning?"

He nodded sadly. "First-degree murder. The judge warned that if I didn't obtain my own attorney within seventy-two hours, one would be appointed for me. I find myself embroiled in a most complex situation from which only someone of your skill can extricate me."

Karen slid a folder from her case and flipped it open. "The police report says you beat Gerald Brock to death, that a patrol officer found you still pummeling his dead body. Doesn't sound complex to me."

The Professor shook his head. "If you've read my statement, you know that's not the way it happened."

Karen had read his statement, but also knew that often, when asked to repeat his version of events, a guilty person exposed himself through inconsistencies. "Tell me what you told the police."

"I found Gerald collapsed in the alley, not breathing. His heart had stopped, but his body was still warm, so I initiated CPR. I was compressing his chest when the officer arrived and arrested me."

"Any witnesses?"

"Not at the time. A crowd gathered after the officer handcuffed me and read me my rights."

Karen picked up another paper. "The autopsy report cites heart attack as cause of death. Brock had a diseased heart. Your blows evidently triggered a fatal heart attack."

"Gerald Brock was my friend." Tears misted his sharp eyes, but he held his chin up and shoulders straight. "I wanted him to live. He appeared dead when I found him. Why would I want to kill my best friend?"

Karen ignored her twinge of sympathy for the gentle old man. "Maybe for his inscribed gold watch the police found in your pocket?"

Herman Gaylord leaned across the table, his face intense with sorrow. "Gerry gave me that watch on my birthday, almost a year ago. The mission had a party for me. Nothing fancy, just cake and ice cream, but Gerry made the occasion special by giving me his watch."

Karen narrowed her eyes and assessed her prospective client. "Why would Brock, a known alcoholic, give you something he could have pawned for booze money?"

The Professor shifted uncomfortably on the small stool. "The watch was Gerry's way of expressing his gratitude."

9

"Gratitude for what?"

"Gerry spent a great deal of time, ah, totally inebri-ated, which left him in a very vulnerable state. During those periods, I watched out for him. The alleys can be very dangerous."

"So Gerald Brock discovered," Karen said dryly.

"I did *not* kill him!"

"If you were such a terrific guardian, then why is Gerald Brock dead?"

The Professor sighed. "I wish I knew. The last time I saw Gerry alive was six months ago."

"Did you two have an argument, a parting of the ways?"

"It was nothing like that. Gerry was extremely ill. I asked someone at the mission to call 911, and the para-medics took him away in an ambulance. I never saw him again until two days ago when I discovered his body in the alley."

"He was hospitalized all that time?"

"That's what's so strange." Gaylord's white eye-brows bunched in puzzlement. "When I attempted to visit him at County Hospital the day after he was taken away, a receptionist at the main desk said no one was there by that name."

Karen jotted a few notes on her legal pad.

"I assure you, I did *not* kill Gerald Brock," Gaylord insisted. "If you wish to administer a polygraph test, I'm prepared to take it."

He met her gaze unblinkingly, a picture of innocence. Obviously well educated with above average intelli-gence, he could be putting on an act. His story would be easy enough to check out.

Her objectivity was slipping, but she couldn't help herself. She *liked* the man. He reminded her of the fa-ther she had dreamed of as a child, the daddy she had longed for while growing up with only her indifferent mother and a nanny. The Professor called to mind *Father Knows Best*'s Robert Young and an older Ward Cleaver. Unless Gaylord was a world-class actor, he didn't seem the type to beat a man to death for a watch.

But then Ted Bundy hadn't looked like a killer, either.

She scrutinized the man across the table, noting again his clear eyes and steady hands. "Are you an alcoholic, Mr. Gaylord?"

He laughed, as if surprised by the question. "I never touch spirits. They cloud the mind."

The mind. He could be mentally ill. A high percentage of homeless were. Brock's murder in the manner described by the police was the work of either a cold-blooded psychopath or a psychotic. Gaylord appeared too rational to be crazy, but a common characteristic of psychopaths was their disarming charm.

"Why are you living on the streets?"

He slumped as if someone had removed his bones. "It's a lengthy story."

"I'll take the time to hear it."

The Professor clasped his well-manicured hands on the table and stared at them as if his thoughts were a thousand miles away. When he finally spoke, she could see the effort it took him. "Eighteen years ago, I was a tenured professor at Duke University. I had everything a man could want. A respected teaching position, a loving and beautiful wife, and three wonderful children."

Karen wrote as he spoke. She'd have her private investigator, Bill Castor, check out every aspect of the man's story.

"One afternoon, I returned home from the day's classes. Diana, my wife, would be returning soon after picking up the children at school. I heard a car turn into the driveway." His hands shook, in spite of the

11

fierceness of a grip that turned his knuckles white. "It was a police car. A uniformed officer knocked at my door."

A tear spilled from his left eye and caught in the crinkled skin at its corner. "My wife, my son, my daughters, had all been killed in a traffic accident when a speeding teenager ran a stop signal."

"I'm sorry," Karen said softly.

Gaylord, the faraway look still in his eyes, seemed not to hear her. "After the funeral, I just walked away. I never went back to my classes, to that house. The memories were too painful. I just kept walking. I slept in barns and open garages, taking a meal here and there at a church or shelter. Five years ago, I ended up in St. Petersburg. The weather was warm, I could sit on The Pier and watch seagulls and pelicans dive for food, and best of all, there was nothing here to remind me of all I'd lost."

He blinked as if suddenly remembering she was in the room. "In almost eighteen years, I never let anyone get close to me until Gerry came along. He needed someone to look after him, and for me, after so long without family or friends, being needed was exhilarating. In many ways, although we were almost the same age, Gerry was like a child. I found myself becoming quite fond of him, something I promised myself I would never do again. And now he's gone, too."

He laid his head on his folded arms and sobbed silently, his thin shoulders shaking beneath the prison-issue blue.

Karen placed her hand on his shoulder, and slowly his weeping ceased. He lifted his head, his face flushed with embarrassment. "Forgive me for subjecting you to this display. I'm not usually emotional."

Feeling the pain of her own losses, Karen shook her

head. "No apologies needed, Mr. Gaylord. I've decided to take your case." She smiled. "A shoulder to cry on is part of the service."

She rose and extended her hand.

"Thank you." He hastened to his feet and clasped her hand in both of his. "I regret I am unable to provide compensation."

"All attorneys do a certain amount of pro bono work each year," Karen explained. "Yours is a fairly uncomplicated case. It shouldn't take much of my time."

When his escort arrived, Gaylord walked to the door, then stopped and turned back to her. "I hope you can discover where Gerry disappeared to all those months. I have a strange feeling about that."

Karen simply nodded and shoved folders into her attaché case. Herman Gaylord should count himself lucky if she was able to win his case. Gerald Brock's six-month hiatus from a St. Pete alley was no concern of hers.

TWO

"I'm sorry I'm late." Dr. Martin Bradford extended his hand.

"At least you found the place." Dr. Philip Stiles gripped Martin's hand and smiled.

Martin resisted the urge to adjust the jacket of his navy pinstripe, one of three off-the-rack suits he owned. He was tall and athletically built, the result of heredity, not exercise, and his square face was pleasant rather than handsome. His soft brown eyes glittered with excitement on occasion. At the moment, they were slits of unswerving concentration as he steeled himself for questions to come.

"I've been looking forward to talking with you, Dr. Bradford," Stiles said. "Correspondence is fine, but nothing replaces a face-to-face meeting, don't you agree?"

Not really, Martin thought. The prospect of this interview, the most important of his life, had kept him awake nights. "As I told you on the phone, I have to be back at the university tomorrow. My return flight leaves at four."

Stiles took the hint. "Then I guess we'd better get to work."

Martin followed Stiles down a long hall and studied him from behind. He was about Martin's age, but smaller and leaner, and his expensive suit and tie struck Martin as odd. Most of the scientists he knew were oblivious to fashion trends.

Then again, Martin thought, this entire interview was odd, starting with this surprisingly massive building, built of concrete and painted white. When he had approached the entrance, he'd noted the almost windowless monster stood some forty feet high and appeared to cover over 200,000 square feet of space. Even stranger was its surrounding chain-link fence topped with concertina wire, and the plethora of armed security guards whose gamut he'd had to run in order to enter. The place resembled a fortress, and Martin wondered why.

They entered a small and unpretentious conference room. Stiles motioned Martin to a chair, took a seat across the table, and laid a manila folder in front of him.

Martin made an effort not to squirm under the scrutiny of Stiles's intense dark eyes and thin-lipped smile.

Stiles opened the folder and scanned the top sheet of a stapled document. "I'm sure you have many questions, but before we proceed, I must ask you to sign a document which clearly outlines the nature of this meeting."

"The one you mentioned on the telephone?"

Stiles nodded. "As I explained, the work we do here is extremely sensitive. The first part of the document is an agreement that holds you to absolute secrecy. You will pledge not to discuss anything that happens within the walls of this building from this moment forward. Not with anyone, including your family. Is that clear?"

"Yes."

"The second part, which we don't discuss until the applicant is here in person, is a settlement agreement. If you break your secrecy pledge, you agree to settle any suit we bring forward as a result of your actions according to the terms already outlined."

"What do you mean, agree to settle?"

Stiles's constant smile seemed forced. "If you mention a word to anyone about what goes on here, in simple terms, you'll be destitute for the rest of your life."

Stiles slid the document across the table, and Martin eyed it suspiciously.

The scientist must have read his expression. "Should you wish to consult with an attorney, we'll be happy to reschedule this meeting. However, there isn't a lawyer in the country who would advise you to sign this document, since it means you are giving up many of your rights as a citizen."

Martin's mind whirled as he juggled the implications of the document and his need to catch his four o'clock plane.

"If you want to work here," Stiles continued, "it's an absolute requirement that you sign this agreement before we even can discuss the nature of the work and the part you play in it."

"This"—Martin stabbed the paper with his index finger—"it's legal?"

"It will hold up in any American court." Stiles stood. "I'll leave you for fifteen minutes. When I return, you may either sign the document or decide to consult with an attorney. If you sign, we can proceed."

"And if I don't?"

"If you want legal counsel, you'll have two weeks to

seek it. Be assured the latter decision will not reflect adversely on the possibility of your employment here."

"I understand," Martin said.

Stiles left. They'd told Martin about the secrecy requirement before they mailed his airline tickets. He'd talked it over with Grace, explained that all he had to do to avoid a problem was keep his mouth shut. It had seemed easy enough. But the way Stiles explained it now, the document before him seemed like a time bomb ready to explode.

Before Stiles had contacted him, Martin had received a call from Tony Trattio, his long-time friend at the university, who blatantly admitted he was recruiting Martin to join him at Consolidated Research Enterprises.

"Would you consider moving to Florida if the salary is twice what you're making now?" Tony had asked. "We can work together again, share some laughs like the old days."

The money, not renewed friendships, had drawn Martin from California to Florida like a magnet.

Now Martin carefully read the document before him. If he signed it, most of his problems would be over, provided he passed the interview test. If he didn't sign it, he was back where he started.

"I'm ready to sign," Martin said when Stiles returned with two women in tow. Martin wrote his signature, the women signed as witnesses and left.

Stiles seemed pleased. "At present, you're a tenured professor of biology at Stanford, right?"

"That's right."

"And you're working on the Human Genome Project?"

"Yes."

"An immense project. How's it going?"

"Slow," Martin admitted.

Stiles's ubiquitous smile returned. "I understand they've cut your budget again."

There were few secrets in the academic community. "That's true, and not just at Stanford. The National Institute of Health and the Department of Energy have had their budgets sliced, too."

"Are you still working on the twelve-year timetable for DNA sequencing?"

"More like twenty," Martin said, "which almost assures the French will beat us to it, maybe even the British, considering the progress they've made in cloning mammals."

Stiles nodded. "The French decision to use longer streams is a mistake in my view. As for the Brits, we'll see who wins the real contest. What's your current focus?"

"I'm searching for the locus of the so-called addiction gene. The work is preliminary, but it could be a step toward identifying people vulnerable to heroin addiction."

"What kind of progress have you made?"

"I haven't proved it yet, but I believe the gene is the same one already linked to a personality trait called novelty-seeking, which includes impulsiveness, excitability, and extravagance."

"If memory serves me," Stiles said, "your original budget was three million. And now?"

Martin shrugged. Grants were public knowledge. "Our budget was reevaluated six months ago. We'd been given a million-six, but now the balance has been adjusted to a million-four."

Stiles scribbled on a yellow pad. "Do you feel your budget is adequate?"

"There are so many worthwhile projects—cancer, AIDS, heart disease—and there are limits to resources."

Stiles's thin-lipped smile tightened. "Diplomatically put. But wouldn't you agree that the completion of the Human Genome Project might provide therapies for the diseases you mentioned, as well as others?"

Martin took a deep breath and exhaled. "The study of genetics can provide answers to many questions, and I believe in the project. But once completed, the project will present us with a thousand more questions than it answers. Sure, it'll point us in the right direction, but I'm not one who believes genetics is the only factor in disease."

"Nor am I." Stiles smiled his increasingly irritating smile. "So you're enthusiastic about your work, but not passionate. Would that be a fair assumption?"

Martin hesitated. "No, I'm very passionate about my work. All I'm saying is that genetics is but one of several areas that need increased attention. As for my work, I brought a couple of papers I've published—"

Stiles waved an imperious hand. "I've read all your papers, Dr. Bradford. That's one reason you're here."

"Yes, of course."

"What I'm trying to determine is whether you are simply putting in time or are a scientist obsessed with finding the answers to questions which can irrevocably change life on this planet."

"Neither," Martin answered quickly, slightly riled by the question. "I'm a professional. I consider myself steady, serious, and extremely careful. Those who are obsessed often take too many shortcuts and make too many mistakes. I try not to make mistakes."

"I see you're married. Does your wife work?"

"My wife was a nurse. She stays at home with the children now. Two boys and a girl."

"How do they feel about a move to Florida?"

"My family has always been very supportive."

"How do *you* feel about it?"

Martin licked his dry lips. "I've never been to Florida before, so I don't know how I'll like it. I've never worked in the private sector, and to be honest, despite the problems with budgets and equipment, I enjoy working in the academic environment."

"Dr. Bradford—"

"It's no secret your company is on the lips of everyone in the profession, that you're hiring biologists from all over the world, but that's *all* anyone seems to know. I'm intensely curious, but now that I'm here, I resent being treated like some graduate student looking for summer employment. While I'm certainly interested in discussing a possible position here, I'm not desperate, so if you don't mind, I'd rather be talked to than interrogated."

His smile never wavering, Stiles wrote more on his yellow pad. "Are you always this assertive?"

"I didn't mean to—"

Stiles waved a hand. "You have an excellent reputation. I'm simply trying to get a handle on how you'll fit in here."

Martin uttered his first lie. "I've never had a problem fitting in."

Stiles's smile seemed more a sneer. "We believe in the team concept. A homogeneous team produces more than the sum of its members by a factor of two. I want to be sure you'll mesh with the team you're assigned to, so I'm asking questions designed to elicit honest responses. To this point, I'm favorably impressed—"

"And I'm still in the dark. Exactly what is your company and what's it doing?"

They eyed each other warily before Stiles answered. "Consolidated Research Enterprises is actually an association of private companies, some pharmaceutical, some biotechnological, some chemical, all tired of government red tape and the slow pace of discovery. We've been in business exactly three years and one month."

"And your budget?"

"At the time of our inception," Stiles said, "we were given a budget of three-point-six billion dollars."

Martin gulped. "Billion?"

Stiles nodded. "And we were assigned the task of completing the sequencing of human DNA within four years."

Martin jerked back in his chair. "Four years! Impossible!"

"On the contrary," Stiles said, brimming with undisguised confidence, "we're almost there."

Martin's mouth fell open. "What?"

"We'll beat the French and the British and do it with proper research, not meaningless shortcuts. When the French make their grand gesture of giving knowledge away, it'll be too late. We'll have patented the discoveries and they'll all remain in American hands."

"But the academic community has always shared—"

"We've found a score of areas that require immediate attention," Stiles interrupted, "but two high-priority projects remain unassigned to teams, hence our recent expansion. Should you be hired, you'll be assigned to one of those projects."

"What kind of project?" Martin asked.

"The first concerns the loci of three genes, not one, located on three different chromosomes, that predispose addiction to drugs and alcohol. We think we've found the loci. I don't have to explain what that entails."

Martin was speechless.

"Second," Stiles continued, "and perhaps more important, we're on the threshold of discovering a way to alter DNA in human beings that would allow certain medical cures to take place without surgery or conventional pharmacology. The implications are staggering."

Martin was even more stunned. A budget of over three billion dollars? A twenty-year project completed in four? Discoveries only dreamed about within reach?

"If you decide to work with us," Stiles said firmly, "the years ahead will be filled with unimaginable adventure. Soon we may actually have it in our power to improve basic human existence. The question is, do you want to be part of that adventure?"

Martin didn't hesitate. "I want that very much."

Dr. Stiles smiled again.

THREE

In the twilight before dawn, Karen watched the tail-
lights of Carl's car recede down the quiet street as he
headed for Helen Ellis Memorial Hospital in Tarpon
Springs. Starting at six, he had a full morning of surgery scheduled.

For years, Carl had awakened hours before her and
slipped away to work, but since her brother's death,
Karen's sleep habits had changed. Now she found herself wide awake long before Carl's alarm sounded, and
she relished the solitary quietness of the house between
the time Carl left for the hospital and eleven-year-old
Andrea and Rahni, their au pair, awakened.

Tying her silk robe snugly at the waist, she padded
into the kitchen, reached into a cupboard, and removed
a large package of unshelled peanuts. After slipping
through the sliding-glass doors that led from the breakfast nook to the patio, she skirted the swimming pool,
then crossed the lawn to the woods that edged the rear
boundary of their property.

They had gathered already, for this had become her
sunup ritual, and the blue jays and squirrels knew a
good thing. Some sat boldly on the split-rail fence,

staring directly at her as she approached, the dew-wet grass soaking her bedroom slippers. The more timid creatures kept their distance, perched on one of a dozen tall pines that reached fifty feet into the air toward the rapidly brightening sky. But once Karen scattered the peanuts, the race was on. Birds and beasts noisily attacked, diving and scurrying in a flurry of activity. The peanuts were gone in seconds.

Some of the less aggressive ones looked at Karen as if to tell her they'd missed out. She shook her head. "You know the deal, half a package a day. You get too fat and you'll all die from clogged arteries."

Grinning, she went back inside. After each morning session, the tangled knot of tension and grief, a remnant from her brother's death and the chaos that had followed, loosened slightly. While her family and colleagues worried over her, Karen knew, given time, she was going to be all right.

Three hours later, after a leisurely breakfast with Andrea, Karen was at her desk, ready to tackle the day's work.

On top of the pile of correspondence lay a report from Bill Castor, her private investigator. She scanned it quickly. He had checked out the background Herman Gaylord had given her a few days before and corroborated that The Professor had indeed been on the faculty at Duke University, that his wife and children had been killed in an automobile accident eighteen years earlier, and that Gaylord had subsequently disappeared. Bill noted he was still checking on the rest of The Professor's story.

Liz Walsh slipped into the room just as Karen set Castor's report aside.

"There's a Travis Weller in the outer office," she said, "who wants to see you."

Karen frowned. "Travis Weller? Does he have an appointment?"

Liz shook her head. "He said I should be sure to tell you that he's here about the death of his father."

The name rang no bells. "Do we represent Weller or his father?"

"No," Liz said, "but that was all he'd tell me. He insisted he won't say more, except to you."

"If there's no one else on my calendar for this morning, show him in."

Karen rose from her desk and crossed to the wall of plate glass that looked eastward toward Tampa. From her sixth-floor observation point, she watched a high, fleecy cloud scud across the deep azure sky and caught the glimmer of Tampa Bay in the distance, beyond a sea of houses and commercial buildings.

"Ms. Perry-Mondori?"

Travis Weller stepped into her office.

She shook his hand and motioned him to a seat in front of her desk, then returned to her desk chair.

"Thank you for seeing me," he said, his face wreathed in a pleasant smile. But above the smile, his dark, penetrating eyes were pinched with confusion and pain.

"You wanted to talk about your father?"

"I understand," Weller said, "that you're very particular about the cases you take on."

"I can afford to be."

"Lucky you." He smiled, not a forced this-is-business smile, but a genuine expression of warmth that made his dark eyes sparkle pleasantly.

The man looked in his late thirties, with curly dark hair sprinkled with gray at the temples. His dark eyes were topped by thick eyebrows and separated by a patrician nose that obviously had never endured a football scrimmage or boxing ring. Tall and muscular, he was dressed in a European-cut gray suit, a pale blue silk shirt with a geometric-design tie, and Italian shoes.

"Like almost everyone in the country," he said, "I've been reading about you and watching your television press conferences for the past year. I'm flattered you agreed to see me."

"Mr. Weller, I don't have much time—"

"I've checked you out," he said with an expression of approval. "I was told you are an excellent attorney with a reputation for absolute integrity. That sparked my curiosity. Those are words rarely used to describe an attorney these days—or anyone else for that matter. I had to see for myself what such a creature looked like."

To her surprise, Karen felt herself blushing. "That's very flattering, but you have me at a disadvantage. You've checked me out, but I know nothing about you."

"Fair enough. I'm a lawyer myself, although I don't practice." He reached into his jacket pocket, withdrew a business card, and handed it to her. "I run a public relations and consulting business in Orlando."

Already she liked him, and that was unusual. She rarely made quick judgments about people, for her psyche was suffused with a healthy cynicism. She'd learned, often through bitter experience, that things were seldom as they first appeared. But something about this man made her like him instantly, and that instant attraction set off an alarm now ringing in the back of her head.

He relaxed in the pastel-upholstered chair, picked up a slim briefcase from the floor next to him, and extracted a single sheet of paper, which he slid across her desk.

"A death certificate," he said simply. "My father's."

"I'm sorry—" Karen began, then caught the name on the document. "Gerald Brock was your father?"

Weller nodded.

"I represent the man who's accused of murdering him."

"Herman Gaylord. I know."

Weller's name had thrown her, but in this day of multiple stepfamilies, different surnames were not uncommon. "If you're attempting to dissuade me from defending Gaylord—"

"On the contrary. I want to help with Mr. Gaylord's defense." He smiled again in his disarming way.

Karen stood behind her desk and placed the flat of her hands on top. "This is highly irregular—"

Weller held up both hands, as if in surrender. "Please, just hear me out. Then if you want me to leave, I'll go immediately."

Karen studied him a moment, but his handsome face offered no clue to his motives. Sinking back into her chair, she punched a button on her phone. "Liz, hold my calls."

"As you know," Weller began, "my father was an alcoholic. He'd been drunk almost thirty years. He was a carpenter by trade, but except for brief periods, it was my mother who supported us. She worked two jobs most of the time, because she had an obsession, and that was to see me through law school."

He took a deep breath. "Her obsession became mine. A law degree would provide me opportunities usually unavailable to the son of a drunken carpenter. I'm not trying to curry sympathy. I just want you to be aware of the salient facts. All this may sound personal, but it really isn't."

"I appreciate your candor," she said.

He nodded, then sighed. "My father's behavior certainly killed my mother, and it almost killed me. After

27

trying everything, I decided to no longer emulate my mother and gave up trying to help him. My father responded by making the grand gesture of disowning me and moving to Florida. He went steadily downhill and eventually became a common street person, living on garbage and begging enough money to buy cheap wine."

Karen nodded. Weller's description of Brock matched Gaylord's.

Travis Weller looked deep into Karen's eyes. "My father and I hadn't talked in over a decade. And now he's gone."

Silence hung in the air until Karen shattered it. "Would you like some coffee? My secretary will bring it."

"I'm fine, thanks. After my mother died, I was very bitter. I took my mother's maiden name, had mine legally changed. I was still in law school at the time. That was thirteen years ago."

He took another deep breath. Talking about his father obviously troubled him. Karen waited.

"As I said," he continued, "I eventually gave up trying to help my father. Even so, I kept an eye on him through an intermediary, an old friend who lives in St. Petersburg. We were friends in law school. My friend would locate my father about once a month and give me a report. There wasn't much to say, actually. It was really a death watch. I guess I was simply trying to alleviate my guilt over my failure to persuade my father to get some help."

Karen listened, wondering where Weller was headed with his story.

The look of pain was back in his eyes. "It wasn't as if I didn't try. I had him admitted to clinics seven times, but it was hopeless. He'd never had the desire to change. I

28

finally realized if I was to have a life of my own, I had to let him go. So, with the help of some professional guidance, I finally managed it. But it still hurts."

"I'm sure it does," Karen said and glanced at her watch significantly.

He didn't miss her unsubtle hint. "I'm coming to the crux of my story. Frances, my friend in St. Petersburg, lost track of my father about six months ago. She checked things out as best she could, but found nothing in the official records to indicate my father was in either a hospital or the morgue. I considered filing a missing persons report but decided against it. I assumed my father had moved to another location and thought I'd best accept the reality and have no further contact. Then, a week ago, the police found my father dead in an alley, beaten to death, they claimed, by another vagrant, Herman Gaylord."

He reached into his briefcase again, but Karen held up a hand to stop him. "I've seen both the police and autopsy reports. Death from heart attack due to blows to the chest. Heart disease is common among alcoholics, and your father's illness, according to the ME, predisposed him to suffer a fatal coronary at the hands of Herman Gaylord."

Despite her words, Weller withdrew his copy of the autopsy and placed it on her desk. "Didn't you notice anything unusual in this report?"

Karen glanced at it. She'd read it through twice before and had found nothing amiss. "It's perfectly clear as to cause of death."

"Look at the evaluation of the liver, pancreas, spleen, and kidneys," he said.

"The ME would have noted anything significant."

Weller shook his head. "Not unless the ME was

aware of my father's drinking history. She knew he was a vagrant, but not all vagrants are alcoholics. Many never touch the stuff."

Karen scanned that portion of the report, and her oversight hit her like a runaway train. All the organs were listed as unremarkable. Normal, in other words. No signs of disease. Amazing for a man who'd been a drunk for thirty years.

She clasped her hands in her lap to hide their trembling. How many other matters of significance had she missed lately? If her mind performed so shoddily, no wonder Carl, Brander, and Liz were worried about her.

Travis Weller handed her another document. "A year ago, the last time my father was treated at the St. Petersburg Free Clinic, they did a complete workup at my request. As you can see from this report, he was suffering from advanced cirrhosis of the liver. His kidneys, pancreas, and spleen were also showing signs of advanced disease. The overall prognosis was not good."

Karen sat, stunned by the discrepancy and her own lack of attention to details.

"That's why," Weller said, "I called Frances's looking out for him a death watch. My father was already living on borrowed time."

Karen looked from the medical report prepared by the clinic to the autopsy report and shook her head. "There's probably some explanation—"

"No," he said, "when I read the autopsy report, I was astonished. I, too, thought there'd been some mistake, so I had his body shipped to Orlando where it was examined by an eminently qualified forensic pathologist. His examination showed that, aside from his heart, my father's other internal organs were like those of a man of forty, a man who'd taken good care of himself throughout his life."

He stared at Karen so intently she could feel the hair on the back of her neck beginning to stand at attention.

"What the evidence shows," he said, "is that my father's terminally diseased liver was restored to perfect health before he died. His less-damaged kidneys, pancreas, and spleen were also restored to perfect health."

"How was that possible?" Karen asked. "Transplants?"

"Such operations would leave telltale scarring," Weller said, "and there was none. I've learned, however, that these organs can sometimes be returned to healthy states in the initial phases of alcoholism, but only if the patient stops drinking. In a case like my father's, such a reversal is impossible."

Karen shrugged. "I'm not a doctor, but I do know something about bureaucracies, both private and public. Mistakes are made on a regular basis."

"True," he said, "and if it's simply a case of bad lab work or a wrong diagnosis, even mistaken identity, I can accept that. But until I have evidence that it's simply a mistake, I'm left with some impossible conclusions."

Karen worked to assimilate the information Weller had given her. The implications were too fantastic to believe, yet his story had the ring of truth.

"I have yet to arrange for my father's burial," he said. "His body remains in storage until this is cleared up. If you want to have a doctor of your choice examine the body—"

"Your father's dead," Karen said gently. "Why don't you put all of this behind you? If some bureaucratic mistake has been made, I fail to see how proving it will help you—unless you're contemplating a lawsuit of some kind, and if that's what you're after, I'm not interested."

"I'm not asking just for myself," he said calmly.

Karen's eyebrows shot up. "Who, then?"

He shifted his tall frame in the chair. "I told you this isn't strictly a private matter. My reason for contacting you goes far beyond personal concerns."

For an instant, Weller had looked so terribly vulnerable, she was touched. Either he was one of the most sincere people she'd ever met, or one of the better actors to come out of Orlando. Either way, she was curious.

"I'll bite. What's your other reason?"

He expelled a deep breath. "What do you know about genetic engineering?"

"Not much."

"But you know what it is?"

"Of course," Karen said, her intelligence insulted. "The news is full of it: altering genes, cloning, all sorts of exotic stuff."

"As we speak, both private and public institutions throughout the world are conducting extensive research. The scientific community has found, and will continue to find, relationships between genetics and disease that will eventually revolutionize medicine."

"Not to mention health insurance," Karen added with a wry smile.

"If the human body could be compared to computer hardware, DNA could be considered the operating system—the all-encompassing software that determines everything the body does. Let me give a small example. Science now knows the gene defect that results in such diseases as cystic fibrosis and sickle-cell anemia. This knowledge is the first step in developing treatments."

"What does any of that have to do with your father's death?"

"One of my biggest accounts," Weller said, "is a

pharmaceutical company heavily involved in biochemical research and genetic engineering. They've invested billions of dollars in research over the years. Much has been discovered in a short time."

Karen ran her fingers through her hair. "This is all very interesting, but—"

"They have advised me that one of the long-term goals of biochemical researchers is to restore damaged human cells through genetic engineering, by modifying one's DNA to the point where cells are instructed to heal themselves. Some small steps have been taken in that direction, but the final techniques are decades, perhaps centuries away."

"At the risk of sounding rude," Karen said when Weller paused to draw breath, "what has any of this to do with me?"

Weller stood, walked to the window and stared out for a moment, then turned and faced Karen with his arms crossed over his muscular chest. "My contacts at Gulf Coast Pharmaceuticals have advised me there is only one logical explanation for what happened to my father. He was the object of some experiment, an experiment that proved successful beyond anyone's wildest dreams. The experiment was done in secret by a party or parties unknown—but suspected—who repaired my father's other organs but destroyed his otherwise healthy heart."

Karen's eyes widened. "If that's the case, then these experimenters, not Herman Gaylord, may be responsible for your father's death."

"That's why I came to you. I have to know. And your client deserves the truth."

"You mentioned suspects. You think you know who did this . . . genetic alteration?"

Weller nodded. "The explanation will have to come from my contacts at Gulf Coast Pharmaceuticals, and they're prepared to do so. Like me, the folks at Gulf Coast are interested in knowing how this was done to my father and why."

"But I'm an attorney, not an investigator."

Weller leaned across her desk. "You're a damn good attorney, one of the best in the criminal defense field, which means you also must have a damn good investigator working for you. I am prepared to pay whatever it takes to find out what happened to my father."

Karen shook her head. "You'll have to talk to my investigator. I don't accept cases for him. But I'm still not convinced—"

"My conclusions are not unfounded," he said earnestly. "When I received the results of the forensics examination I had ordered, I was stunned. I even had a DNA check done on my father's body to make sure the organs checked during the autopsy actually *belonged* to my father. They do. There's no mistake about that. The only possible explanation has to involve genetic engineering."

"As I said, I'm not an investigator—"

"Yes, but judging from your track record, you'll make certain there's no stone unturned in your defense of Herman Gaylord. If genetic engineering, not that pathetic old man, caused my father's death, you'll want to know. While your PI is checking that out, why can't he share his findings with me?"

"Possible conflict of interest, for starters," Karen said. "Not to mention this is a pro bono case—"

"Not anymore." Weller reached into his briefcase and pulled out an envelope. "I will pay all the expenses incurred in Mr. Gaylord's defense. Here's a check for fifty thousand dollars. Whatever it takes, I'll pay it."

Karen looked at the envelope lying on her desk as if it would bite her.

Weller pulled out a folder from his seemingly bottomless briefcase and handed it to her. "Here are people you can talk to. You can examine the body yourself. You can talk to the pathologist who performed the second autopsy, to the people at the clinic where the original prognosis was made, to Gulf Coast Pharmaceuticals. I've given you everything you'll need."

Karen hefted the thick folder before placing it on her desk and sliding it and the sealed envelope back toward him. "I'm not accepting, not without checking all the legal ramifications, but suppose I did accept? Why me? With all due respect to my inflated reputation, if there's a chance that your hypothesis is correct, wouldn't you be better served by a larger firm with a wider range of resources?"

"I picked you because of your background, for one," Weller responded quickly. "You're used to working alone and getting results. You're anti-establishment as well, and I mean that as a compliment. I also know I can count on you to be discreet, and the fewer people who know about this, the better, for now. Finally, although I don't know you personally, I trust you, Ms. Perry-Mondori, and there are few people I trust in this greedy, grasping world."

Karen smiled. "You're quite a salesman. You should have stuck with law. I can imagine the impact you'd have on a jury."

He grinned and slipped the envelope with the check into his jacket pocket. "If you decide not to accept, I'll simply ask you not to reveal any of the details. On the other hand, should you agree to take this on, you're probably the one person who can produce results."

Karen shook her head. "I still think someone is jumping to conclusions. As you said, billions are spent on research throughout the world. It's inconceivable that someone or some group could have developed this . . . treatment in complete secrecy. For openers, there'd have to be a money trail somewhere. For another, a discovery like this is worth mega-billions of dollars. Why keep it secret?"

"I wish I had the answer," Weller said. "All I know is this: those who examined my father's organs are experts. They're convinced of their conclusions beyond all doubt."

"I'm not questioning their expertise—"

"If your investigation produces another answer, I will be happy to accept it. I'm actually hoping there *is* another explanation."

"I *have* no investigation at this point," Karen reminded him. "There are legal technicalities that must be researched before I can even consider your request."

"And if you find the legal technicalities present no obstacle, will you help me then?" His smile held a boyish appeal.

Karen rose, circled her desk, and opened her door. "Leave a number with Ms. Walsh where I can reach you."

With a sigh of resignation, Weller lifted himself from his chair and walked toward her. At the door, he bent to face her eye-to-eye. "Don't forget, Ms. Perry-Mondori, Herman Gaylord stands to benefit the most from your association with me."

Karen shut the door behind him, returned to her desk, and tried to sort through the jumble of information Weller had told her. Her glance fell on the thick folder still on her desk. She grabbed it and raced for the reception room to return it, but Weller had already gone.

Back in her office with a fresh cup of coffee, Karen leaned back in her chair, opened Weller's folder, and began to read.

FOUR

After four days of earnest deliberation, Martin and Grace Bradford made the wrenching decision in favor of the career move—if Consolidated Research Enterprises would have him. The overriding factor in all their discussions was the money the new job would provide, and what that money could buy for their children's future.

At the same time, well aware of what they expected to be giving up, they made a pact. If, after five years with Consolidated, the family was unhappy with their new lifestyle, they would return to California. And if they did move back, the couple was confident that Martin, then forty-two, would have no trouble finding some kind of position with a university in northern California, perhaps even Stanford again. In the meantime, they would have saved enough money to insure that their three children would attend college. It seemed like a no-lose proposition.

As the mating game with Consolidated continued, Martin made another trip to Florida, this time with Grace in tow. While he huddled with Dr. Stiles, she looked over Tampa, Orlando, and Osolo, where Consolidated was located.

With Martin's meeting concluded, and with an early morning flight scheduled, the couple, sure the question of Martin's employment would remain unresolved, had arranged to spend the night at a cheap motel in Tampa. But when Martin arrived at the motel about an hour after Grace, he was beaming.

He waved a manila envelope in the air, threw it on the bed, then took Grace in his arms and smothered her with kisses.

"Is that what I think it is?" she gasped, coming up for air.

"Yup," he said, squeezing her tightly. "It's the contract. I'm in."

She squeezed back. "That's wonderful. I'm so proud of you!"

He kissed her again. "Maybe we should check out of this dump and into a nice hotel. It's time to celebrate."

She laughed. "A bed is a bed. Let's keep the dump and have a good dinner. Should I call the kids?"

Martin thought for a minute. "Let's wait until we see them. They may have a few questions."

Grace nodded. "So, when do you start?"

Martin handed her the contract to look over. "This time, Consolidated is *requiring* that my personal attorney review the contract before I sign it. And I have to provide proof that I've consulted with my attorney prior to putting my name on the dotted line."

"Why would they need that?" she asked.

"I don't know, but I'm sure Aaron will have the answers."

The next day, Martin sat across the desk from his long-time friend and lawyer, Aaron Rich, but on this day Aaron looked anything but friendly. As always, his white hair was combed from one side of his head to another in a futile attempt to disguise his baldness. He was tieless, his shirt collar unbuttoned, a picture of calm. But Aaron was far from relaxed. He clasped his stubby hands in front of him, leaned forward, and fixed Martin with a withering stare.

"It was good of you to let me see this wonderful contract before you signed it, but why the hell didn't you talk to me before you signed the goddamned *secrecy* agreement?"

Martin laughed. "Because I knew what you'd say."

"What kind of reason is that? That's what I get paid for. When one of your kids is sick, do you refuse to see a medical doctor because you know what he'll say?"

"Aaron—"

"Don't *Aaron* me," Rich said, waving a hand in the air. "I've never seen such a contract, and I've been at this awhile. Do you realize what you've done?"

"I think so," Martin said, suddenly defensive. "If I reveal any of the company's secrets, I lose everything I own. No big deal. I can keep my mouth shut."

"Really?" Aaron shook his head. "God protect us from the lame, the halt, and the incredibly naive."

Martin frowned. "Why are you so angry?"

"Because the secrecy agreement is not as simple as you perceive." He flapped the document in the air. "This so-called employment contract is pretty standard stuff and, at first reading, looks terrific. It's clear and concise, and on the surface, one of the best I've ever seen—except for one small item."

"Which is?"

Aaron threw him a hard glare. "Should the company decide not to honor any part of the contract, you're precluded from doing a damn thing about it. You can quit. That's it."

"I don't understand. The contract clearly states—"

"You don't understand?" Aaron threw the contract on his desk. "Is that what you said?"

Martin just stared at him.

"Take a good look." Aaron picked up the contract and handed it to him. "This contract incorporates the secrecy agreement you signed. Page fourteen, paragraph eight."

Martin found the offending clause. "Which means?"

"Let's suppose that once you begin work, the company decides to cut your salary in half. Can you sue? No. Suppose they drop the medical benefits or require you to work seven days a week. Can you sue? No. Or the company comes along and says it wants to increase the rent on the house it's so kindly provided, thereby breaking the lease agreement. Can you sue? No."

Martin shook his head. "Why would they do such a thing?"

"Maybe because they just feel like it. More likely, if business is down and they want to trim the staff, they can do whatever the hell they want."

"But the contract says—"

"The contract says," Aaron interrupted, "you've already agreed you'll never divulge *anything* the company does. If you walk into court and say they broke the contract, they can immediately file a cross-complaint, claiming you've violated a secrecy agreement. Since you've obviously previously agreed to the terms of a settlement, you'll lose. Big-time."

Martin swallowed hard.

"And another thing," Aaron said. "This contract is drawn under Florida law. They'd never get away with this in California, but Florida's different. Employers hold almost all the cards in Florida. There is precedent for upholding a contract like this."

"I can't believe it," Martin said.

41

"Believe it. You have no recourse for misrepresentation, fraud, or anything else. If you go to work for these people, you're at their complete mercy, worse off than the poor bastards who come up here from Mexico to work the fields. You'll be risking everything. If anything goes wrong with this job, you can take your leave. Period."

"They couldn't get away with that stuff," Martin said. "They'd lose everyone who works there."

Aaron took a deep breath. "I'm not saying what Consolidated will or will not do. The point is, they are in a legal position to do whatever they please. They've invoked a clause which relates to something called 'National Security.' By doing that, they preclude the possibility of your fighting the contract on any of several grounds. In sum, you have no rights should anything go wrong. That's not a smart way to do business."

Aaron leaned back in his chair and looked at the ceiling for a moment. "Aside from everything you've heard from your friend Tony, what do you really know about these people?"

"They have a lot of money—"

"You don't *know* they have a lot of money."

"Well, no, but—"

"In fact, you don't know a damn thing about them. No one does. I tried to do a credit check and drew a blank. Dun and Brad has them listed but almost no pertinent information on them. No suppliers, no rating, zip. Florida public records show them as a privately held company owned by another based in the Netherlands Antilles, but aside from that, another zip. Their reference to 'National Security' may be legitimate, but it can also be a hoax. No matter. It takes more money than either of us has to test it in court."

"There has to be information on them somewhere,"

Martin argued. "You just haven't looked in the right places."

"I checked with a database I subscribe to, and the best they could come up with was forty-two news articles, all of them innocuous, mostly about the number of scientists going to work for Consolidated. Two articles related to some computer company having sold them some newfangled supercomputers."

"That's something, anyway," Martin said.

Aaron shook his head. "A week after the first article appeared, the computer company made a retraction. Said they'd never heard of Consolidated. Obviously, they were told to shut up."

Martin slumped in his chair.

"I know you're trying to do the right thing." Aaron's once-angry eyes now filled with compassion, his sharp tone turned soft and soothing. "Hell, I can see what's running through your mind. You think the extra money will insure your kids' future, and that's a worthy thought. But these people aren't being straight with you."

Martin shifted, pushed his fingers through his short hair, rubbed the back of his neck, and wondered what to make of Aaron's advice.

"It's very odd," Aaron continued. "A company this big should leave footprints. These people leave none. A company this large should be in a public corporation, but this one is private. I even checked with Washington. Consolidated has not applied for a single patent. What the hell have they been doing for three years?"

"I think I can answer that," Martin said.

"Please do."

"The way I have it figured, they're trying to short-circuit the system. Normally, once a patent is granted, the owner of the patent still has to apply to the Food and Drug Administration before the product can be tested on humans. Often, something as complex as a genetic engineering process can take ten to fifteen years to be approved. By that time, the patent has almost run out. A company doesn't have much time to recover its research and development costs."

Aaron nodded.

"Dr. Stiles told me the people behind Consolidated were fed up with red tape. His words. So, I'd say they're waiting for one of two things—or both. The development of products that can be brought to market quickly, or a change in the patent laws. In any case, they're damn sure interested in patents, because the French are doing parallel research and intend, or so they state, to give the knowledge away. That would be devastating to Consolidated."

Aaron grinned, leaned back in his chair, and stared at Martin.

"What's so funny?"

Aaron looked at the ceiling. "See if you can figure it out."

"Figure out what?"

For a moment, Aaron said nothing. Then he sighed. "You've just violated the secrecy agreement you signed."

Martin blinked. "But I—"

"Relax. I'm just making a point. I'm on your side, Martin. What's this got to with the French? Who exactly are you talking about?"

"Francois Houle, a geneticist with the Center for the Study of Human Genetics in Paris, believes it both immoral and economically repressive to allow genetic engineering discoveries to be patented. He's employed different techniques in an effort to map the human genome before we do."

Aaron waved a hand. "So, in essence, you want to help some company beat this guy and make billions in the process. Is that what you're saying?"

"Thank you so much," Martin said caustically.

Aaron shook his head. "Don't get mad at me, Martin. You *asked* for my advice. If you'd rather not hear what I have to say—"

Martin hung his head. "I'm sorry. Continue, please."

Aaron stared at him a moment. "We'll leave the question of ethics aside. As for Consolidated, I checked the public financial ratings of every publicly owned pharmaceutical company in the country. No mention is made of any involvement, financial or otherwise, in Consolidated. By law, publicly owned corporations must reveal their investments in other companies. I can only assume that their failure to do so indicates that no such investment has been made. If that's the case, who the hell is really behind Consolidated? Do you know?"

Martin shook his head.

"So it's possible that everything that you've been told is pure bullshit. And if it is, there's nothing you can do."

Martin sat numbly.

"Aside from the money," Aaron said, "what's a bright guy like you doing even considering this deal?"

Martin had expected Aaron to be upset, but not to this degree. "There's the opportunity to be a part of one of the greatest breakthroughs in the history of science. Combine that with a doubled income, and you've got serious temptation."

Aaron considered him for a moment. "Here's the bottom line. You have a contract that is absolutely worthless. As for the work, if they decide you'd be better off being their janitor, you can't do a damn thing about it. I realize things have changed in corporate America, but no ethical employer would present a prospective employee with such a no-win situation. It smacks of feudalism, and I don't like it. If you need the money that bad, why don't you join the private sector? Surely they must be looking for experienced people like you."

"The research being done by private companies has flattened out. I talked to two companies a few months ago, and they were totally uninterested."

Aaron stood up, stretched, then stuffed his hands in his pockets. "The thing that worries me is this last document, the one where you were *required* to seek counsel. That's a very tricky document, one that reinforces Consolidated's legal position should anything go wrong. It means you're an adult who has made an informed decision after consultation with your own lawyer. The final nail is in the coffin."

"Aren't you being overly dramatic?"

"I smell a setup, that's for sure. Why else would they make all these preparations?"

"I don't know," Martin said. "After listening to you, I feel depressed about the whole thing. Your advice is not to take the job, right?"

"Right." Aaron's voice hardened. "If I were you, I'd run away from this as fast as my legs would take me."

Martin didn't run. He told Grace what Aaron had said, and together, they assessed the situation. But Aaron's warning didn't really matter, when they saw enough money for university educations for their kids. Martin pictured himself involved in exciting new discoveries, and Grace saw her long-frustrated husband finally achieving the gratification he'd sought for so many years. There would be hardships, the loss of friends, the dramatic change in lifestyle, and, according to Aaron, a strong possibility they were making a terrible mistake. But they thought the chance was worth taking.

If it all went bad, it was only a few years out of their lives.They were young, resilient, and still very much in love. It would all work out, one way or another.

They were almost sure of it, Aaron's counsel notwithstanding.

They were wrong.

FIVE

Sunday morning, as dawn turned the eastern sky a soft mauve, Karen scattered the last of her peanuts to the waiting squirrels and turned back toward the house. Carl, dark and handsome, his tall, muscular body wrapped in a short silk robe, waited for her on the patio.

She padded across the grass toward him. "Why are you up so early on your day off?"

"I was about to ask you the same thing." He pulled her into his arms and kissed the top of her head.

With her arms around his waist, she placed her head against his chest. "I come out here this time every morning."

"Since when?"

"Since Claire died."

Remembering, she felt chilled, in spite of Carl's warmth. First her brother's suicide, followed by the media frenzy over its supposed cause, had destroyed his reputation as a United States Senator, and taken its toll on the entire family. Then her sister-in-law's stroke and her nephews' trial for murder. The final blow had been Claire's death a few months ago.

Carl looped his arm around her shoulder and led her

inside to the kitchen. "You should never have kept working. You need some time off."

"Why?" She pulled from his embrace and began making coffee. They'd had this discussion several times before, but hadn't resolved the issue.

"Two major cases in less than a year, both involving your family, that's why. You're exhausted—"

"I'm fine." She smiled to reinforce her words and dumped ground coffee in the filter-lined basket. "I'm getting ample sleep, not skipping meals. What else would Dr. Mondori prescribe?"

"I wish I knew." Carl lounged at the table in the breakfast nook. "You've changed, Karen.".

His statement surprised her. "Changed? How?"

A tender smile lit his face and softened his words. "You've always been intense, especially about your work, but until recently, I've never known you to be so introspective."

She turned on the coffeemaker, then crossed the kitchen. Sitting on Carl's knee, she placed her hands behind his neck and stared into his dark Mediterranean eyes. "Losing Robert in such a cruel way, then watching his boys go to pieces, opened my eyes about a lot of things."

Carl nuzzled her neck. "What things?"

Karen paused, framing her thoughts carefully. "The fragility of life, my own limitations at changing the course of events, the ephemeral nature of happiness." She brushed his dark hair, now lightly sprinkled with gray, back from his forehead. "I'd thought about those things before, but only intellectually. Now I *feel* them, and those feelings have become an integral part of me. They color everything."

His face tightened with worry. "Are you depressed?"

49

"No, not that. But life has taken on a bittersweet quality I can't seem to shake."

"Maybe counseling—"

She stopped his words with a finger on his lips. "I have a better solution."

He appraised her with raised eyebrows. "A new case?"

She laughed. "How can I keep the mystery in our marriage when you read me like an open book?"

"What is it this time? Another murder defense?"

"Let me pour the coffee"—she hopped from his lap—"and I'll tell you all about it."

While the sun rose higher over the pines and filled the kitchen with golden light, Karen filled him in on her conversation with Herman Gaylord and her visit from Travis Weller. When she finished, Carl looked thoughtful.

"If Weller's right, the medical implications of organ regeneration by genetic engineering are staggering," he said, "but according to reports of the latest research in *JAMA*, such a process is decades away."

"That's what I suspected," she said. "Weller's claims were too fantastic."

"But can you imagine? Nerves regenerated. Discs repaired."

"It could put you out of business," she said with a teasing grin.

"Have you run Weller's proposition by Brander?"

"I won't bother Brander with the legal complications of such an arrangement until I decide whether I'm interested in pursuing Mr. Weller's line of inquiry."

Carl raised his eyebrows. "From the glint in your eyes, I'd say you're interested already."

"I want to check out Weller's information first."

"Will you have Bill Castor poke around for you?"

"Maybe later. I want to dig into this myself."

Carl made no comment.

She took his silence for disapproval. "Just a few interviews shouldn't take too much time. I have to talk with most of these people about Herman Gaylord anyway."

"I hate it when we have so little time together," he said finally. "In the past year and a half, it seems you've been away more than you've been home. Andrea misses you, too."

Karen had made up her mind, but at Carl's objection, she wavered. "I *could* send Bill, but I really want to get to the bottom of this myself. If Weller's jerking me around with fallacious stories, the sooner I find out, the better."

Carl reached across the table and laced his fingers through hers. "Discussing this case, you had your old fire back, but I don't get the advantage of those sparks if you aren't around."

She sidestepped the issue. "Rahni has the weekend off and Andrea spent the night with Tiffany. She won't be home until lunchtime."

Carl stood and pulled her up next to him. "I know a perfect way to spend what's left of the morning."

He was kissing her when the phone rang.

"Let it go," he murmured against her ear.

"It might be Andrea or an emergency at the hospital." She pulled away with a sigh and picked up the kitchen extension.

"Ms. Perry-Mondori?" a Spanish-accented voice asked.

"Yes."

"This is Maria Rodriguez, administrator of Bay Biscayne Rehabilitation Center in Miami. Martha Perry has you listed as her next of kin—"

"My mother's a patient in your facility?"

51

"You didn't know?"

Karen couldn't understand why she felt surprised. She never heard from her mother—unless it served Martha's interests. "Why is she there?"

"She's recovering from hip replacement surgery, but . . ." The woman paused.

"There's a problem?"

"I must ask you to have her moved to another rehab center."

"Why me? Can't this be arranged with my mother?"

Ms. Rodriguez cleared her throat with a nervous cough. "Your mother refuses to go."

"Are your facilities inadequate for my mother's care?"

"Absolutely not. It is your mother who is the problem."

Tell me something I don't know. "You'd better explain."

"Since Mrs. Perry arrived a few days ago, a nurse, an orderly, and a physical therapist have resigned. Several others are threatening to leave if they must continue caring for her."

Karen sighed. "My mother can be a difficult woman."

"Forgive me, Ms. Perry-Mondori, but describing your mother as *difficult* is like calling Hurricane Andrew a sea breeze."

"Can you recommend another facility?"

"Bay Biscayne is your mother's fifth rehab center since she left the hospital ten days ago. At this point, finding another facility in Miami with quality care willing to take her will be almost impossible. That is why I called you."

"But I'm not familiar with rehab centers in your area."

The administrator hesitated. "Perhaps your mother could stay with you during her recovery?"

The prospect staggered Karen. "Give me your number, please. I'll call you back."

"Your mother's ill?" Carl asked when she hung up the phone.

Karen sank into a chair at the breakfast table. "She's recovering from hip replacement surgery, and in her own inimitable fashion, making life hell for everyone around her. If the administrator is telling the truth, Mother's already been kicked out of every decent facility in the Miami area."

"I don't find that hard to believe," Carl said. "What did the administrator suggest?"

"That Mother stay here while she's recuperating."

"Good God! You're not—"

"There has to be another way. Maybe I can arrange for nursing care and a visiting therapist at Mother's house."

Carl shook his head. "Your mother's acid tongue would make short work of them, too."

"It would serve her right."

"I agree, but do you really want your mother alone and immobile in that big place of hers in Miami with no one to care for her?"

"Of course not."

"She can't stay here," Carl said with unshakable conviction. "You've already been through too much to have to put up with her. Besides, Rahni would quit."

"We're running out of options."

"If she came here, we could put her in Manor Care. Maybe between the two of us, we could run interference between her and the staff."

Karen gave him a wry smile. "Are you implying that if she has us to pick on, she might leave them alone? That's a happy thought."

He kissed her gently. "Nothing about this situation is happy. I'll get dressed and contact Manor Care. You arrange Martha's transportation."

"She won't fly. The only time she's flown in the last thirty years was when Robert died."

"Charter an ambulance. She can afford it."

With a sense of foreboding she couldn't shake, Karen returned to the telephone to call Maria Rodriguez.

Early Monday, Karen drove to the office of Frances Scott, Travis Weller's law school friend who'd kept tabs on his father. Her practice was located a block off Central Avenue near the waterfront in downtown St. Petersburg on the floor above a Cuban deli. The spare but clean suite was permeated by the smell of onions and spicy sausage. Sticky heat seemed to radiate from the thinly carpeted floor, the painted walls, even the high ceiling.

Ms. Scott was about the same age as Travis Weller, medium height and slender, and reasonably attractive. Judging by the fact that her sixtyish secretary kept her face buried in the latest issue of the *National Enquirer,* the solo practice wasn't a busy one. Frances Scott seemed friendly enough and offered Karen a cup of coffee. Karen declined.

The female attorney swung her chair around and slapped the growling window air-conditioning unit. The rumbling sound jumped ten decibels. "Got to get me a new one, I guess. This thing is on its last legs."

She turned back to Karen. "So you're representing Herman Gaylord for the murder of Gerald Brock? Travis almost dropped his teeth when he saw that autopsy report, but he never really explained. What got him so excited?"

Karen shrugged. "I think he's just trying to tidy up some guilty edges."

"So what can I do for you?"

"Travis said you'd been keeping an eye on his father for him."

The woman grinned. "Glad to do it. I'd do anything for that man, even if it means hanging around the back alleys. Never should have let Travis get away. Biggest mistake of my life." Her eyes gleamed. "Did he tell you we were once an item?"

"He skipped that part," Karen said.

Scott stared at the ceiling, a wide smile on her face, her arms behind her head. "God! All through first year law. It was incredible. That man couldn't get enough. He'd get me on the backseat of my old Ford during lunch and screw my brains out. Broad daylight. Didn't matter to him. After study group, we'd head to a small park on campus, and wham! I was so tired that first year it's a wonder I made it."

She focused her small brown eyes on Karen. "Never should have let him get away. He never married. Probably couldn't find a woman to keep up with him. Must be balling all the women he works with, while I married a man who thinks sex is dirty. Jesus—"

"About his father," Karen interrupted, fighting hard to resist the urge to leave.

"Yeah, I figured I'd keep an eye on his father for him. What the hell, you never know. Gave me an excuse to meet with him occasionally. Wouldn't want to miss an opportunity like that." She winked suggestively.

"He was here recently," Karen said coldly, shifting uncomfortably in her chair. Crude women like Frances Scott made her skin crawl.

"Yeah, but with his father murdered like that, it just wasn't the time, you know? He was only here a couple days. I helped him with the paperwork. We never got a chance to really talk, if you know what I mean."

55

"He said you last saw his father alive six months ago?"

"Brock was drunk, as usual," Scott said. "I said hello, then sent a fax to Travis."

"Where was Brock when you saw him?"

"His usual hangout, an alley a few blocks west of here, off Central. He was sitting in a puddle of his own urine, and this other guy, another vagrant with gold-rimmed glasses, was trying to pull him out of it."

"Was that the last time you went to check on him?"

Scott shrugged. "A month later, he was gone. I asked around at the shelters to see if anyone knew where he was, but they said no. I checked with the city, all the services. No sign of him."

"Did you ever talk to Herman Gaylord?"

"The drunk who killed him? No."

Karen grimaced. "And that was the last time you checked?"

"I called Travis and told him, and he asked me to check again, but there was still no trace of him. Travis finally told me to forget it, so I did."

"Until Brock died."

"The cops called me," Scott said. "I'd left them my name and address, just in case."

"Had you filed a missing persons report?"

"Travis didn't want me to. I just asked some people to put a flag beside the name in case they got a lead. As it turned out, I didn't know he was dead until a day after the murder."

Karen stood up. The stench of onions was getting to her. So was Frances Scott. "Thanks for your help."

"Anytime. What's the deal anyway? Travis practically hated his father. Is that why he's helping the lawyer for the guy who killed the old man?"

56

Karen shrugged. "We all have our demons, Ms. Scott."

"That's the truth. And Travis is one of mine, I don't mind telling you." She winked again. "You should give him a try yourself, and see what I mean."

"Do you always talk about your friends this way?" Karen asked, red-faced.

Frances Scott stiffened, and a cruel sneer twisted her lips. "Let me guess, you're a lesbian, right? Men don't turn you on? Hell, that's okay, gals like you don't bother me, as long as you keep your distance."

Karen glared at her. "Are you just depressed, or have you had this self-destructive urge for some time?"

Before the woman could reply, Karen turned on her heel and strode out of the office.

A half hour later, Tom Palmer, a burly St. Pete cop with a bushy walrus mustache and arms as thick as telephone poles, was showing Karen the spot where Gerald Brock was murdered.

"Right there beside the Dumpster," he said.

The alley, one like any other, was littered with garbage, dirty, smelly, and dark, even in the broad day-light of a humid Florida morning. A slender, shallow river of water, flushed into the alley by clattering air conditioners, trickled its way to a storm drain.

"You called the paramedics?" Karen asked.

"The guy was dead. I stopped Gaylord from beating on the still warm body, cuffed the suspect, and called the Crime Scene Unit."

"And Brock's body was taken to the ME's office?"

"Yeah, and the case was turned over to the homicide detectives."

Karen nodded. "You say you responded to a call?"

"Right. Somebody said there was somebody sick in the alley."

"Who called?"

"No name. Happens all the time around here."

The alley ran behind a series of seedy shops, religious missions, and employment agencies. Men in various stages of sobriety shuffled in front of the employment agencies, their chests puffed out, their short sleeves rolled to their armpits to display their biceps, all with the hope of being hired for a day's work by a moving company or warehouse. If they registered with the agency, the agency got a cut of their pay. If they failed to register, they were told to move on. Those who refused were forcibly removed.

"Had you ever seen Brock before?" Karen patted her sweaty brow with a handkerchief. It was over eighty degrees with humidity to match, unlike the air-conditioned air of the office and courtroom Karen was used to. Palmer, his body long since acclimatized to the outdoors, appeared dry as a bone.

"This isn't my usual zone," the cop said. "I was driving by when the squeal came, so I answered it."

"Any witnesses, besides you, to Gaylord's alleged attack on Brock?"

"Nobody else was around when I arrived. Then a crowd of about twenty gathered, contaminating the crime scene."

"And no one saw anything before that?" Karen asked.

"We talked to some of the people. As usual, nobody claimed to know Brock or Gaylord. But they both sure looked like regulars. According to some lawyer in town who'd been keeping tabs on Brock, he'd been here for years."

"Frances Scott?"

"Yeah," he said, "that's her. She knew Brock's son."

Karen nodded. "Since this isn't your zone, I'd like to talk with someone familiar with it."

"Billy Tabor works this area." The cop looked at his watch. "You come by the station at three. He'll be there. I'll tell him to expect you."

Karen stuck out her hand. "I appreciate your help."

"No problem. Mind if I ask you a question?"

"Go ahead."

"Both these guys were obviously vagrants." Palmer scratched his head. "You're a high-profile defense attorney. Why take *this* case?"

Karen smiled. "If a vagrant is wrongly convicted, the rest of us are at risk of potential abuse by the system. I want to make sure Gaylord gets a fair trial, no matter how little or how much money he has."

Palmer grinned and rubbed his chin with a meaty hand. "Couple of the guys down at the station said, even for a defense attorney, you got class, Ms. Perry-Mondori. Looks like they were right."

Nine hungry men sat at a long table and shoveled food into their mouths. For most of them, it was the only meal they'd have all day, a meal provided by three portly women in their sixties with unflagging energy and compassion-filled eyes. They dished out food from large aluminum trays and offered a smile and encouraging word to each man.

The men ranged in ages from early twenties to late seventies. Some had been on the streets for decades. Karen could see it in their eyes, that vacant stare of the lost. The younger ones looked either afraid or hostile, the macho pose struck to ward off enemies both real and imagined.

The man sitting next to Karen farted loudly. No one said anything. Karen gagged.

"Anyone here know a man named Gerald Brock?" she asked.

No one answered.

"How about Herman Gaylord? The Professor?"

The men kept eating.

"Twenty dollars to anyone who knew either of them."

Still nothing.

Karen left the table and headed for another. Eventually she asked the same question to almost everyone in the room before one old man stuck up his hand.

"Yeah, I knew both of 'em."

Karen took a seat beside him. "They were friends of yours?"

"You bet. We been friends a long time."

"I'm looking for them," Karen said. "Can you tell me where I can find them?"

The man smiled crookedly. "You give me the money, and I'll take you right to them."

Karen got up and left.

The reaction was much the same at the next mission, but at the third, Karen finally found someone willing to talk. He said his name was Charlie Bond, and he looked reasonably healthy, perhaps a relatively recent arrival to the ranks of the homeless.

"Yeah, I knew Gerry," he said. "I knew The Professor, too, and there's no way he killed Gerry."

At least this one knew Brock was dead and Gaylord had been charged with the murder.

"What do you know about them?" Karen asked, testing, the twenty-dollar bill still folded in her hand.

Charlie licked his cracked lips, then stuck a half-smoked cigarette between them and flared a match. "The Professor was from one of the Carolinas. Can't remember which. Gerry was from Central Florida, I think."

Karen nodded. "Anything else?"

"The Professor didn't have no family, but Gerry had a son. A real bastard. I can't remember his name. Gerry said his son threw him out on the street. That's why he started drinkin', 'cause his own son threw him out of his own fuckin' house."

"How did the son manage that?" Karen asked.

"He was a lawyer. Fuckin' lawyers can do whatever the hell they want. They rule the world, the bastards."

Karen took a deep breath. "Why did Gerry's son throw him out?"

"Maybe he wanted Gerry's money. Gerry had money, you know. Then his own son takes it all away and throws him out on his ass."

"What do you know about The Professor?"

"Nothing. He was always quiet, always reading a book or a newspaper he scarfed from a Dumpster."

The smell of urine tweaked Karen's nose. Around fifty, Bond was dressed in filthy clothes with a week's worth of beard on his craggy face. His eyes blinked constantly, and he wheezed as he talked, almost a death rattle.

Karen handed him the twenty. "Gerry disappeared six months ago. Do you remember that?"

"Yeah. One day he just wasn't there. The Professor was mighty upset. He worried about Gerry like the man was his kid or something. Tried to find him. No luck."

"Did you ever see Gerry again?"

The man shook his head slowly. "I never saw him dead neither. Just heard about it."

Karen nodded. "Were you present at a birthday

party for The Professor last year, when this shelter served ice cream and cake?"

"Yeah." He wiped his nose with his sleeve. "Gerry gave him a gold watch. Real gold. It had belonged to Gerry's daddy."

"Why would he give away an expensive watch that had sentimental value?"

"Gerry was afraid he'd get desperate and pawn it. He knew The Professor never drank, so he'd take good care of it."

Karen's pulse quickened. "Would you testify to that?"

He looked skeptical. "To lawyers?"

"The police say The Professor killed Gerry for his watch. With your testimony that Gerry gave him the watch, The Professor has no motive for murder."

"The lawyers'll think of something else. The bastards always do."

"If you swear to witnessing the gift, it'll make their job harder."

Charlie's eyes glinted. "There's always that. I'll think about it."

"Where was the last time you saw Gerry Brock?"

"Right here. He was eatin' lunch and talkin' about baseball. The Professor, he just listened. We was talkin' about the Devil Rays and how we almost didn't get a team. Gerry said it was the lawyers screwed things up. First the White Sox, then the Mariners, and the Giants, he said. The lawyers fucked up those deals, like they always do."

Bond fixed his gaze on Karen. "Gerry hated lawyers, just like me. You a lawyer?"

"No," Karen lied, straight-faced.

"A cop?"

"No."

"What the fuck are you, then?"

"A friend of The Professor's."

Bond shook his head. "Too bad he's in jail. He ain't killed nobody, much less Gerry. Must be the fuckin' lawyers keeping him there."

Karen changed the subject. "Do you have any idea where Gerry was for those six months he was missing?"

Charlie shook his head. "No idea at all, and I ain't lyin'. Funny thing. It's the third time it's happened."

"Excuse me?" Karen said.

Charlie grew more excitable. "I had two other friends disappear just like Gerry. Didn't come back neither. Just took off is all. That's what I thought happened to Gerry. They do that, you know. Have a fight with somebody or a chance to work somewheres else. They just take off."

He smiled for the first time, exposing yellow stubs of teeth. "Don't have to worry about breakin' no lease."

"These other friends, when did they leave?"

Charlie shook his head. "Don't know. Got no mind for time. Coulda been a month, maybe more."

"Do you remember their names?"

"Albert Smith was one of 'em. And Jack . . . Bayless. He and I were pals. Then he took off."

"Anything unusual about their leaving?" Karen jotted down the names in a small notebook.

"Just that neither of 'em ever talked about leavin'. Most times, when a man's fixin' to take off, he tells a buddy. I would. Al and Jack was just like Gerry. Just up and took off without a fuckin' word. Weird."

"And you've never seen them since?"

The man shook his head. "You reckon they're dead, like Gerry?"

"I hope not." In spite of the man's propensity for

63

four-letter words and his aversion to lawyers, Karen felt a pang of sympathy. Charlie Bond had had nothing but his friends, and now they, too, were gone.

"Thanks for your help." She slipped him another twenty as she left.

SIX

Officer Billy Tabor was an hour late. There'd been a bad accident on I-275, and he'd been involved in traffic control. When Karen introduced herself, the policeman shook her hand. "Can we make it short? My wife's got dinner on the table."

"I'm inquiring about Gerald Brock and Herman Gaylord. Sergeant Palmer says you might have known them."

"Yeah, I knew them."

They walked out of police headquarters toward the employee parking lot.

"This is real bullshit," Tabor said. "They used to let us take the patrol cars home. Then they had this idea they could save a few bucks by making us leave them for the next shift to use."

"About Brock and Gaylord. You knew them?"

"I told you. I know most of them down there. We have to roust them every so often. Don't want them gettin' too comfortable."

"Was either of them ever arrested?"

"We dragged Brock in here a couple of times, but he was never booked. These days we don't have the money to spend on drunks. Got our hands full with violent kids and the druggies."

"What happens when you pick up one of these homeless drunks—let's say one's passed out?"

"We don't do so much as touch them anymore. Not these days. If they're passed out, we call the paramedics. They take them to County Hospital. HRS handles the paperwork. The drunks get checked over. If they're really sick, they get treated. If they're just drunk, they get released, unless they're unconscious, in which case they get a bed for the night and released in the morning."

"Is County the only place they go?"

"Yeah, it's a public hospital."

"Would there be a record?"

"Of course. The whole damn city's ass-deep in paperwork."

"Brock had been missing for six months," Karen said."Any idea where he might have been?"

"Nope. These vagrants come and go. That's why we call 'em transients."

"No idea at all?"

"None."

"You ever hear of an Albert Smith or Jack Bayless?"

Tabor smiled. "Sure. They're both regulars. At least they were. They both took off."

"Do you know when?"

Tabor gave her a sharp look and dug in his pocket for his keys. "I told you I gotta get home. We better finish this another time."

"I'm almost done."

Tabor's eyes narrowed. "What's this all about?"

Karen smiled. "I'm representing Herman Gaylord, who's been accused of Brock's murder. I'm trying to piece together the last few months of Brock's life. A man I talked to said that Smith and Bayless simply disappeared. Since Brock was out of sight for six months, I thought there might be a connection."

Tabor scratched his head. "I doubt it. These people are nomads. They wander all over, come and go all the time. But I know someone who might help you."

"Who?"

"Fella name of John Green. He, Gaylord, and Brock were real close. They worked the odd job together. Even slept together most of the time. Used the same ratty sleeping bags John found in some Dumpster. John's still around. At least he was a couple of days ago. Should find him in one of the missions. There's one called the Holy Trinity that has cots. Opens at eight p.m. Won't let in anyone who's drunk. Kind of a reward for staying sober the whole day."

"And I'll find Green there?"

"He's one of the few who isn't an alky. He's a little nuts is all."

"One last question."

"Go ahead."

"How many cases like Brock have you had in the last few months? Not just you, but the entire department?"

"Dead, you mean?" The cop shrugged. "Can't rightly say."

"A guess?"

He thought for a moment. "In Pinellas County alone, I'd guess four or five a month."

"All of natural causes?"

"Yeah, if you want to include the homicides, you're up to around twenty-five a month."

"But," Karen prodded, "in the case of homeless drunks dying of natural causes, you find as many as five a month?"

"I'd say that's about right. More in the winter than the summer. They come down here from the North lookin' for a break from the cold."

John Green sat on the cot and picked his nose incessantly as Karen asked him questions. His eyes kept jerking in their sockets, and drool ran from one corner of his mouth. But he was sober.

"The Professor's lawyer, eh?" he said when Karen introduced herself. "Ain't it just like The Professor to go and get himself some uppity-up attorney. If it was me in trouble, every lawyer in the state would run the other way. Ain't that a pisser?"

"You were saying you knew what happened to Gerald Brock."

"He got sick is what happened. The ambulance came and hauled him off to the hospital. I went over there that night and asked to see him, but they said he wasn't there. Matter-of-fact, they said he'd never been there. I figure they just threw him out on the street."

"When was that?"

"About six months ago."

"Which hospital?"

"County. Where else?"

"How did you know where he was?"

Green scratched beneath his tattered shirt as if something was biting him. "That's where they take folks like us. The only place'll have us. Somehow Gerry got separated from The Professor and me that day. The Prof and me were having lunch . . . right here, as a matter of fact . . . and Gerry was drunk. They wouldn't let him in. They's real stiff about that, you know. When I came out, the ambulance was pulling away from out back of the grocer's place. The Professor had found Gerry and called 911."

"But Gerry wasn't at the hospital?"

"No. I hadda walk all the way over there. Took me over an hour. I talked to the people in the emergency room. They said he'd never even been there. They accused *me* of being drunk." He shook his head in dismay. "I never drink. It's not healthy."

"And you never saw Gerry again?"

"Not ever. The day he died, I heard about it later, and about them arresting The Professor. What a crock! He wouldn't hurt a fly, much less Gerry. I never saw either of them, though. All I know is Gerry was back after all that time. Then he was dead. Crazy."

"What about a man named Albert Smith? You know him?"

Green shook his head.

"Jack Bayless?"

Green smiled. "Yeah, him I knew. Wop from Atlanta. Bayless ain't his real name. Some long eye-talian name with a lot of o's and i's. Crazy bastard, that one. You lookin' for him, too?"

"No, but do you know when Bayless disappeared?"

"Yeah. Come to think of it, it was about a week before Gerry." Green's eyes finally stopped jerking. Now they were fixed on Karen's. "What's going on around here, miss? Should I be worried?"

Karen patted the man's shoulder. "I don't think so. This is all just routine in preparing for The Professor's trial."

"Routine? A classy dame like you slumming it and asking questions? That ain't routine. Nobody gives a shit about us. Never have, never will."

Karen looked around the room. "I'd say there are some people here who care. A clean bed and a good meal is not all bad. And it's free."

"It ain't free. You gotta listen to their bullshit for an

hour or so. Lotsa guys would rather starve than listen to that bullshit. 'Just give yourself to Jesus and everything will be fine,' they keep telling you. Crap. I seen guys who did that, gave it a try, and nothing changed much."

"There's another way of looking at it," Karen said.

"Yeah? What's that?"

"Maybe they didn't try hard enough."

Green made a face. "You're one of *them*."

"Not me, but I like to keep an open mind. You just never know."

The following day Karen drove to Orlando. She parked her rental car in one of the slots reserved for visitors at a tall, glass-walled structure a block from the office complex of United Cable Network, formerly owned by the late Walter Stockman, who had caused her family so much grief. When she entered the building, a receptionist looked up from the curved plastic desk.

"I'm here to see Dr. Robert Griffin."

"Your name, please?"

"Karen Perry-Mondori. Dr. Griffin's expecting me."

The receptionist picked up the phone, spoke to someone in muffled tones, then replaced the receiver. "Dr. Griffin will be with you momentarily. Please have a seat."

Karen sat in one of several chrome and vinyl chairs and waited. Gulf Coast Pharmaceuticals was a large, successful company, but one would never know it from the waiting room, austere to the extreme, with threadbare carpets and cheap furniture. She presumed the corporation had decided to spend its money on other pursuits, such as advertising and research. It certainly wasn't trying to impress the hoi polloi. Then again, maybe shareholders and supplier reps used another entrance. On the third hand—

"How very good to meet you, Ms. Perry-Mondori." A man had burst through the door to her left. He smiled and extended his hand. "I'm Robert Griffin."

Karen got to her feet and shook the man's hand. "Thank you for seeing me."

"It's my pleasure. Come this way."

Griffin was about fifty, short, thin, and balding. The thick glasses he wore made his eyes appear unnaturally large. He wore a rumpled blue suit with a white shirt and a multicolored bow tie that might have been a more fastidious man's idea of a joke. Obviously, the doctor had no proclivity for sartorial splendor. He seemed friendly enough, almost effusive. Certainly not the typical lost-in-thought scientist oblivious to anything and everything taking place in the outside world.

"In my position as vice president of Gulf Coast," he told her as they traveled the hallway, "my responsibility is scientific discovery. Marketing and public relations are left to others, so I'm not often asked to meet with outsiders."

"If this is an intrusion—"

"Not at all," he assured her with a big-eyed smile. "I view this meeting as a special treat."

He ushered Karen into a small conference room that overlooked the parking lot. She took a seat at an oak table.

The doctor sat across from her. "I was delighted to receive your call. How can I help you?"

"As I explained on the phone, Mr. Weller believes his father was the object of some bizarre experiment, one that might even have caused his death. The State of

71

Florida, however, believes my client killed Weller's father. Weller tells me you concur with his theory. I'd like more information."

The doctor nodded enthusiastically. "I do concur with Mr. Weller's conclusions. I know it sounds inconceivable, but after examining the data personally, there's no doubt whatsoever in my mind."

Karen leaned forward. "What makes you so sure?"

"I fancy myself a bit of a detective. Not the kind you employ in your law firm, of course, but I'm a detective all the same."

Karen groaned inwardly and hoped she hadn't driven all the way to Orlando to confer with an amateur Sherlock Holmes.

Griffin removed his glasses and cleaned the Coke-bottle lenses with a wrinkled handkerchief. "For one thing, my work is the purest kind of detective work. Research always is. For another, I'm a voracious reader of mystery novels. I pride myself on my ability to figure out who did the evil deed within the first few chapters."

"That must make finishing them boring."

Griffin squinted nearsightedly, then slipped his glasses back in place. "I love the challenge. Besides, it's great exercise for the mind. Do you read, Ms. Perry-Mondori?"

She nodded. "Mostly nonfiction."

"Ah, you prefer reality to fantasy?"

"I'm not sure there is such a thing as reality."

"Philosophy, then?"

She shifted in her chair. "Dr. Griffin, I've had a long drive through horrendous traffic. Can we return to the matter at hand?"

"Of course. You've already had an opportunity to examine Mr. Brock's body?"

"I did."

"And you talked to the forensics man?"

"Yes."

"And?" Griffin asked.

"He was very persuasive."

"But you're still not convinced, are you? I can see it in your face."

"Let's just say that I find this all a bit unusual."

"It is that, Ms. Perry-Mondori. So you left me for last. No offense, of course."

"I hope not. I've examined all the documents Mr. Weller inadvertently left with me, and I've read your statement."

"And it still seems preposterous, doesn't it?"

"It does."

"Yes, of course it would. But the facts are irrefutable. Mr. Brock's organs could not have been restored to health any other way. Advanced cirrhosis of the liver is not a remissible disease. It's progressive, in fact."

"Maybe so," Karen said. "But the archives of medical science are filled with documented cases of people who've enjoyed remissions of brain tumors, heart disease, leukemia, any number of things. None were supposed to have happened. When confronted by *this* reality, medical science simply throws its collective hands in the air and says, 'We have no explanation.' It's the kind of thing that keeps faith healers in business. Not all of them are fakes, Doctor. What makes this case so different?"

"This case is different because we *know* Mr. Brock's DNA was altered."

"How?"

"It's what we do. DNA research is one of our biggest interests."

"So, your tests are conclusive?"

"Absolutely. There's no mistake, I assure you."

Karen rubbed her chin. "From what I've read, DNA can sometimes be altered spontaneously . . . naturally, without outside influence."

Griffin nodded. "I see you've been doing your homework. Good. Very good. If you read deeply enough, you will soon learn such alterations occur over a very long time span. Millennia, in fact. In the case of Mr. Brock, the changes occurred, at most, within a few years, according to documentation, but we have reason to believe they occurred within a few months. Occurring naturally in that short a time is quite impossible."

"Nothing is impossible."

Griffin's face hardened. "Really? You can flap your arms as hard as you like, but your feet will never leave the ground for more than a few milliseconds. Some things *are* impossible. Take my word for it."

"I meant to say nothing in medical science is impossible."

"Exactly," the doctor said with a grin.

Karen laughed. "Touché. You *are* quick, Doctor."

"I better be."

"Still, in reference to Mr. Brock, there could be another explanation, one in keeping with the documented cases I spoke of earlier for which there appears to be no reasonable interpretation. Isn't that also a possibility?"

"If it is," Griffin said, "I wish I could find it. I prefer, if you will, to consider the alteration of Mr. Brock's DNA by means of deliberate manipulation as the most likely reasonable explanation. I prefer it because I have seen genetically altered cattle that grow faster to larger weight, because I've seen genetically altered ears of corn that are impervious to the ravages of most insects and disease. I've seen enough to convince me that what

74

occurred to Mr. Brock was *not* a natural or spontaneous event."

Karen was resolute. "If I'm to convince a jury that flawed genetic engineering, not Herman Gaylord, killed Gerald Brock, I'll need more than your conclusions. You have yet to perform a successful experiment that would duplicate what happened to Mr. Brock. Nor has anyone else to your knowledge. Your own report states that such a treatment is fifty to a hundred years away. What makes you think some person or company or country has developed a process now? And if they have, why would they pick a subject like Brock? And why would their research be kept secret? That's the biggest question."

Griffin shrugged. "We don't have the answers. That's what we're hoping you can find out. In representing the man accused of killing Mr. Brock, you have the perfect reason for this kind of investigation."

"Bear in mind, Doctor, mine is a murder investigation, not a scientific one."

The doctor stood and paced the floor for a moment, hands thrust deep in his pockets. "I may have a clue for you. As I said, I'm a devotee of mysteries. I've given a tremendous amount of thought to this problem, and I may have focused on a real possibility."

Karen slumped in her chair. Amateurs like Griffin needed to be tolerated, especially if they had information that might help her client, but she wasn't a woman who suffered fools gladly. "Okay, I'm listening."

"Has anyone mentioned the name Consolidated Research to you?"

"No. Should they have?

"Not really. I expect they left it to me."

"What does Consolidated Research have to do with Gerald Brock?"

"Perhaps everything. During the past few years, a new company has entered the field of genetic engineering, a company located in Osolo, not an hour's drive from here, called Consolidated Research Enterprises. They came out of nowhere, are privately funded, and have been hiring the cream of the crop in the molecular biology field for several years."

Karen's interest quickened. "Osolo isn't far from St. Petersburg, either. What else do you know about this company?"

"Not much. The strange thing is, they never publish the results of their work, and no one who works for them ever attends conferences or meets with past employers. It's as though their scientists are forbidden to discuss their work, which is contrary to the usual way things function in the scientific community.

"In fact," he added, "two of our people went to work for them during the past year. Despite our best efforts, we've been unable to even contact our former employees."

Karen shrugged. "So what? They're working for a competitor, right? I would *expect* people working for competitors to keep quiet."

"So would I. But you can be a competitor and still be concerned about common issues. In any business enterprise, there are common goals, concerns about ethics, government regulations, legislation, all sorts of issues. Competitors rally together when something is afoot that could affect the industry as a whole. The car companies have their associations, the tobacco and oil companies, just about any industry you'd care to mention." He smiled. "Even the American Bar Association. As do we. But Consolidated is not a member of our association, or any association, to our knowledge.

"Each time there's a change of national leadership in

Washington, the government's priorities change along with it. Just when we think we have a handle on the political agenda as it relates to matters concerning our industry, we're forced to readjust. Those of us in the industry have, through our many associations, been heavily engaged in the effort to affect priorities. We've hired lobbyists and public relations firms, all of whom are well connected. It's the way business is done these days. For Consolidated not to be a part of this important effort is most peculiar, and we know they've not hired a single lobbyist."

"How do you know that?"

"Because we've contacted them all."

"Go on."

"We know Consolidated employs more scientists than any one company in this field, here or abroad. We know it's spending more on research than the rest of us combined. And yet, not a single government grant has been given to these people."

"That's unheard of," Karen noted with growing interest, "and highly unlikely."

"In fact, there's not been a peep from Consolidated on any issue affecting the industry as a whole. And keep in mind, the company is located about sixty miles from where Mr. Brock's body was discovered."

Karen shook her head. "How could you possibly know they employ more scientists than any of you? How could you know what they spend on research?"

Griffin smiled again. He seemed to be enthralled by the investigative process. "It's not that complicated. As for the first question, we simply polled the members of our association and asked how many of their people had left to work for Consolidated. The number was shocking. As for the research money, we all use essentially the same equipment in our work.

Our suppliers have refused to divulge any information about their dealings with Consolidated, but their sales must be enormous to support a facility with so many scientists."

Karen stood. "I have the feeling what you're really after is industrial espionage, and I want no part in that."

Griffin shook his head. His owlish eyes expressed a seriousness that had been lacking until now. When he spoke, his voice resounded with sincerity. "Let me assure you, we're more concerned about the welfare of this country."

"How so?"

"If Consolidated does have the knowledge I think it has, we're looking at a situation where one of the most powerful discoveries in the history of mankind is being controlled by a private corporation, a corporation owned and operated by people unknown to us."

"This is America, Doctor. Free enterprise is king."

"Since it's a private company, it's unregulated and completely unfettered as long as their people don't publish and don't make public what they're doing. Frankly, that terrifies me. What happened to Mr. Brock terrifies me more."

Karen wrinkled her brow in confusion. "But wasn't the regeneration of Brock's organs a good thing?"

"Not if he was killed in the process. Let me assure you, if, after you've made your investigation, you are reticent to discuss information you feel might fall under the heading of industrial espionage, you will encounter no pressure from Gulf Coast Pharmaceuticals. On the other hand, if you find Consolidated responsible for Brock's death . . ."

He left the sentence unfinished.

Karen extended her hand. "Nice meeting you, Doctor."

Griffin shook her hand, his eyes filled with uncertainty. "What are you going to do?"

"I'm going to think about this. After that, we'll see what develops."

Griffin nodded. "As I've read in the newspapers, you're a cautious woman about the cases you accept. But the man accused of killing Brock is merely a homeless drifter. The issue here is much greater than one vagrant's innocence or guilt. Is there a special reason for your reticence?"

"No," Karen said flatly.

"In that case, I'll look forward to hearing from you."

"You won't."

"No?"

"Herman Gaylord is my client. Anything I have to report will be given to him. What he does with it is his business."

"I see. Well, you're a stickler for detail, and that's fine."

"Have a nice day, Doctor."

Outside the building, Karen climbed into her car and pulled into traffic. She hated to admit it, but Travis Weller had been right. This case *was* intriguing. For more reasons than he knew.

As it had on other occasions, the challenge, the curiosity, and the cynicism combined to form a motivational force. Together, they sent a stream of unanswered questions whistling through Karen's consciousness.

She wanted answers to those questions.

She phoned Travis Weller when she returned to her office. "I've met with Dr. Griffin."

"You believe my father was murdered by these people and their genetic experiments?"

"It's possible."

"Then you'll investigate?"

"I'll do whatever necessary to clear my client."

"And you'll share your findings with me?"

"As far as they relate to your father and don't create a conflict of interest for my client."

"Good." Weller sounded pleased. "Then I'll deposit a retainer with your firm."

"Absolutely not. Let me make myself perfectly clear," Karen said sharply. "*You* are not my client, and I have no fiduciary responsibility to you. Any information I might share will be of my own accord and will not compromise my duty to Herman Gaylord. If that $50,000 check from Gulf Coast Pharmaceuticals is burning a hole in your pocket, I have a suggestion for what to do with it."

"What?" Weller's tone was wary.

"Donate it to the Holy Trinity Mission in St. Petersburg. And I have one other suggestion."

"Yes?"

"You should find another location for your father's body, one as few people know about as possible."

Weller hesitated. "Why?"

"I can't give you a good answer. Let's just call it being careful. Once I get started on this investigation, people's ears might pick up signals. I wouldn't want anything to happen to the one piece of evidence you have at the moment."

"I'll take care of it."

"Good."

"And good luck, Karen. I'll look forward to hearing from you."

"I'll be in touch."

As she hung up the phone, a score of questions still rattled around in her head. She was by no means convinced that this wasn't a small case of hysteria created by a set of botched tests.

At the same time, there was always a chance that Griffin was right.

SEVEN

Martin Bradford was more aroused and stimulated than he'd been in months. Grace, pleasantly surprised by this rare exercise in self-control, responded in kind, alternating between complete passivity and unbridled passion.

In the beginning, he'd been a terrific lover, very giving, very adventurous, always concerned with her pleasure above his own. Then, after several years of marriage, he'd become completely wrapped up in his work. He was still a good, if infrequent, lover, but he seemed impatient, eager to perform what was now more a ritual than an adventure.

Now, tonight, it was like the old days. It was a rare performance—guileless and lustful—and she was thoroughly enjoying it. She felt unusually relaxed and sexy, uninhibited and free, relishing the giving and getting, her mind unfettered by the normal cares of the day. Muted candlelight caressed her eyes, while in the background, the soft sounds of Mozart tickled her eardrums.

Now he was tasting that special place that drove her absolutely wild, flicking his tongue and kissing her with utter abandon. She responded by arching her pelvis, urging him on, moaning in ecstasy.

"Martin," she gasped.

He knew what to do. He moved forward, inserted himself inside her, then locking her in a tight embrace, he rolled over on his back. She was now on top of him, her back arched, feeling his every movement as she moved up and down rhythmically. His hands caressed her breasts, his fingers gently squeezing her nipples.

She moaned again and pressed herself down on him as she came with an uncommon force that seemed to last an eternity. The release left her feeling slightly faint.

"God!" She fell against him, her chest heaving, her breath coming in short bursts.

He let her rest for a minute, his soft hands stroking her silken skin from the back of her head to her thighs. Hot hands, but dry and smooth as velvet.

She looked into his eyes. "Incredible," she said huskily.

"I'm not finished yet," he said with a wide grin.

"No. No more. I can't take—"

He stopped her voice by kissing her on the lips, then gently rolled her over on her back. Smiling, he said, "This shouldn't take long."

Still naked, he left the bedroom and returned with two glasses of liqueur. Grace was feeling more mellow than she could ever remember, her now-languid body gleaming with perspiration, her hair splayed against the pillow, her blue eyes filled with love.

She stroked his hair. "I hope whatever it was that turned you on remains. Anything special?"

He laughed. "I just feel good."

"You still can't tell me?"

He shook his head. "You know the deal."

"But I'm your wife," she protested. "I can understand

their need for security, but this is a little obsessive, don't you think?"

He sighed, then giggled. "It's more than a little obsessive, it's impossible. I can't *not* tell you."

She sat straight up in the bed and leaned against the padded headboard. "So tell me."

His expression became serious. "You must promise to keep it within these walls. I mean it, Grace. Not a word to the kids. Remember that contract. If any of this leaves this room, we could be destitute."

She made a face."I'm aware of that. What, do you think I'll post a note on the supermarket bulletin board? They all work for Consolidated, anyway."

He slapped her gently on the thigh, his eyes glowing with excitement, and sipped his liqueur. "All right. I'm working on something absolutely incredible."

"What?" Her excitement quickly matched his own.

He took a deep breath. "For three years I've been working on the theory that genetics and addiction are related. Now these people have actually found the link."

Grace's jaw dropped. "They've found it?"

"Absolutely. When I started work at the university, we thought the gene lay on just one chromosome. Then, as we progressed, we began to think that two chromosomes were involved. Here, they're sure three chromosomes affect it, and they know where they are."

"My God!"

He could barely contain himself. "They're already doing the experiments. On humans."

She was shocked. "How is that possible?"

"Nobody's saying anything, what with this obsession for secrecy . . . though I'm beginning to understand it. In any event, I saw a man today—a volunteer, a lifelong drunk—and he was completely devoid of any craving whatsoever."

"Incredible!"

"He's been with them for less than four months. I was there when they offered him a glass of wine. He drank it. Then they offered him a second glass, and he simply shook his head. He's no longer an alcoholic, and he's not on any kind of medication. There's been no psychotherapy, just gene therapy."

"How did they do it?"

Martin laughed. "It's really quite simple when you know where to look, and these people are years ahead in DNA mapping. It's astonishing. With this patient, for example, they took a small tissue sample, located the three affected chromosomes, clipped out what they thought were the defective DNA strands, cloned the remainder, then combined it with the same DNA strands from a donor without the defect."

"They used cloning?"

"Uh-huh. They divided the new combination and cloned it again. They now had DNA that was roughly fifty percent the original patient and fifty percent donor. You follow?"

"I follow."

"They kept dividing and modifying or inserting the healthy DNA until they were left with DNA that was ninety-nine-point-nine percent the original, with the exception of the three defective genes which were now perfectly normal. Now with no possibility of rejection, they cloned the new DNA and inserted it into the patient."

"How does that work?"

"It's like new software for a computer. The new DNA is minus the defect that creates the craving for alcohol. But the secret is in the modification. They've found a way to modify existing DNA so that it has, in effect, new instructions. The new DNA replicates inside the body and quickly replaces the existing DNA. The actual changes are minuscule, just enough to do the job, but now, the entire body is affected. It's like creating a completely new human being from within."

"No wonder you're excited." Grace's eyes glowed with pride. "It's unbelievable."

"It's like a miracle. Without those defective genes and with the new instructions, the man's craving for alcohol is gone, and he's normal. The addiction is cured. It's like the guy *never had* a hunger for alcohol."

His voice rose as his enthusiasm grew. "They wanted me to see this right away so I could appreciate the light at the end of the tunnel. Part of what they call 'the indoctrination process.' They give it to new people a step at a time. I guess they figure we'll go nuts if we get too much too fast. But I can guess what's going on. They must be doing all *kinds* of experiments. It's mind-boggling to think where this can lead."

Grace pursed her lips, her enthusiasm now dimmed. What should have been exhilarating now seemed the opposite.

Martin noticed her changed expression. "What's the matter? Did I fail to explain it properly?"

She didn't answer. "You say this man volunteered?"

"Yes. There's a wing of the facility that serves as a hospital. They didn't let me up there, but they brought this guy down so I could talk to him."

"Isn't this a departure from normal research methods?"

"You mean using volunteers this soon?"

"You usually work with lab animals until you have a complete study. That's what you were doing at Stanford. Have they gone through all that?"

"I don't really know."

"They couldn't have, could they? They're skipping steps. They haven't had time to do everything."

"There's no question," he said, "but if someone is an alcoholic, their life is pretty grim, and their future bleak. For them to agree to be part of a study that could cure them of the disease is not that big a risk."

"It isn't?"

"Not really. I mean, the ones who volunteer are about to die anyway from damage to their livers. At the very worst, if something goes wrong with an experiment, what have they really lost?"

Grace looked pale. "What have they really lost? Is that what you said?"

He shook his head. "I didn't mean it the way it sounded. I've not heard of any unacceptable side effects. The man I talked to was happy as a clam and feels better than he's felt in years."

She gnawed at her bottom lip. "Martin . . . they showed you a success story. You said yourself it was experimental. I was a nurse long enough to know that experimental procedures are almost never successful the first few times. It's a process of trial and error."

"So?"

"So what about the failures? You said the man had been there four months. That's not long enough. Hell, three *years* isn't long enough, and Consolidated's only been in business that long."

"What are you saying?"

"I'm saying I'm frightened. This sounds so risky, so abnormal, not like any research I've ever heard of."

"It isn't," he replied seriously.

She sipped her drink. "What happens to him now?"

"Who?"

"The man you saw. The happy-as-a-clam man."

Martin shrugged. "I don't know."

"Can he leave if he wants to?"

He frowned. "I'm sure he can. Why not?"

"Security," she said simply, leaning back against the pillow.

Martin leaned over her and kissed her lips. She pushed him away.

"I shouldn't have told you," he said softly.

She took his hand. "No, you should have. It's not just that."

"Then what?"

She stared at the ceiling for a moment, silently cursing herself for exhibiting her concern. She wanted to be supportive of her husband. The decision to take the job was a joint one, as were all their decisions. They were a team in the best sense of the word.

At the same time, they kept little from one another, and while she didn't want to spoil his obvious euphoria after three days on the job, there were things that needed to be said.

"What *is* it?" Martin asked, pushing now for an answer.

She sighed. "Maybe it's just a natural letdown after all the excitement, I don't know. It's just . . . well . . . here we are in a house we aren't even allowed to buy for five years. That's one thing. The weather is dreadful, and that's another. The kids can play for only a few minutes before they're drenched in sweat. They want to stay inside all the time."

"That'll pass," he said quietly. "We haven't even unpacked all the stuff. Once we get organized, you'll feel better. And once the kids make some new friends, they'll feel better. You have to give it some time."

She sighed again. "I will, but that's not all of it. Today when I went to the market again, I really looked at the faces of the people, both the customers and those working there."

"And?"

"They looked odd. I mean, they seemed to have no emotion. You know how I like to get to know people where I shop. I always introduce myself and make a few funny remarks, just to let them know I'm a friendly sort. Today, like the other day, there was simply no reaction. No anger, no happiness, no smiles, no conversation. It was weird."

"Maybe it just seems that way because you're the new kid on the block."

"Maybe. Consolidated keeps telling you that this project is not to be discussed with anyone. All right, I can understand the need for some of it, but it seems the people in this town have been told they can't discuss *anything*. We both know the company owns all the stores and leases them out. Everybody is beholden to Consolidated no matter where they work. The company owns the schools, the hospital, the bank, everything—lock, stock, and barrel."

"That isn't necessarily bad," Martin said defensively.

"But who the hell *are* these people? You don't even know that! But it's possible for them to know everything there is to know about us, right down to what we eat. It's a closed society, and that makes me very uncomfortable."

"But Grace—"

"And then, when you tell me about those volunteers, that makes me even more anxious, because I've lived with your work long enough to know that shortcuts are being taken here. You told me it would be years before some of this knowledge would be tested on humans, and, even then, it would have to be supervised very carefully."

"I'm sure Consolidated knows what they're doing."

She shook her head. "This is all coming too fast for

me. I don't mean to sound like a shrew. I'm just scared, that's all. This is so different from what I'm used to. It's like living in another world."

He smiled at her. "It is that. Look, it will take some time before we really settle in. As far as the people go, strangers are always given the cold shoulder for a while. We've experienced that everywhere we've ever gone. And this is the South. Redneck country. Down here, they're even more reticent."

She forced a smile, for his sake. "Maybe you're right."

"As for the company, they told me from the get-go that they were ahead of everyone else. Frankly, I think what they're doing is right. You never really know a procedure will work until it's tested on humans. Normally, we spend too many years covering our asses while people continue to suffer. Look at the situation with AIDS patients. The FDA refused to let them try various drugs even though they were at death's door. That makes no sense to me. As far as I'm concerned, if we try these things on human beings who have no other hope, where's the harm?"

"I don't know . . ."

"Consolidated asks for volunteers who would die if they remained untreated, who have nothing to lose by being a part of this. And the man I talked to today is delirious with joy. Without Consolidated, he'd probably be dead."

She looked into his eyes. "What's his name?"

"Who?"

"The man you met today, the patient."

Martin thought for a moment. "I don't know. They never mentioned a name."

Grace allowed a small smile of irony to reach her lips. "Don't you find that rather impersonal?"

Martin shrugged. "Not really. They're probably protecting his identity at his own request."

"Do you really believe that?"

"Yes."

She turned away from him and closed her eyes.

The next morning, less than an hour after Martin arrived at work, Dr. Stiles's secretary telephoned Martin and asked him to report to Stiles's office. Martin doffed his white lab jacket and walked from the small lab to which he'd been assigned to Stiles's office, located near the front of the massive building.

Stiles's secretary smiled at him and told him to go right in. Stiles, sitting behind his desk, stood and waved Martin to a seat.

"So," Stiles said, "I trust you found yesterday's demonstration interesting."

"I did indeed."

"Remarkable, isn't it?"

"Very."

"Tony tells me you've settled in rather well."

Martin nodded. "Yes. It's terrific to be working with an old friend like Tony. He's showing me the ropes as best he can, but there's much to learn in a very short time."

"You're impressed?"

"When you talked to me about this work, I was excited, but now that I see what's going on, I'm even more enthusiastic. It's remarkable. You didn't exaggerate anything."

Stiles smiled. "And you thought I had?"

"Well, most people tend to embellish things a little when they're trying to sell something." Martin leaned forward. "Was there something else you wanted to see me about?"

"Now that you're here and part of the team, I wanted to reemphasize the importance of maintaining absolute confidentiality. I underscored the importance before you agreed to accept your present position, and I reiterated it the moment you arrived."

"I'm aware of that."

Stiles placed his hands together in a steeple. "I know you are, but I must caution you again. You are not to discuss your work with anyone, not even your wife."

Martin felt a chill go down his spine. "I assure you, I've talked to no one."

Stiles smiled. "I'm sure that's true, but we've found that most new employees have a tendency, confronted with so many stimulating concepts, to blurt things out to their spouses. It's natural, I suppose, but dangerous, nevertheless. I just wanted you to be aware that it's a serious concern to us and will not be tolerated."

Martin stiffened. "I *am* aware. I haven't mentioned anything to Grace."

Stiles smiled again. "Good. Let's keep it that way. I realize this may sound overly cautious, but we're inflexible on this issue. If we ever discover you have talked to your wife or anyone else, your work will be terminated forthwith, and you'll be held to the agreement you signed. You'll be left penniless. You understand?"

"Yes."

Stiles's smile faded, and he fixed Martin with a cold stare. "We are sometimes prone to forgive the first lapse, but that's it. There will never be a second warning."

Martin fought his rising temper. "You're giving me a warning?"

Stiles stood and his smile returned. "No, I just want you to be vigilant at all times. I can't emphasize enough how important it is that you keep what goes on within these walls a secret."

The cold chill in Martin's spine intensified. Looking into Stiles's eyes, Martin saw a glimmer of something, as if the man were imparting more than just his words. It was as if he *knew*. Martin's mind began to whirl.

"I understand," he said, his voice timorous.

Stiles nodded. "Good. You can go back to your work now. I'm glad we had the chance to talk. I think you'll fit in very well here."

When Martin returned to the lab after his disturbing conversation with Dr. Stiles, his mind was still spinning. He sat at his workstation and tried to think. But thinking was difficult. All around him, machines hummed and clattered, their multicolored diodes flashing green, red, yellow, and orange.

This lab was only one of about forty, all in varying sizes, that took up about half of the building's main floor. This one was the smallest by far, less than thirty feet by twenty feet, windowless, the air filtered, purified, and maintained at a constant temperature of sixty-eight degrees with humidity at thirty-eight percent. Filled with equipment, the lab had room for only eight scientists including the team leader, Tony Trattio.

Martin, his face still stinging with undisguised anger, sat at his workbench and stared hostilely at Tony.

Tony glanced at Martin, then returned his attention to the machines. "Problem?" the weary-looking scientist asked.

"Can we talk?" Martin said.

"Sure."

"Not here."

"Then it'll have to be later," Tony said. "I'm in the middle of a sequence."

"Fine."

"Why can't you tell me here?"

"That should be obvious," Martin said.

Tony gave him a curious look. "What's bugging you this morning?"

Martin glared at him. "Later. Your house. Let's say after dinner."

"Why not dinner? I'll throw some steaks on the grill."

Martin shook his head. "No. After dinner."

Tony shrugged, mumbled, "Suit yourself," and returned to his work.

EIGHT

Everyone else was asleep, but tired as she was, Karen was agitated by what she'd learned from Robert Griffin that afternoon and knew any attempt to sleep was futile. Despite the fact that she had an early morning flight to Miami, she climbed out of bed and padded on bare feet to her home office.

She turned on her computer and accessed a private agency out of California that dealt in information. For a hefty monthly fee, plus line time, associate members of the agency—insurance companies, credit bureaus, private investigators, law firms, even some government agencies—could retrieve stored information on almost any person or company in the world.

The service was Orwellian, all-encompassing, and the largest private database in existence, quasi-legal, a result of people's insatiable desire—sometimes need—to know anything and everything about other people. It was also fallible, because the data was simply accumulated, not checked for accuracy, and it was also expensive.

Once on-line, Karen tapped the keys and asked for information on Consolidated Research Enterprises. The information appeared on her screen in less than a minute.

CONSOLIDATED RESEARCH ENTERPRISES:
Incorporated as a for profit corporation, Delaware, March, 1997. Origination, unincorporated DBA CRE, New York City, 1992 (see below).
P.O. Box 84773
23659 Orlando Road
OSOLO, FLORIDA 32934
(407) 555-9822
Type of business: Medical Research
Ownership: Private. Wholly-owned subsidiary of CRE Corporation, N.A., Willemstad, Netherlands Antilles
Annual revenues: Unknown
Number of employees: Unknown
CEO: Dr. Walter Schatt (see listing under this name in International Personnel Records—Berlin, Germany)
CFO: B. H. Gollems (see listing under this name in International Personnel Records—Paris, France)
Directors: Unknown
Officers: Unknown
Public spokesman: Dr. Philip Stiles (see listing under this name in U.S. Personnel Records—New York)
Officer for Service: Dr. Philip Stiles (see above)
Long-term debt: None listed.
Short-term debt: None listed.
Financial report: Not available.
Facility: The company operates from a concrete building located in Osolo, Florida. Building estimated to be 234,000 square feet in size. Company-owned. No mortgages recorded.
Land: Company-owned. No mortgages recorded.
Property assessment: $2,377,330.
Property taxes: $67,000. Payable to Kilmer County. None outstanding.

Bank: First National Bank of Osolo. Company-owned.
The company also owns 585 single-family homes
having an assessed value of $120,000 each for a total
of $70,200,000, two 220-unit apartment buildings
with an assessed value of $11,499,000 each, and an
18-store shopping mall with assessed value of
$13,844,000. Company also owns one combined el-
ementary-high school. No assessed value. All property taxes paid to Kilmer County. No mortgages
indicated. Possibly held offshore.

Credit Rating: N/A

Suppliers:	High	Low	Terms	Payments	+30
A	6m	0	OD	AA	n/a
B	120m	0	OD	AA	n/a
C	37m	0	OD	AA	n/a

No credit rating is available as all suppliers payable
on delivery. Payment as agreed. Unusually high ex-
penditures are noted. No information supplied by
company. Supplier info is sequestered at supplier request. All buildings were constructed by offshore
contractors. No other information available.

*****End of report*****

Karen printed out a hard copy of the information,
studied the pages for a minute, and shook her head.
CRE was a huge company, but the way they did business was extraordinarily secretive. For a company of
this size to have no recorded debt whatsoever was unheard of. There was no mention of customers, just suppliers, as if everything was coming in and nothing
going out.

To be sure, CRE was a medical company, but even research companies had clients. CRE appeared to have
none. The number of company-owned dwellings indicated they provided single-family housing for at least

585 employees, and the assessed value of the houses indicated the residents were upper level management, probably scientists. The company-owned apartment buildings were probably for the service and clerical staff. In total, a staff of at least a thousand people, generating a cash flow of millions of dollars a week—without a penny of debt.

Unless the debt was all offshore.

As Griffin with his funny bow tie had said, it was highly suspect.

Tapping the keyboard again, Karen called up information under the personnel listings:

Stiles, Philip W., M.D.
236 Alpine Way ·
Osolo, Florida 32934
No phone listed in directory (including unlisted)
Born: August 11, 1949, New York
SS# 059-44-9483
Marital status: Married
Annual income: Unknown
Assets: Unknown
Liabilities: Unknown
Bio: Born in New York City. Father George, lawyer; mother Gladys, homemaker; no siblings. Graduated from Columbia with an M.A. Graduated Harvard Medical School with M.D. Interned at Bronx Community Hospital. Resident at Mount Sinai, Los Angeles, until hired by Consolidated Research Enterprises in 1989. CRE unincorporated at that time. Located in office in Manhattan. 374 West 59th Street. Moved to Florida upon completion of the Osolo facility.
Credit report: N/A. Subject has no credit cards or

charge accounts. Does not own car. Not listed in any mail order data base.
*****End of report*****

Schatt, Walter, M.S., Ph.D. (Biology)
Born: Berlin, Germany
Present address: 3773 Rue Grosbear, Paris, France
German National
Born: April 29, 1942, Berlin, Germany
Annual income: Unknown
Assets: Unknown
Liabilities: Unknown
Marital status: Single
Bio: Studied at Cape Town University, South Africa. Graduated with Master of Science. Received Doctorate in Biology 1978. Taught at Cape Town University 1978 to 1989. Hired by Consolidated Research Enterprises in 1992. Has resided in Paris since then. No records of ever entering the U.S. No other information.
*****End of report*****

Again Karen printed out the information, then accessed the records of B. H. Gollems, listed as the Chief Financial Officer for CRE. Gollems's records were as incomplete and obscure as the others. Gollems was shown to have been born in Paris in 1937, graduated with a Doctorate in Molecular Biology in 1967, taught at the University of Paris until he was hired by CRE in 1989. He lived at the same address as Schatt.

"Impossible," Karen said.

"What is?"

She jumped at the sound of Carl's voice. "What are you doing up at this hour?"

"You weren't in bed. I was worried about you."

"I'm fine—but this case is driving me crazy." she filled Carl in on what she'd learned from Dr. Griffin and showed him the data printouts.

"Impossible, isn't it?" she asked when he'd finished reading.

Carl looked thoughtful. "You know what this whole setup reminds me of?"

"What?"

"Remember the time your brother told us about CIA 'black projects,' set up around the country and operating right under people's noses without their knowledge?"

"I remember." With an ache in her heart, she recalled that particular conversation in the big, homey kitchen of Robert's Virginia house. As a U.S. senator, he'd been privy to a great deal of fascinating information, some of which he'd shared with her and Carl on their visits there. "But why would the CIA be interested in molecular biology and genetic engineering?"

Carl wrapped his arms around her, pulled her close, and kissed her forehead. "More likely CRE's operating some kind of elaborate tax dodge. But you can puzzle over this in the morning. Right now, you need your sleep."

The adrenaline that had kept her going ebbed. "You're the doctor."

With their arms around each other, they climbed the stairs to bed.

The following afternoon, Karen made no sound as she traversed the padded vinyl flooring of the Miami rehabilitation center. Martha Perry was unaware when Karen stepped into the room.

Karen paused in the doorway, taking in the antiseptic

whiteness of the room with only a faded beachscape on the wall as an attempt at cheerfulness. Her mother gazed out the window, her face, tight with fear and etched with pain, for once showing every one of her seventy-five years.

As if sensing someone was watching, Martha turned and flinched at the sight of her daughter, settling her mouth into its familiar disapproving grimace. "What the hell are you doing here?"

"Nice to see you, too, Mother." At one time, her mother's rebuff would have hurt, but Karen had long ago accepted that she would never win her mother's love or acceptance. Martha Perry thrived on dishing out rejection to her children. With her brother Robert now forever beyond the reach of her mother's vitriolic disposition, Karen bore the full brunt of her mother's disapproval.

As a child, Karen had longed for her mother's love, but Martha Perry, while providing her daughter with food, shelter, and clothing, had been unable to furnish the love and affirmation Karen had so desperately longed for. All her mother's energies had centered on developing her chain of Florida department stores. Fortunately, Martha had supplied a competent and loving nanny for Karen, the result of an indiscreet affair, and Robert, son of the alcoholic husband whose weakness had soured his wife for life. Her interest in her children sparked when they reached an age to participate in the family business, but when both chose the law instead, they earned their mother's undying animosity. From her mother's current attitude, Karen surmised that hostility was alive and well.

"You didn't answer my question," Martha snapped.

"Carl and Andrea are fine, in case you're interested."

"How did you know where I was?"

"The administrator called. They're releasing you."

The fear Karen had noted earlier flashed briefly in her mother's eyes. "But I'm not ready. I can't walk yet."

"You should have thought of that while you were tongue-lashing every person on the staff."

"Staff, huh." Martha's mouth puckered as if from a bad taste. "Bunch of blacks and spics. I won't have them touching me."

Karen bit back an angry reply. All her life she'd fought against her mother's prejudices, but Martha Perry clung to them like some cleave to faith. Nothing Karen said now would change her.

Martha narrowed her eyes. "Where are they taking me?"

Karen moved closer, slightly disconcerted by the alien experience of looking down on her tall and stately mother. In her three-inch heels, Karen was barely over five feet tall. "You have two choices. You can return home, or you can come back to Palm Harbor where Carl's arranged for your care."

"Palm Harbor! That's ridiculous. Who'll run the stores?"

Karen sighed. She and her brother had never been able to compete with their mother's first and only love. "Who's running them now?"

"I am. By phone."

"This may come as a shock, Mother, but we have telephones in Palm Harbor."

"I can't go traipsing halfway across the damned state. That's the stupidest thing I've ever heard, and you're a fool to suggest it."

"All right, then. There's an ambulance waiting outside. I'll just have them transport you home."

"But my bedroom's on the second floor. How will I get around? Who'll bring my meals, empty my bedpans? I know it won't be you, Miss High-and-Mighty Attorney. You'd never stoop to waiting on your mother. If you'd gone to work in the store, like I wanted you to—"

"You're right, it won't be me." Karen nipped that age-old complaint in the bud. "In addition to a housekeeper, you'll need a trained nurse and a therapist to help with your rehabilitation."

She knew she had her mother over a barrel. Martha lived alone, not so much out of choice as by virtue of alienating immediately everyone who'd ever worked for her. Only her store employees garnered any consideration or respect. Anyone else, Martha treated as she did her children, lower than dirt.

Martha folded her arms over her breasts and glared at her. "What's this place in Palm Harbor? Hell, it's probably the most expensive one you could find."

"You can afford it."

With Martha's fortune from her stores and her portion of the multimillion-dollar settlement of Robert's wrongful death, she was a millionaire several times over.

"And I suppose Carl will be getting a kickback?" Martha's grimace was evil.

Knowing her mother was purposely goading her, Karen held her temper. "The only kickback Carl will receive is the resentment of people who are doing him a favor if you treat the staff there as you have here."

"I suppose I have no choice." Martha curled her lips in defiance. "But I don't have to like it."

Karen sighed. She hadn't expected this confrontation to be easy, but she'd hoped for better. "No, Mother, you don't. You can add this to the mega-list of all the things you hate."

"Why, you ungrateful—"

"An attendant will be here in a few minutes to pack your things and prepare you for the trip."

Martha cocked an eyebrow. "Aren't you coming with me?"

Karen suppressed a shudder at the idea of a six-hour drive, cooped up in an ambulance with her mother. "I have a plane to catch."

"Of course," Martha said with a sneer, "you're in a hurry to get back to those rapists and murderers you consort with. It's a wonder I can hold up my head in polite society."

"On second thought," Karen said, knowing her threat was empty, "maybe I should have the ambulance take you home and leave you there alone."

"You'd do it, too," Martha screamed, "leave your own mother alone to rot while you splash yourself all over the headlines—"

Karen walked out and closed the door on her mother's tirade. Taking a deep breath, she headed for the entrance and the rental car that would take her to the airport. She issued up a silent prayer as she went, thanking God for Carl and Andrea, who more than made up for her mother.

After checking in with her office the following morning, Karen drove to downtown St. Petersburg. Her mother had arrived safely at Manor Care the previous evening and had managed to pass the night without causing a staff member's resignation. Karen sighed. Knowing her mother's temperament, it was only a matter of time.

She pulled into the parking lot of EMS headquarters. Upon her initial inquiry at the front desk, the receptionist called someone from public relations, and in a minute, Karen was ushered into the office of a black woman named Denise Walcott. Ms. Walcott had Karen's business card in her hand.

"Have a seat, Ms. Perry-Mondori," she said crisply. Then, smiling, she added, "This is the first time I've met such a famous defense attorney. You're something of a legend around here."

Karen returned the pleasant smile, shook her hand, and took a seat. "Thanks for seeing me. The job's not quite as exciting as it's depicted in the newspapers and on television. Mostly lots of detail work. Like this visit."

"How can I help you?"

"My client has been charged with the murder of Gerald Brock. I'm gathering information about the circumstances of Mr. Brock's death."

Ms. Walcott nodded. "I understand, but I'm not allowed to impart any information on our clients."

"Look," Karen said with a conciliatory smile, "I can get a court order if you want, but you could save us both a lot of time by letting me see Brock's file."

The woman sighed. "While these bureaucratic policies may seem like simple red tape, they do protect the people we serve."

"I see."

Ms. Walcott stared at her a second. "But . . . tell me about this case."

Karen nodded. "Brock was a homeless drunk for many years. He died in an alley of a heart attack, precipitated, according to the State, by a beating by my client. My client is a gentle old man who claims Brock was his friend."

"Did Brock die at the scene?"

"Yes."

"I don't understand why you need our records, then."

"I've learned that Brock fell ill another time six months ago and was transported by one of your ambulances to County Hospital. Would you have a record of that? That's all I'm asking. I'm not trying to make it tough on anyone."

The woman stared for another moment, then turned to her computer. "About six months ago?"

"It could be a month or two either way."

"And his full name?"

"Gerald Brock, no fixed address."

Ms. Walcott's fingers flew over the keyboard. In seconds, information filled her screen. "I have it. He was sixty-three. Is that the one?"

"That's him."

"He was transported to County Hospital on December tenth. He was semiconscious, intoxicated, and complaining of acute abdominal pain. Too young for Medicare and never registered for Medicaid. In spite of that, he was accepted by County, as is required under the law." She pointed to the screen. "I see we wrote off the ambulance charge."

"Was he admitted?"

"That wouldn't be in our records, but I do have the record of a transport two weeks ago if you need it. Mr. Brock was declared dead at the scene. Once again, we wrote off the charge. That's one reason people with insurance get charged two hundred dollars for a one-mile trip."

"Do you have a time on that December call?"

"Certainly. Two-thirty p.m."

Karen made a note. "Do you have a signature?"

"The receiving nurse was Mabel Cook."

"While you've got your computer humming, can you check a couple other names?"

The woman frowned. "What exactly are you looking for?"

Karen smiled. "As I said, Brock was a homeless drunk. He was never heard from after your people took him to County, not until six months later when he was found dead in that alley. About the same time Brock disappeared, two other homeless men vanished. I'm not sure there's a connection, but if there is, I want to follow it up. You can't blame me for being curious, especially if the answers to my questions might help clear my client."

Ms. Walcott hesitated. "I guess not, though I'm not supposed to be giving out that kind of information without some sort of authorization. I could get in serious trouble."

"I can appreciate that," Karen said with a consoling smile. "If the information you give me is needed in court, I promise I'll come back with the appropriate official requests."

Ms. Walcott turned back to her computer. "What were those names?"

"Albert Smith and Jack Bayless."

The woman entered the names and waited. "Yes, I have a record. Smith was taken to County in November. Three p.m. on the twenty-fourth. As for Jack Bayless, he was transported to County on the second of January. One-thirty p.m. I have nothing else on either patient."

Karen made a note of the information. "You've been a big help."

"Do you know what happened to these other two?"

"I'm not sure at this point. Neither Smith nor Bayless

has been seen since your service took them to County. Brock was, but not alive." Karen stood and held out her hand. "Thanks for being so cooperative."

Ms. Walcott's forehead wrinkled in concern. "I'd like to know."

"Know what?"

"What you find out. I find this troubling. If there's some sort of problem at County Hospital, I want to know about it."

Karen smiled. "How long have you been doing this kind of work?"

"Ten years. Why do you ask?"

"It's encouraging that you still care after ten years on the job, that's all. I'll be happy to keep you informed."

Karen left the EMS office, returned to her car, and pulled out her cell phone. Bill Castor answered on the third ring.

"Karen, are you okay?"

"I swear, if people don't stop coddling me, I'm going to scream."

"Sorry. I know you've been through tough times, and if I can't convince you to leave your husband and run away with me, I can still care whether you're all right."

She pictured the chagrined expression of her private investigator with his boyish grin and was instantly sorry she'd snapped at him. "I have the perfect cure for the blues."

"A new case?"

"It's a puzzler. I need you to snoop around for me without giving my connection away. If you'll meet me at The Pier for lunch, I'll fill you in on the details."

"I'm on my way."

Karen pulled out of the parking lot and headed for The Pier on St. Petersburg's Tampa Bay waterfront. She needed to know if Gerald Brock had somehow ended up at Consolidated Research Enterprises after checking into County Hospital. If anyone could dig out that information, it would be Bill Castor.

NINE

Martin Bradford could hardly eat his dinner. Grace and the kids, aware of his moods, left him alone for a while, but after the kids settled in front of the TV set in the den, Grace took his hand.

"I hope I didn't upset you by what I said last night."

He shook his head and proffered a weak smile. "I'm just a little down, that's all. Just tired."

She chewed on her lower lip for a moment. "I complained about everything, and I'd promised I wouldn't do that. I'm sorry. I meant to tell you this morning, but you were out of the house too fast."

"It's okay."

"No, it isn't. We've only just arrived, not even completely unpacked, and I'm complaining already. I hate doing that. Besides, it really isn't that bad here. I just miss Palo Alto. Give me a few days and I'll be fine."

"I know you will."

"Then . . . will you please cheer up? You look like the world has fallen around your ears."

"I'll be fine," he said. "Tough day, that's all."

"Can you talk about it?"

He gave her a fierce stare. "You know I can't."

"Because of what I said last night?"

"Because I can't talk about it, that's all."

She pouted. "It *is* because of last night. Does that mean you'll never discuss your work with me again? Because I asked you some questions about ethics, and it pissed you off?"

He slammed his hand on the table. Sudden anger contorted his face, his eyes flashed, and his body tensed.

"Grace," he yelled, "this has nothing to do with you, understand? If I fail to slaver over you twenty-four hours a day, it doesn't mean you've screwed up, committed some terrible deed, or otherwise pissed me off. It simply means I'm tired."

She stared at him in shock. He had never talked to her that way.

"Just let it be, will you?" he persisted.

Hurt, she refused to answer, rose, and quietly started clearing the table.

"I'm going out. Over to Tony's." He shoved to his feet, left the room, and let himself out the front door.

The humid night air enveloped him in its sticky, invisible cloak, and by the time he reached Tony's house a few blocks away, he'd worked up a sweat. He rang the doorbell at a walnut-stained front door almost identical to his own. Tony answered and waved Martin inside. Martin demurred.

"Let's just take a walk," he said without emotion.

Tony put his hands on his hips. "What the hell's the matter with you. You've been in a blue funk all day."

Martin gave him a hard stare. "Can we talk about it outside?"

Tony hesitated briefly, then turned and called to his wife that he'd be back in a few minutes. He stepped outside. Martin was already ten paces ahead, walking quickly in the twilight.

Tony caught up to him as they reached the street. "So, what's so important?"

"Just keep walking."

They walked to the far end of the complex, where the street ended in a fifteen-foot-high pile of dirt, with bits and pieces of lumber, cement blocks, empty paint barrels, and other assorted construction residue.

Martin finally stopped, turned, and faced Tony. His eyes blazed, his jaw thrust forward, and his hands formed fists. Without a word, he brought one fist up suddenly, striking Tony flush on the jaw. Tony dropped to the ground in a heap.

Martin was on him in a flash, clutching Tony's shirt, hauling him up, his angry face inches from Tony's.

"You bastard!" he yelled.

Tony, his eyes wide with surprise and fear, held up a hand to ward off further blows. "What in God's name is the matter with you?"

"Stand up!" Martin yelled.

Tony shook his head. "Why? So you can take another swing at me? No way. I'm a scientist, not a fighter. You want to tell me what's on your mind or not?"

He sat there, wiping a trickle of blood running down from the corner of his mouth.

Martin glared at him, then sighed. "Why didn't you tell me?"

"Tell you what?"

"That these assholes bug our homes, tap our phones, monitor every move we make."

"What the hell are you talking about?"

"You've been here a year. You must know what's going on. You sucked me into this job, Tony. I want to know why."

Tony shook his head. "You're crazy. Where the hell did you get this?"

Martin leaned over the fallen scientist and raised his fist. "Enough bullshit. I want answers. If I don't get them, I'll break your ugly head with my bare hands. I mean it. Start talking." Tony rubbed his jaw, then managed a weak smile. "You hit like a mule, Marty, you know that?"

Martin raised his fist again.

Tony put up his hand. "Hold it."

"Start talking."

Tony nodded, then got to his feet, both hands extended in supplication. "I don't know what brought this on, but you're way outta line. You must be paranoid. Jesus Christ! None of that stuff goes on around here. Why would it?"

Martin rolled his eyes skyward. "I know my house is bugged. You have to know as well. Don't try to deny it. Just tell me the truth. I'll deal with it. But if you keep lying to me—" He raised his fist.

"All right," Tony said softly.

Martin waited impatiently, opening and closing his fists.

Finally, Tony started talking. "I had no choice, Marty. They'd read some of your stuff in the journals. They knew we once worked together and came to me and said I had to get you down here. If I didn't, I'd be in deep shit. Besides, you were always complaining about your perpetual lack of money, so I figured I was doing you a favor. You have to admit the money's good."

"Forget the damn money," Martin yelled. "What goes on here? Who *are* these people?"

"Don't get excited," Tony pleaded. "You're doing what you always wanted to do, right? You have the best equipment, the best help, the opportunity you've continually dreamed about. Just keep your nose clean and you'll be fine."

"Just answer my questions!"

Tony rubbed his chin and sighed. "Okay, okay. It won't change anything, though. You have to learn to live with it. You signed a contract."

"The hell with the contract."

Tony laughed. "You think so? They can make it stick, my friend."

Martin shook his head. "I won't tolerate having people listening in on personal conversations. This is America, for God's sake. I don't have to take this."

"Yes, you do. You never heard it from me, but we now work for the U.S. Government. They funded this entire project, and they'll crush anyone who tries to mess with them. Believe me, others have tried and failed."

Martin staggered back a step, as if he'd been slapped in the face. "You can't be serious."

"Believe it, Marty. Two months ago, we had a guy try to make waves. He went to Tampa to some TV station and spilled his guts. It hit the national news . . . for all of five or six hours. Stiles invited the TV reporters and some syndicated columnists to come out and have a look for themselves. Stiles produced documented evidence that the disgruntled former employee was crazy, took the reporters on guided tour of the facility, and convinced them that we're strictly kosher. End of story, except the guy who talked is now in some kind of psycho ward. Don't know if he'll ever get out. They play for keeps, pal."

Martin shook his head in disbelief. "This is a nightmare."

"Call it what you want, but there's nothing you can do. If you try to leave, they'll come up with something to make it appear you broke your contract, enforce the contract, and you'll be flat broke. Try to talk, and they'll find a way to discredit you. No one will believe you."

"Why in God's name do they monitor our homes?" Martin's voice was now a plaintive whine.

"They want to keep tabs on everything you say, and the bugs they use are undetectable, the latest hi-tech stuff. You'll never prove it's being done. Besides, they only do it for a few months. Once they're sure you're with the program, they knock it off. I haven't been monitored for six months."

"How do you know?

"They said so."

"They said so?"

"After the initial indoctrination period, they bring you in, tell you everything that's been happening, and explain the reasons why. Then they tell you you're off the hook."

"And you believe that?"

Tony stared at him for a moment. "Yeah. What the hell, they don't have the manpower to do it constantly."

Martin shook his head in stunned amazement.

"Look," Tony said, "it's not as bad as you make out. As long as you keep your end of the bargain, they won't interfere. They don't really care much about your private life. They just don't want anyone talking about what we do, that's all. And in the beginning, they make sure you understand that. Makes sense, if you really look at it with an unbiased eye."

"Unbiased?"

"Right now you're bent out of shape about little things. You're clouding the bigger picture."

Martin could hardly believe what he was hearing. "You think bugging a man's home is okay?"

Tony shrugged. "You don't get it. It doesn't *matter* if

it's okay. It's what *is,* and there's nothing you can do about it. Don't ask me to hold your hand."

"But we're little better than slaves. That's what we are. We do as we're told or we lose everything. This is the twenty-first century, for God's sake."

"Yeah, it's the millennium, and from the moment we unlocked the secrets of human existence, nothing could be the same. That incredible power is too enormous to be entrusted to money-grubbing private companies or foreign countries who might try to use that power against us. We have to own the technology and protect against anyone else gaining access to it, perhaps for our very survival. Surely I don't have to explain to you what we have here."

"This is unreal," Martin muttered.

"Once you really accept the stakes, you'll accept the small invasions of privacy as necessary. You'll also accept the terrific pay and benefits, and you'll realize you're helping to make this country stronger than it ever was."

"Stronger, maybe, but not better, not like this."

"You've only been here a few days," Tony said soothingly. "Once they let you in on everything that's being done, which they will eventually, you'll see why it has to be this way. There's no other way to protect the knowledge."

"Others will discover what's been discovered here," Martin said. "They may take longer, but no one can stop progress."

Tony smiled. "We can't stop it, but we can sure as hell make sure we have it first. And once we've perfected the systems now being tested, we'll be decades ahead of anyone else. They'll never really catch up."

Martin stepped closer. "Perfected? You said perfected. You mean to tell me that these experiments are still fishing expeditions?"

"Some are, yes."

Martin grabbed Tony's arm. "I saw a man yesterday, an alcoholic. He was cured."

Tony's gaze dropped. "Temporarily. The problem we have right now is the side effects. For some reason, the change in the DNA sets up a chain reaction within the body which eventually destroys the immune system. We're working on it. We hope to have the kinks out in a couple of years or less."

"So this guy is . . . doomed?"

"He was *already* doomed. Without the procedures, he would last a few months, all of it in excruciating pain. This way, he has a few months of pain-free living, quality living, and then he dies of some infection in a matter of days."

"And you approve of that?"

Tony grimaced. "Dead is dead. So the guy dies of bacterial heart disease in a matter of days. Do you seriously propose that an agonizing death over a period of months is somehow more noble? Bullshit. Without these experiments, we'll never perfect the process. And we always pick people who have everything to gain and nothing to lose. So don't try to muddy the waters with some long speech about ethics. We're scientists, pal. We have a mission."

"Bacterial heart disease?"

"That's what kills them in the end. The effects on the immune system are almost like AIDS, except quicker. The immune system shuts down in a rush, and some bacterial infection attacks, usually the heart. When the infection hits, it's all over in days. Like I said, the subject is better off. That's why we use terminal cases in

117

our experiments, usually homeless people with nothing to lose. No matter what eventually happens to
them, they have a better life than they had."

Martin's jaw dropped. "You mean . . . they aren't
volunteers?"

"No."

Martin hung his head. His voice was barely a
whisper. "How many people have you used in these
experiments?"

"It really doesn't matter."

"How *many*?"

Tony stared at him. "Maybe sixty."

"Jesus!"

It was more a wail than an exclamation. Tony gazed
at the sky before speaking again. "We'll save millions of
lives by the time we're through. Can't you see that?"

Martin didn't answer. "None of this work has been
officially approved, has it?"

Tony laughed. "We're working for the government,
pal. Whose approval do we need?"

Martin stood silently, his face contorted in pain.

"Marty," Tony said, "if we try to work within the present constraints, we'll get nowhere. The Frogs will beat
us to it, and they intend to give the knowledge away.
That would blow every biotech firm in the country out
of the water. That's why the government set this up.
The answers are here. We just have to find them before
someone else does. Can't you understand how important this is?"

"You're saying the ends justifies the means. God!
That excuse has been used for every illegal and immoral act ever perpetrated by man. The government
said this would never happen again after the flap with
the human plutonium experiments." A chilling thought
struck him. "What the hell else are they up to here?"

Tony sighed. "What's the biggest problem facing this country today?"

Martin didn't answer.

"Don't tell me you haven't thought about it. You're the kind who worries about everything."

Martin sank onto the rubble pile and held his head in his hands. "I don't know."

"How about drug abuse? How about smoking? We lose 430,000 people a year because of smoking alone. We lose about 200 billion dollars a year in wasted resources because of drug and alcohol abuse. Half the AIDS cases are related to drug abuse. Half the auto accident fatalities are caused by alcohol abuse. Half the crime in this country is drug-related, not to mention illegitimate children, spousal abuse, you name it. We have a program here that can eventually stop all of that."

"What program?"

"Nothing very complicated. Samples from every blood test taken in the nation get sent here eventually. We even get tissue from the umbilical cords of every baby born. We use some of the teraflop computers to maintain a database. In a few years, we'll have cataloged sixty percent of the population. We'll be able to identify those who are susceptible to genetic diseases, those likely to become addicted, be it to drugs, booze, cigarettes, or whatever. The addiction genes aren't discriminating.

"By the time we have that information cataloged, we'll have found a way to alter the DNA in the addiction gene. Then we can treat people, put an end to addiction, and, with it, about seventy percent of the problems that exist in this country. And that's not all. We can eliminate a dozen childhood diseases, prevent the wrong people from having too many kids, thereby breaking the cycle of child abuse and other horrors, and eventually reshape this entire country."

"A brave new world." Martin's voice was bitter with irony.

"Think of it," Tony said, as if mistaking his comment for approval, "no more ghettos, no more crackheads, no more battered kids, no more crime in the streets. We can create a society that's the strongest and smartest in history. We can truly be the most powerful nation on earth."

Martin slowly shook his head. His eyes were misting as he balled his hands into fists, unclenched them, then made fists again. "This is as bad as the Nazis during World War II. The same kind of sick thinking. It's monstrous. We're supposed to be a nation of laws. CRE can't arbitrarily ignore all the laws and do whatever the hell they please."

"Yes, they can."

"Well, I can't."

"You damn well better, and in short order. There's no other way, pal. You either cooperate or face the consequences. And the consequences are much more unacceptable than the stuff you'll learn to live with. Trust me."

"Trust you?" Martin glared at him. "I did that once. Obviously, I made a big mistake."

He brought his fist back to strike Tony again, but as he did, he noticed the headlights of a car approaching at high speed. The car stopped twenty feet away. Two men got out and walked toward Martin and Tony. Both were tall and heavy, smartly dressed in suits and ties.

One jerked a thumb at Tony. "You got a problem here?"

"No," Tony said. "Everything's fine. We were just talking."

"Well, your wife's worried. She gave us a call. You better head on home."

Tony nodded and walked away without another word. Martin, still fuming, held his ground.

One of the men planted his large feet in front of Martin and placed his hands on his hips. "Dr. Bradford, right?"

"Who the hell are you?"

"Security."

Martin felt trapped in some never-ending, macabre bad dream. "Security? What happens now? I get put up against a wall and shot?"

The man laughed. "You're overreacting, Doctor."

"The hell I am. My house is bugged. You assholes know every move we make. It's some Kafka-esque nightmare made real."

The smile remained fixed on the security man's face. "You're just upset, Doctor, and not thinking clearly. You have to understand that we do have to protect our interests. There's stuff going on in this facility worth hundreds of billions of dollars. That's *billions*, Dr. Bradford. If one of our scientists decided to get greedy and sell some information to a competitor, he'd make enough money to live like a king for the rest of his life—except he'd never live long enough to enjoy it."

Martin shuddered. The man's threat wasn't even thinly veiled.

"This country has invested a fortune in genetic research," the man continued, "and the results of that investment will change all of medical science for eternity. At the moment, most of the information is unprotected by patent. If somebody got their hands on the knowledge we've gathered, all that money would be down the drain."

Martin scowled. "Are you saying money's what this is all about?"

"The security here is tighter than the Manhattan Project, and for good reason. The end result of the work going on here will have a greater impact on the world than the bomb did. You must realize that. The company has to take every possible step to insure that the information stays here. That's why the contract you signed is so tight."

"I understand the need for security," Martin said, "but you people have no right to do what you're doing."

"That may be true," the man said, his patience exhausted, "but we're gonna do it anyway. If you don't like it, you can take a hike. The only problem is, you'll be very poor. Or worse."

Martin moved his head from side to side in shock. His nightmare continued.

"Here's what we suggest," the man from security said softly. "Go home. Chill out. Then think about how much money you're earning. Think about the education your kids will get. You can take it from me, no one will bother you as long as you keep your big mouth shut about what goes on here. All the company wants is for you to keep your word. Is that too damn much to ask?"

Martin gazed at him, too stunned to speak.

"As long as you keep your word, you'll be left alone. You'll be part of the greatest adventure in science. You'll live well and retire rich. Your family will reap the rewards of your work, as will you. Think of the positives, not the negatives. Forget about the taps and the bugs and a whole lot of stuff that doesn't really matter. Concentrate on your work. You do that and you'll be fine."

The man started walking toward the car where his partner waited, then turned back to Martin. "On the other hand, you mess with us, you'll regret it. You, your wife, your kids. Understand?"

The pair drove off, leaving him sitting in the dirt, his heart pounding, his hands shaking, his mind a whirling cauldron of conflict.

What had he done?

Adrenaline was surging through his veins, but he felt exhausted. When he finally gathered the strength to return to the den of his own house, he flopped in a chair and held his head in his hands.

Grace was there immediately. "What did Tony say?"

Martin looked at her vacantly. "Tony?"

"You went to see him, didn't you? You said you couldn't talk about it, but from the way you look, something happened. Tell me."

He sighed. "There's nothing to tell. We just had a discussion about something that happened at work today."

"What something?"

"Nothing really. An argument about procedures. Nothing serious. We got it straightened out."

"Then why do you look like you've lost your best friend? Your face is white, your hands are shaking. What's going on?"

He stood up and walked to the small bar, poured himself a finger of Scotch, and downed it in one gulp. "There's nothing to worry about. Everything will be fine. But you have to do something for me, Grace."

"Yes?"

"I can't discuss my work, okay? So don't ask me. Ever again."

She went to him, put her arms around his waist, and

hugged him. "Something awful has happened. Why can't you discuss it with me?"

He put his arm around her shoulder. "You'll have to get used to this. I know it's tough, but you have to. This is the private sector, and these people are motivated by things other than simple knowledge. They have secrets, and those secrets are worth money. They do what they must to protect those secrets. And that's all I can say. Don't ask me to explain it again, okay?"

He wanted to cry, but he couldn't. It wasn't Grace he was concerned about. He was worried they'd hear him if he cried.

He refused to let the bastards hear him cry.

TEN

Two days after putting her private investigator on Herman Gaylord's case, Karen, working late and alone in her office, answered a call from security.

"There's a Bill Castor wants to see you," the guard said. "Okay if I send him up?"

"Sure, Frank, no problem."

A few minutes later, Bill bounded into her office, looking as fresh and boyish as ever, his eyes sparkling like a kid's at Christmas. "You're not going to believe what I've uncovered," he said with a satisfied grin.

"Try me." His enthusiasm was infectious, and she felt her exhaustion slipping away.

"Day before yesterday, I spoke with Dr. Iverson at County Hospital. Something rotten is going on there."

"Iverson admitted that?"

Bill shook his head. "I had to trick it out of him."

"How?"

"I posed as an aide to Senator Keith—"

"That's illegal—"

"Hear me out, and I think you'll agree this is one instance where the end justifies the means."

"Let me be the judge of that. What did you discover?"

"Iverson's a dour-looking man, short and thin, with

a pencil mustache almost an afterthought above his thick lips. He's bald, wears glasses, and dresses more like an undertaker than an administrator. And he was nervous as hell.

"I told him Senator Keith had received a complaint about the hospital and wanted me to talk to him personally before bringing in the FBI."

Karen's eyes widened. "The FBI—"

Bill held up a hand to interrupt. "Save your indignation for the end of the story. Then it won't be aimed at me. I told him one of the senator's closest personal friends and political supporters was a woman named Valencia Goldblatt, heir to the Goldblatt tobacco fortune, who lives in Naples and is a long-time friend of the Keith family. She's also a major contributor to the senator's electoral committee."

"Is she for real?"

Bill shook his head. "But Iverson didn't know that. I told him that, as happens in the best of families, there were some black sheep in the Goldblatt clan. In this case, a second cousin, Gerald Brock."

Karen groaned and shook her head. "You're really stretching credibility here."

"Iverson didn't think so. He bought the whole shtick. I told him it appeared that Gerald Brock was last seen alive in the emergency room of this hospital, drunk, sick, brought here by ambulance. After that, he disappeared for six months until he was found in an alley, allegedly beaten to death by another vagrant. My job, I told Iverson, was to determine what happened to Mr. Brock during those six months he was missing."

"And Iverson cooperated?"

"In a manner of speaking. He called in Dr. Samuel Eagleton, the ER physician on duty the day Brock was admitted. The arrogant son of a bitch insisted that Brock must have sobered up and left."

"There was no record of his treatment?" Karen asked.

"I pushed Eagleton hard on that. He said that many times they'll treat a patient, but the patient, feeling better, will leave before they can write up a report. There were three such patients, John Does, listed in the records for that day."

"Sounds reasonable enough."

"No way. These guys were too edgy. They were definitely hiding something. I accused them of exhibiting a pattern of unacceptable practices and threw the names of Smith and Bayless into the mix and gave him the dates EMS said they'd been admitted."

"Were they in the records?"

"Nope. Not a trace. But Dr. Eagleton and Nurse Mabel Cook were on duty that day, just like the day Gerald Brock was brought in. I threatened to have the FBI investigate unless Iverson could provide me with answers to what happened to those men. Iverson almost had a stroke."

"So he came through with answers?"

"He begged me to give him until today to find out. But when I went back to the hospital to meet with him again, he had two very large men in business suits and grim expressions waiting in his outer office. I smelled trouble and ducked out before they saw me, then waited in my car and watched the entrance. It was close to an hour and a half before the two men left the building, angry looks on their faces, got into a Chrysler, and drove off in a hurry."

"You followed them?"

"That's what you pay me for, isn't it?" he said with a grin. "I followed them discreetly all the way to the small town of Osolo and then to a fortresslike building about two miles from the town. They parked their car and entered the building. I drove back to my office then and fired up my computer. The car I followed is registered to Consolidated Research Enterprises of Osolo."

"So CRE and County Hospital are connected somehow, but none of this helps clear Herman Gaylord," Karen said with a sigh.

"There's more," Castor said. "I disguised myself as an older man and drove to Iverson's house late this afternoon. Iverson didn't recognize me from yesterday. He was too flustered after I identified myself as FBI."

Karen felt the blood leave her face. "You didn't."

"I told him Senator Keith had asked me to investigate the circumstances surrounding Gerald Brock's six-month disappearance. Iverson was sweating bullets, swearing calling in the Bureau was overreacting. Claimed he'd conducted a complete investigation, that Gerald Brock arrived at the hospital by ambulance, was given a cursory examination, and deemed to be in no danger. A simple case of indigestion. But before the emergency-room doctor could write up a report, Brock left the hospital."

"That's it?"

"He said he'd personally talked with three people who saw Brock leave minutes after he was examined."

"Why didn't anyone try to stop him?"

"He insisted they don't force people to accept treatment. He claimed the same situation for Smith and Bayless."

Karen shifted in her seat. "You're going around in circles, Bill, and getting us nowhere."

"It gets more interesting now. I told him Roger Davis had been scared off by the two men in his office. Iverson claimed the goons were distributors for a medical supplier. He almost passed out when I told him their car was registered to Consolidated Research Enterprises. Said I had to have been mistaken, that he'd have their names and the company they work for if I'd stop by his office tomorrow. Believe me, he couldn't get rid of me fast enough after that."

"You left?"

"Yup. And waited down the block while Iverson made a phone call. Then I went back and retrieved the tape recorder I'd used to tap his phone."

"You *what*? Karen leaped to her feet and eyed him with disbelief.

Bill slouched wearily but unconcerned in his chair. "We're not dealing with the good guys here. This whole setup stinks, but it's buried so deep, the only way to uncover it is to play by their rules."

She took a deep breath, sagged into her chair, and struggled for calm. Beyond the green expanse of glass that reflected the interior of her dimly lighted office, the twinkling lights of the city stretched toward Tampa Bay. Her straightforward, pro bono case was turning into a complex maze of dangerous twists and turns where she could lose her way—and more—if she didn't tread carefully.

"Wiretapping and impersonating a federal officer," she said with alarm. "You could go to jail and I could be disbarred."

Bill leaned forward. "You know the illegal stuff's not my style. You wouldn't have had me working for you all these years if it was. But this case is more than gaining Herman Gaylord's freedom. We may be looking at mass murder."

Karen propped her elbows on her desk and cradled her head in her hands. "Okay, tell me the rest."

ELEVEN

Bill Castor pulled a tiny tape player from his pocket, placed it on her desk, and pressed the PLAY button.

A man's voice answered the phone's ring. "Yes?"

"Stiles? It's Iverson. The fucking FBI was just here."

"The FBI? They came to the hospital?"

"No, they came to my home, dammit. Some agent came right to my house."

"What did he want?"

"He was checking the Brock thing."

"The FBI came to your home asking about Brock? Are you serious?"

"Absolutely. Makes no sense to me, either."

"What did the agent say?"

"He was trying to find out what happened to Brock. He says Senator Keith's flunky made a complaint to the senator. Can you believe that? He says the guy came to the hospital yesterday, saw your two people in my office, then called the senator. He says he thought they were waiting for him, for crissakes. It's crazy. This makes no sense at all."

Stiles's voice was calm. "Take it easy. You know how politicians think. Didn't you say all this started with some crazy bitch in Naples?"

"That's what Davis said."

"It's stupid enough to be true. Jesus. Just relax. Once the FBI makes their report, that will be the end of it."

"But he knew about your people."

"He knew?"

"That's what I'm trying to tell you. He said they were from Consolidated."

"How would he know that?"

"He checked the tag on their car. The guy's a regular detective."

"What did you tell him?"

"I told him he was mistaken. I said they were a couple of salesmen working for a medical equipment distributor. I said I couldn't remember their names."

"Good move. How did you leave it?"

"He's coming back in the morning. He wants their names and the name of the company. Jesus, I've never heard of such a flap over a goddamn drunk."

"Don't panic. What time is he coming to the hospital?"

"Tomorrow at ten."

There was another pause. "All right. I'll have them there, but this time, they'll have ID showing they work for a medical distributor. They'll handle it. Don't worry."

"What I don't understand is why the FBI would be involved. Don't these people have an 'A' list or something?"

"Listen . . . probably less than twenty people outside Consolidated know what's going on. We have to keep it that way. This Davis character must be trying to earn brownie points. You did fine. I'll set it up and talk to you in the morning."

"All right."

"If anybody wants to know anything before you hear from me, tell them you aren't talking until you consult your lawyer."

"I find this all very distressing."

"These things happen. We were unlucky that Brock was distantly related to some nut with influence. We'll take care of it. The senator is simply going through the motions for a valuable cash cow. Once he gets a credible report, the matter will die."

"I hope you're right."

The line went dead, and Bill shut off the machine.

Karen leaned back in her chair, breathing hard and thinking furiously. She remembered what Griffin at Gulf Coast Pharmaceuticals had said about Consolidated. From the sound of this conversation, it was much more sinister than even Dr. Griffin had imagined.

"But that's not all," Bill said.

"Please, don't tell me you've broken another law."

He shrugged. "While still in my FBI makeup, I paid a call on Mabel Cook."

"The admitting nurse at County?"

"Right. She refused to tell me anything, but implied that if I wanted to know what was going on, I should ask my superiors."

Karen blinked in surprise. "She implied this whole project is FBI?"

"Not necessarily. She said I'd have to go much higher than my immediate superiors. That means this CRE project could be under the auspices of any arm of the government, possibly even the military."

"They'll discover quickly the FBI agent is a fraud," Karen said with a worried frown, "and they'll come looking for you."

"Not to worry. I was so well disguised each time, no one would recognize me."

"You've put me in a hell of a spot. I can't condone your methods. If you break the law again, our business relationship is terminated, understand?"

Her ferocious attitude didn't daunt him. His youthful grin transposed to an expression of paternal concern. "You had to know, Karen. You're messing with the big guys. If you're not careful, they'll eat you alive. If they're killing people with their experiments, God knows what they'll resort to in order to keep it secret."

She was too exhausted to argue further. "Send me your bill. I'll let you know if I need anything more from you."

"Come on." He rose to his feet. "It's the middle of the night. I'll walk you to your car."

"I'm flying to Virginia tomorrow," Karen announced the next evening over dinner.

"Again?" Carl asked with more than a hint of pique. "You've spent more time in Virginia over the last two years than you have at home."

He hadn't bothered to hide the irritation in his voice, and it stung her with unaccustomed fierceness. They were having dinner at Mulberry Street, their favorite spot, a small Italian restaurant on U.S. 19 where they'd had their first date. It hadn't changed over the years. The food was still terrific, the atmosphere convivial, and the waiters remained as efficient as fighter pilots. Usually Karen and Carl sang along with the strolling guitarist, but not tonight. Neither was in the mood for song.

As they drank Ruffino and ate veal, she quietly told him all she'd learned about CRE.

"It looks like you were right," she said. "If this isn't one of those CIA black projects Robert described to us, it has to be something similar."

133

Carl's expression was grim. "If they're experimenting on human beings, their project flies in the face of medical ethics and everything I believe in . . . but I'm not willing to risk *you* in order to expose this. You have a responsibility to Herman Gaylord, Karen, but you haven't pledged to save the world."

"Someone has to expose what's going on there."

"But not you. Bill Castor's right. These guys are dangerous."

"All the more reason for me to go to Virginia and speak to Gordon Talmadge. He was Robert's friend, he knows me, and in his position as an assistant director of the CIA, maybe he can tell me what's going on—and offer me some protection."

Carl's dark eyes filled with pain. "We've never interfered in each other's work, but this is different. I'm begging you to drop this. I don't want to risk losing my wife, or have my daughter lose her mother."

"Suppose I do leave it alone?" A dull ache began at the back of her neck. "More people might die in experiments before someone speaks out. How could I live with that?"

He didn't answer. They finished their meal in silence, but the delicious cuisine had lost its flavor.

The Fort Lauderdale cop turned the body over on its back, pressed his fingers to the carotid artery, then shook his head. "No pulse. The body's stone cold. Probably been dead for hours."

His partner shrugged, walked back to the patrol car, and called the crime scene team.

They were near the Seventeenth Street Bridge, investigating a report called in by a passing boater. The caller had said he'd seen what he thought was a body under the bridge as the rising sun illuminated the skin of a single hand. By the time the police arrived, the entire body was bathed in light.

The man looked to be in his sixties, shabbily dressed, and smelling of alcohol. The policemen touched nothing, but set up crime scene yellow ribbons to mark the site, then waited.

The Crime Scene Unit van arrived, and three uniformed and one plainclothes cop examined the scene. Another detective interviewed the two cops who had discovered the body. Photographs were taken, the ground around the body checked, and more cops soon arrived to keep traffic moving as the morning rush hour approached. It would take hours to complete the task, but the detective in charge of the operation was already sure of his facts.

"No foul play," he told the cop who'd found the body. "Probably been dead six hours. The ME will be here soon. Then we'll know."

"Probably a heart attack or stroke," was the reply. "He was still clutching a bottle of cheap wine, but it was almost full. No blood anywhere. Gotta be natural causes."

The cop shook his head in puzzlement. "That's the third one this month. This one have any ID?"

"Nothing. Just like the others. It's like heart attacks have become contagious among the city's drunks. Weird."

"Jesse," the cop asked, "did you ever identify the other two?"

"Nope. Probably won't with this one either. Kinda sad, but what the hell, can't let it get to you. Too many other things to worry about."

The cop scratched his head. "Why here? We hassle the hell out of these people. They usually go all the way down to Miami. It seems odd we'd find three in a single month, don't you think?"

The detective scratched his nose. "Let me do the thinkin', okay? You got better things to do with your time."

TWELVE

Martin Bradford sat in the soft, leather-covered chair and stared at the woman with the lovely gray eyes. Marsha Ivey was also a doctor, a psychiatrist. About forty, she smiled often, a pleasant smile that seemed genuine rather than forced. Her voice was low and soothing, and as she spoke, her eyes twinkled with warmth.

The room, like all of the offices in this building, was windowless. Draperies covered one wall, an attempt to give some cheerfulness to the small room, subtly lighted and decorated in various tones of brown.

"Dr. Stiles has told me how upset you are," she said. "Under the circumstances, you have every right."

Martin lifted his eyebrows. "Really? The impression he gave me was just the opposite."

"That's why he asked me to talk with you." She had a becoming lilt to her voice. "The good doctor may be a genius in his field, but he isn't the most sensitive person around here. At any rate, you're here to talk about your problem, not his, and I'd like to address that directly. You feel you were hired under false pretenses, am I right?"

"That's certainly part of it."

She nodded. "And so you were. Perhaps, if I give you some background, you might be able to deal with your situation better."

"I don't think I'll ever be able to deal with it. The only reason I'm still here is because I'm trapped. I have no alternatives."

She continued to smile. "If you're worried that our conversation is being recorded, let me assure you that what goes on in this room stays in this room."

Martin laughed out loud.

Rather than being upset by the outburst, Dr. Ivey settled back in her chair and nodded again. "It's natural for you to feel as you do. You think you've been betrayed, and in some ways you have. At the same time, if you are given an opportunity to comprehend the circumstances under which you were hired, it may explain some things. May I proceed?"

Martin was unimpressed. "Do whatever you wish."

She considered him for a moment, then stood and stuffed her hands into the pockets of her tailored suit jacket.

"I don't have to tell you how momentous this research is. It's been your life for many years, so I won't insult your intelligence by giving you chapter and verse on that score. But there are some things you may not have considered, and I have a feeling that when you include them in the mix, you'll feel a lot better."

Martin gave her a vacant look.

"If you'd been told your every move would be monitored for the first few months of your employment here, would you have taken the job?"

"Of course not."

"Nor would any of the others. And if you look around, you'll notice that almost everyone working here has come to terms with the very special needs that

Crime in Store Limited
14 Bedford Street
London WC2E 9HE
TEL: 0207-379-3795
FAX 0207-379-8988
Reg. No. 03147051
VAT Reg 676009132

Wed Mar14-01 10:40am
Acct#SCOTTSU Inv#160406 CL:G

Title/ISBN	Qty	Price Disc	Total Tax
CLASS ACTION			
0340751657	1	5.99	5.99
Items	1 Total		5.99
	PmntOnAcct		7.99
	Switch		13.98

IF WE HAVEN'T GOT IT IN STOCK, WE
CAN ORDER IT FOR YOU!

attend this entire project. But had they been told the full circumstances of their initial days of employment, not one of them would have accepted the position. And where would that leave us?"

"You miss the point," Martin said earnestly. "This is America. If you don't trust professionals, you shouldn't hire them in the first place. To bring someone in under false pretenses, especially when they've signed a contract that makes them not much more than slaves, is unconscionable."

"Those are pretty strong words," she said with a smile and sank back into her chair.

"Not strong enough. It's illegal, wrong, dishonest, and immoral, and yet there's nothing any of us can do about it. If others have come to grips with that, so be it, but I sure as hell never will."

Again she smiled. "You haven't given me the opportunity to finish stating my point. We've simply agreed that had you been told everything, you would not have come here. Can we agree on that?"

"Yes."

"That in itself is but one reason you were not told. And while you find it unjustifiable, you can understand why you *weren't* told, can you not?"

"No."

She looked puzzled. "No? Didn't we just agree that you would not have accepted the position?"

"Yes, but—"

"We'll get to the 'but' in a minute, but for now, can we agree that not telling you is, while immoral, a legitimate business decision for someone charged with the responsibility of getting you here."

"It's wrong, any way you want to look at it."

She leaned toward him. "Is it really? Let's pretend you are a patriotic American working for the Pentagon.

You are given the awesome responsibility of starting up and heading a new enterprise that is more important than any project ever undertaken by your country, up to and including both World Wars. You are given intelligence that frightens you and makes success imperative, for failure could mean the very end of civilization. Would you still be concerned with ethics, or would you feel that success for the project requires unusual methods?"

This time it was Martin who smiled. "You've been watching too many movies." His smile dropped away. "You can't be serious. A moment ago you promised not to insult my intelligence."

"And I intend to keep that promise. Is it so hard for you to imagine the potential for evil that exists when dealing with genetic engineering?"

"No," he said, "but again, you seem unable to grasp the simplicity of the problem. Before I was hired, I was given a contract to sign. I signed it. I pledged not to discuss my work with—"

"And you broke your pledge."

Martin leaped to his feet, the last vestige of self-control gone, his rage spilling out like hot lava. "I discussed it with my wife," he screamed. "Big deal! You would never have known had you not bugged my bedroom, you fucking bunch of Nazis!"

Dr. Ivey stood to face him. "Exactly! We would never have *known*."

Martin glared at her for an instant, then threw up his hands in disgust. "Talking with you is like talking to a wall. You people are mindless, evil automatons." He sank back into his chair like a limp rag.

Dr. Ivey remained standing. She took a moment to compose herself. "Can't you see what really happened here, Dr. Bradford? You were new. We had to know if you could be trusted. How else could we find out? And you failed the test. As did at least half of our newcomers—at first. Let me repeat that. Half of our scientists who come here fail the first test."

Martin stood. "I want to leave. Now. I don't care anymore. I'll do the work, but I don't have to listen to this."

They glared at each other until Dr. Ivey's face broke into a another fatuous smile. She pointed to his chair. "You really do have to listen. Please sit down. We have a lot to discuss."

Reluctantly, he sat. So did his antagonist.

"I realize how difficult this is," she said softly. "I've been through it a hundred times. Your anger is understandable, and I empathize. At the same time, you came to work here for some legitimate reasons, and it is those reasons I'd like to address right now."

He tried to shut out her words, but it was impossible. She was smooth, her voice filled with sincerity, her entire demeanor the epitome of caring. As he listened to her verbalize his innermost hopes and dreams, he felt she was treating him as one might treat a recalcitrant child, reiterating the fact that he'd broken his pledge not to discuss his work with his wife, then proceeding to exonerate him for being human.

As she continued talking, he felt his anger begin to recede, for as much as he despised what had happened, as much as he resented being treated like a child, he found himself beginning to like this woman. She seemed genuinely interested in his welfare. Her silky, soft voice and pleasant manner were mesmerizing.

"So you see," she said, "it's absolutely vital that the scientists who work here go through something like boot camp. They have to be shown, not just told, how important it is that security be maintained. Listening in on your personal conversations is an affront to your dignity and an abuse of your rights as a citizen, but in the context of the project requirements, it's the only way we can introduce you to the cold reality of the stated need for unconditional adherence to the code of silence.

"In a military operation, certain rights are abrogated, and that is to be expected. This project, while it might not appear to be, *is* a military operation to a large degree. And until you actually became part of the project, it was impossible to impart that information."

Bewildered, Martin frowned at her. "A military operation? I don't understand."

"I know, but you will in due course. For the moment, I want to remain with the issue of security, our need to maintain it, and your quite reasonable outrage. Can you understand the method to our madness?"

"I've never questioned the need for security. I signed the damn contract, didn't I? At the same time, no matter how you dress it up with rationale, having my home bugged and my phone tapped, and God knows what else, is not something I can accept."

"I understand," she said. "You think that there should be some other way we can determine if someone has broken his contract."

"A person is supposed to be presumed innocent until proven guilty. Isn't that the way it works? Then, if a person has broken the rules, he pays the price."

"You find that acceptable?"

"Yes."

"Ah, but suppose the breach of contract is so serious the entire project is endangered. No matter how great the punishment, the damage has been done. The project is destroyed, and the entire country suffers. Isn't it better, from the standpoint of the nation as a whole, to insure that the contract isn't breached in the first place?"

Martin shook his head. "You keep talking about the country, about the military aspects, and a whole laundry list of—"

"Just answer the question. From the standpoint of protecting the integrity of this project, isn't it better to prevent a security breach *before* it happens?"

"Yes, but—"

"There you go with the 'but' again," she said, smiling. "You sound like a lawyer."

"And you sound like an inquisitor."

"Touché. I don't mean to be harsh, but your work here is very important. I'm sure you'll agree that a man chafing under the yoke of injustice is not able to do his best for himself or the team. Would you agree?"

He sighed. "Yes."

"Good. Then you can see why I'm trying to give you as many reasons as I can to make the anger disappear . . . for now, at least. There will come a time when you'll know much more about the work that goes on here and the need for such stringent security measures. At that time, many things will become clear to you. In the meantime, if you're to be productive and as happy as can reasonably be expected, you need a set of principles you can live with, and I'm trying to provide them."

He couldn't help it. He smiled at her. She was so relentlessly amiable.

Despite his earlier sense of outrage, he was in a much better frame of mind when he arrived home that evening. Grace, her face transmitting the now-constant worry, kissed him on the forehead and squeezed his arm. "I've got your dinner in the microwave."

"Where are the kids?"

"Over at Tony's. They wolfed down dinner and dashed off. Marie rented some new Disney video and they're all watching it. You look tired. You okay?"

He smiled. "I'm tired, but I feel more comfortable than I did this morning."

She sat on his lap and placed her arms around his neck. "The kids won't be back for an hour."

He couldn't help it. Knowing that every word was being overheard, he blushed.

Grace's eyes opened wide. "My God, Martin, after all this time, you can still blush at the thought of making love to your wife? I'm touched."

She stood, reached down, and started to unbuckle his belt. He stopped her.

"What's the matter?" she said. "I know you're tired, but if I wait until after dinner, it'll be too late. And I've been thinking about you all day." Her eyes mirrored the lust in her heart, a lust now tinged with the fear of rejection.

"I'm tired."

"Too tired?"

He avoided her gaze. "I'm sorry."

She walked to the microwave and turned it on. "Your dinner will be ready in five minutes. Do you want something to drink?"

He stood, crossed to the microwave, and switched it off. "Let's take a walk."

Confused, she let him take her hand and lead her out of the house into the street.

"Where are we going?" she asked.

"Just to the end of the street. You said the kids would be an hour. Leave the door unlocked if you like. Better yet, leave a note. This might take some time."

Her heart began to pound. Martin looked so serious,

so forlorn, so mysterious. What was he trying to tell her and why couldn't he discuss it in the house?

She dashed into the house, scribbled a note for the kids, attached it to the refrigerator door with a magnet, then joined Martin in the street in the windless, thickly humid night.

He said nothing until they reached the end of the complex, a jungle of sand and debris. He pointed to a concrete block. "Have a seat."

Grace sat.

He threw back his head and stared at the distant stars. "I've been trying to figure a way to break this to you without upsetting you, but there's no way. And I'm just not strong enough to keep it to myself. So, while I know this is going to be tough to accept, I have no choice."

She was stunned. Horrible images raced through her mind. Whatever it was, the secret he was about to confess was something terrible. She could see it in his face.

"This project," he said, "is more complicated than I ever dreamed."

His horrible secret was related to his work. Relief flooded her.

"You remember when I told you I can't discuss anything about the work?"

She couldn't speak. She nodded.

"This is going to sound crazy, but . . . there are some things CRE really wants to keep secret. And to make sure that happens, they put all the scientists through a kind of test at first, so everyone fully appreciates how important it is not to discuss the work—with anyone."

She was feeling better now that the terrible images had fled. "What kind of test?"

He dropped his chin to his chest and rubbed the toe

of his shoe along the sand. "I know this is going to be tough for you to accept."

Grace rose from the block, moved to him, and gripped his arms. "And you think because I once had a nervous breakdown, I can't handle it?"

He gave her a weak smile. "It's not that I think you can't handle it. I just hate to saddle you with unneeded stress. And this is a bit more than anyone needs."

"You're talking in circles." She was growing impatient. "Are you worried about this test?"

"It's not that simple."

She resumed her place on the rough concrete block.

He plunged ahead. "Our home is bugged, and our phone is tapped. They hear everything that goes on. They may even be able to hear us now. That's the test. That's how they make sure we don't discuss the work."

The sense of relief she'd felt moments earlier was replaced by a dreadful sensation of foreboding.

"There's more," he said. "They read our mail, both incoming and outgoing. Everything we do is monitored. And I'm not even allowed to leave Osolo without permission until I've been given clearance. You can, but I need a pass."

She simply stared at him.

"I know how awful it sounds, but the project is so important, they're forced to take these unusual measures. And once they're sure I can keep quiet, they'll loosen things up. It's only temporary, but I wanted you to understand how things are."

She finally got her mouth working. "Are you telling me they can hear us in our own bedroom?"

"I'm sorry."

She was on her feet. "And you're saying this is okay with you?"

"I'm saying we have to learn to live with it. Consolidated is a secret project being run by the government. A very important project. They have to protect it, no matter how it inconveniences the rest of us. If word gets out—"

"This is incredible." Grace shook her head in disbelief.

He took her in his arms. "I'm not supposed to be talking like this to you, but I had to. Don't let me down."

"Let you down? You're saying you can live with this?"

"I have to. We have to."

"Why? It's monstrous. Can't we just quit?"

"Is that what you really want?" he said.

"If you call Stanford right now, they might take you back." She pulled away from him and wrapped her arms around herself. "This is more than I can handle, Martin."

"I understand."

She looked at him with fear in her eyes. "If we go and you never discuss your work, they'll leave you alone, won't they? They can't enforce the contract if you don't divulge anything?"

"I'm not really sure."

She covered her face with her hands. "I can't live like this."

He reached for her again, drew her close, and whispered softly in her ear. "Give me a couple days. Maybe leaving is the best solution. But I need to convince Consolidated I won't break the contract. That will take a few days."

She pulled away and looked into his eyes. "You want to get away from this, too, don't you?"

"Yes."

"Then let's do it. Let's call Aaron. Maybe he can help us. Don't say anything to these people until you talk to Aaron. Okay?"

He didn't answer. He just held her close.

THIRTEEN

Karen's flight was late arriving at Washington's National Airport, due to heavy thunderstorms in the Tampa Bay area that delayed both incoming and outgoing flights.

She'd experienced some rough going of her own before leaving home. Carl remained indignant over her insistence on pursuing this investigation and putting herself in danger. For the first time in their marriage, he hadn't kissed her good-bye when she left.

Her heart ached at the memory of his handsome face, tight with anger, but she shoved aside her regrets and concentrated on her purpose. If she hurried, she could catch an early morning flight home tomorrow.

By the time she rented a car and drove to the Virginia suburb where Talmadge lived, it was almost eleven p.m. The trip was bittersweet, as she remembered driving the same route less than two years ago with Carl, her brother Robert, and his wife Claire. Now both Robert and Claire were dead.

She parked the car in the street fronting the triple-gabled stone house and saw lights glowing behind the drawn draperies. Gordon was expecting her and waiting up. She walked to the iron gate and pressed a button on the intercom.

A muffled male voice issued from the aluminum-covered speaker. "Yes?"

Karen looked up into the lens of a barely visible security camera. "Karen Perry-Mondori to see Mr. Talmadge."

"One moment, please."

The electronically controlled gate swung open, and Karen stepped through. As she neared the front door, she saw Gordon standing on the step, a cigar firmly planted in his clenched teeth, a wide grin on his jowly face.

"Karen, what a sight you are for these old eyes," he said as she approached. "I haven't seen you since a few days after Robert died. Terrible business, that. How are you?"

Karen reached the man, surrendered to his welcoming embrace, and kissed his weathered cheek. "I'm just fine, Gordon. And you?"

"Managing. What is this all about? When you called, I almost fell off my chair."

"I wanted to see you, and I have some questions you might be able to answer."

Gordon was only slightly taller than Karen and thick through the middle, a testament to years of little exercise and fatty food. His bald skull gleamed in the glow cast by the coach lights flanking the entrance of his grand house nestled among tall pines and cherry trees.

He'd been her brother's friend and more—a surrogate father, mentor, guru, and confidant. Now, with his career near its end, the lines of his face were softer than Karen remembered, perhaps a reflection of inner relief, a looking forward to the years ahead, time to be spent pursuing less stressful—and less controversial—interests.

"I'm flattered you've sought me out," he said.

Karen smiled with genuine affection at her brother's old friend. "I need your counsel."

"Indeed. Well, come in and have a drink. I have a bottle of Talisker I've been keeping for a special moment."

Karen followed him into a walnut-paneled room, Gordon's private home office, a room she had visited last with her brother beside her. It brought back memories, both pleasant and poignant.

Gordon poured the Scotch over ice, handed her a glass, then sank into a soft, leather-covered chair beside hers. He held his glass aloft. "To absent friends."

Karen knew he was referring to Robert. "To absent friends," she managed to utter past the lump in her throat.

"So what's this about needing my counsel? Kind of short notice, I must say."

"It was a spur-of-the-moment decision," Karen explained. "I hope I'm not keeping you up too late."

"That's not a problem. Sleep has always been hard to come by for me."

"I haven't been sleeping too well myself lately." She sipped the smoky-tasting whiskey, then set her glass on a low table beside her chair.

Gordon leaned forward. "You going to tell me what you're doing here in the shank of the evening, dropping in from out of the blue like some long-lost relative, me not having seen or heard from you in almost two years . . . or am I expected to toss out a few queries?"

Karen smiled. "You always did like to get to the heart of a matter. You haven't changed."

"More than you think," Gordon said sadly. "Had the prostate removed six months ago. Stage three, they said, but they got it out in time. At least, that's what they tell me. Another few months, and I'd have been looking death squarely in the eyes. Hell, who'd have guessed that both Robert and Claire would go before me?"

"How's Margaret?"

Gordon lit a cigar, drew a mouthful of smoke, and exhaled. "She's visiting her sister in Oregon. Another world-class chatterbox. The two of them make a great pair. So what's on your mind, Karen?"

Karen took a deep breath. "I'm representing a man accused of murder, a homeless vagrant who allegedly killed another transient. But there're unanswered questions about the victim's death that need clearing up. In my investigation, I think I've stumbled on what Robert once referred to as a 'black project.' I'm hoping you can confirm this for me."

Gordon's eyebrows shot up. "And if I can?"

"I don't know. If there's a reasonable explanation for what's happening, I can wash my hands of this line of investigation. If it turns out I'm treading on toes—"

"Don't waffle with me." Gordon's voice boomed in the high-ceilinged room. "Tread on toes? That's your specialty. You certainly were a thorn in Walter Stockman's side after Robert died. You like nothing better than to turn up rocks and expose what lies beneath. Were it not for your straight-shooting reputation for unimpeachable ethics, you'd have your own talk show on Court TV by now."

"Gordon—"

He held up a hand. "That's intended as a compliment. So, where is this suspected black project?"

"Florida. A company called Consolidated Research Enterprises. They're heavily involved in genetic research, and from what I can see, they're putting people's lives at risk. Is this the way our own government is supposed to operate?"

"Consolidated Research, you say?"

"Does the name ring a bell?"

Gordon shook his head. "Never heard of them. I doubt it's a black project at all. Most of those are in the Nevada desert, away from prying eyes. Florida, with unlimited access, would be last on my list of preferred sites. What makes you think it's a secret government project?"

Karen took another sip of the whiskey. "Things don't add up."

"What things?"

"My sources are confidential. I can't say right now."

A bemused smile graced the older man's lips. "I see. And what happens if I confirm your suspicions?"

Karen shrugged. "If they're not harming anyone, I'll drop it."

"Of course you will."

"I mean it. I'm too exhausted after my fight with Stockman to be tilting at windmills. When I began my investigation, I was under the impression Consolidated was some large private company, and that's a completely different deal. But if this is some secret government project, so be it. If I can still clear my client of murder, I'll bow out gracefully."

Gordon reached for the bottle of Talisker, poured himself another finger, and peered into Karen's eyes as if assessing, thinking, calculating.

"I don't know anything about Consolidated," he said, "but I'll ask around. If they're as obvious as you say, they can't be a big secret. But if it *is* what you think, you'll tell me everything you know. Deal?"

"I'll tell you everything I can without jeopardizing my client."

"Right. Where are you staying?"

"I don't know. I came directly from the airport."

"Stay here."

"I don't want to impose—"

"Nonsense. Our guest room is ready and waiting. And we have a new cook, one who can actually produce edible meals. Breakfast is at seven sharp. What do you say?"

She smiled. "I'll get my bag."

Breakfast was delicious: eggs Benedict with real Canadian bacon, fresh home-baked sweet rolls, and Kona coffee. Roughly two thousand cholesterol-laden calories to start the day, all of it gracefully served by a slightly built Peruvian woman of sixty who looked completely out of place in her starched uniform.

After she had cleared the table, Gordon put down his coffee cup and lit a cigar. "Can you believe it? I'm not allowed to smoke in my own office?"

Karen grinned. "The correlation between second-hand smoke—"

"Nonsense," Gordon bellowed. "Just the crazy rantings of a bunch of fanatics. This whole damn country is being run by fanatics from the right and the left. Nobody's in the middle anymore. Common sense is out the window. And the damn doctors are the worst of all."

"Don't tell me you're investigating the AMA?" Karen teased.

"One week you read that coffee's bad for you, then the next damn week it's *good* for you. The same with red meat and wine and any number of life's little pleasures. Reminds me of that old Woody Allen movie where the nebbish wakes up two hundred years later to find that all of the things he thought were bad for his health have now been proved beneficial."

Karen laughed. "Maybe you're upset with the medical community because of your surgery, but look on the bright side. They probably saved your life."

Gordon exhaled blue smoke and nodded. "Maybe. Speaking of the medical profession, what's so important about this Florida outfit?"

"I'm not sure. If what I'm hearing is correct, they're engaged in some pretty wild experiments involving human subjects. I suspect one of their experiments— not my client—killed the man whose murder he's been charged with."

"How do you figure that?"

"The victim's son insists his father, a long-time alcoholic, suffered from cirrhosis of the liver. He'd been checked a few years ago and given a limited life span. When he was found dead in an alley a few weeks ago with my client beside him, my client was accused of attacking him and precipitating a fatal heart attack. During the autopsy, the ME discovered his liver was in perfect condition. The victim's son thinks he was the subject of an experiment involving genetics."

Gordon's thick eyebrows rose. "How so?"

"According to the son, the only way his father's liver could have been treated would be to alter the man's DNA in some way, so that the cells could be instructed to renew themselves."

"Can they do that?" Gordon took another drag on his cigar.

"According to my information, which is sketchy at best, it's theoretically feasible, but the actual techniques are decades away."

"So you think this Consolidated outfit has found something ahead of its time?"

"That's one possible answer. It would explain a lot of things."

"And you think the government is involved?"

"Perhaps. In looking into this, I've learned that there's a pattern of men, usually homeless alcoholics, being transferred from a public hospital in St. Petersburg to Consolidated's facility in the town of Osolo, not far away."

"You're sure of this?"

"I'm sure. The victim in my current case is the only one ever seen again. The others are still missing. It doesn't take a rocket scientist to put two and two together."

"Their procedures must be pretty loose for you to have discovered this much."

"They are. There are people at the hospital who act as if this is some kind of secret government project."

"They talk openly?"

"Not exactly, but they're pretty sloppy if it's supposed to be hush-hush, and the company itself has a credit report that screams like a Klaxon."

"In what way?"

"No debt. No private company operates without debt, short or long term. Not one this size, anyway."

"And you found all this out in how many days?"

"A few."

Gordon shook his head in amazement. "You're good. I should have had you working for me and the CIA all these years. Okay, I'll check into it. If it's a secret project, I'll sound the alarm. Somebody needs their ass kicked if it's this haphazard."

"And somebody needs to let my client off the hook if Gerald Brock's death is due to something they've done."

He stood and grabbed his attaché case from the sideboard. "You stay put. Relax a little. Use the pool. I should have an answer for you by dinner tonight."

Karen thought of Carl, waiting at home, fuming. But

if she left now, the entire trip would have been wasted. "Sounds good to me."

She was sitting in the shade of a large magnolia beside the pool when two men stepped out of the house and approached her. They were young, barely thirty, dressed in suits and ties and looking very official.

One of them leaned toward her and flashed his credentials. "Mr. Talmadge would like to talk with you."

Karen lifted herself out of the lounge chair. "Where?"

"At his office. He said to tell you he has the information you're after. He'd like to tell you personally."

"Okay. I'll get my purse."

The agent nodded. "You're Karen Perry-Mondori, right?"

"Yes."

"The same Karen Perry-Mondori who defended Uccello, the Mafioso, and blew open the South Florida drug ring?"

Karen gave him a puzzled look. "Why do you ask?"

The man stuck out his hand. "I just want to shake your hand. They teach that case at Quantico."

Karen grasped his hand. "Really? They teach that case?"

"They sure do."

Karen smiled. "I'm flattered."

They drove her to Langley, took her through a security check, then up to the fifth floor to Gordon's office, where he waited with another man he introduced as Fred Gardner, an FBI assistant director. Karen suspected that an FBI man inside the CIA building meant that the project she'd inquired about was not only a black project, but a very important one.

In his late forties, Gardner was of average build and round-faced with thinning black hair swept back from

his expanding forehead. His eyes held the cold, penetrating gaze of the professional.

Gordon Talmadge, for his part, seemed rather embarrassed. Karen didn't need a road map to see where
things were heading, but she didn't hold the circumstances against Gordon. Her brother's friend, who was
once a consummate spymaster, had been reduced now
to not much more than a glorified clerk. He was
holding on for his pension, nothing more. Old loyalties
had long since ceased to exist, effusive gushings of kind
words to the contrary. Karen knew that, but she also
knew that Gordon would react to the questions Karen
posed. The answers were important enough to warrant
the risk.

"Thanks for coming," Gordon told her, getting as
near as possible to a smile. "If you have no objection,
we'll talk in one of the conference rooms."

"Fine with me," Karen said.

It was a small room, windowless, with drab green
walls, a thinning gray carpet, a square metal table, and
four plastic chairs. Light from two ceiling-mounted
fluorescent fixtures exposed the dreariness of the room.
Karen sat in one chair, Gordon in another, Gardner in
the third, and a female secretary took up the fourth, her
fingers poised over the small keyboard of a shorthand
machine.

"We want all of this on the record," Gardner explained.

"Okay."

Gordon began by saying, "You were off base, Karen.
Consolidated is not a black project."

"No?"

"No. But Mr. Gardner would like to know what you
know. It sounds like something the FBI should be
looking into."

"We'd like to know who the hell they are," Gardner

added. "It's not healthy to have foreign interests working on American soil without us knowing about them."

Karen looked at the man. "Maybe it's a black project anyway. Maybe they don't *want* you to know about it."

Gardner tensed. "I don't think that's the case. If it's a black project, I'd know about it, I can assure you."

"Okay."

"Fred wants you to fill him in on exactly what you know," Gordon said. "You don't mind?"

"I'll tell him what I can," Karen said calmly, although she was beginning to tense inside. "As long as it doesn't violate attorney-client privilege."

Gardner grunted, then nodded to the secretary. "First, tell me in your own words everything you told Mr. Talmadge last night."

Karen sighed, then related the story of Herman Gaylord, leaving out the names of Gerald Brock, Travis Weller, and Dr. Griffin at Gulf Coast Pharmaceuticals. She was finishing up when a young agent opened the door. An older man was with him.

Gardner was apoplectic. "I told you I didn't want to be disturbed," he screamed at the young agent.

The shocked agent's jaw dropped. "I was told you wanted to see Dr. Iverson as soon as he arrived. I was just—"

"Get out of here and take the doctor with you." Gardner looked ready to kill. "You wait in my office, hear?"

"Yessir."

The two men left. Karen leaned back in her chair and sighed.

Gordon looked embarrassed. "Well, so much for the cover story."

Karen suppressed a smile.

"I need the name of the alleged victim and the name of his son," Gardner said.

"The victim's name is a matter of public record. I won't reveal his son's name without his express permission."

"Look, you're in deep trouble, Ms. Perry-Mondori. You've had someone impersonating an FBI agent. That's a felony. So don't give me a hard time."

They'd moved quickly. Too quickly. But as sloppy as they were, there was a chance they didn't know everything. Karen tried to bluff through it. "I don't know what you're talking about."

"No? You never heard of an FBI agent by the name of Frank Jackson."

"No." Bill Castor hadn't told her the name he'd used, so her answer, if not totally accurate, was truthful.

"You're sure?"

"Positive."

"How about a man named Roger Davis? Iverson seems to think you must know him. True?"

Karen shook her head. "I can honestly say I've never heard of anyone named Roger Davis."

"This man was pretending to work for Senator Keith. That's another felony."

"Are you accusing *me* of posing as Frank Jackson and Roger Davis?" Karen asked. "Because if you are, maybe I should abandon my law practice and earn my living as a master of disguise."

Gardner scowled. "This isn't funny. We want to know the name of the victim's son and anything else you know, and that will be that. Except . . . we want you to forget everything you've learned about Consolidated Research Enterprises."

Karen's eyes flashed with anger. "Even if it means an innocent man is convicted of murder?"

"We could bring legal pressure on you," Gardner threatened.

"Suit yourself," Karen said. "Let's go to court. You tell the world why I'm being prosecuted, and I'll tell the world what I'm investigating."

Gardner smiled. "You *are* a hotshot. I've heard your name mentioned at the Bureau a lot. People think you're pretty bright. Well, I don't think you're so goddamn bright. In fact, you're pretty stupid if you think we can't settle your hash without the press getting wind of it."

Gordon finally reacted to Gardner's onslaught. "This is not the way to do this. Karen came to me on her own to bring this to our attention. She's made it quite clear she's not interested in making waves, so stop treating her like some criminal. I won't stand for it."

Gardner looked at Talmadge for a moment, then turned his back on the man without a word.

"I want the name of the victim's son," he repeated to Karen.

"Why is it so important to you? And why don't you look for this information through ordinary channels?"

Gardner sneered at her. "C'mon, Ms. Perry-Mondori. We need to impress upon you and the victim's son that this investigation should come to an immediate end."

"That would be a mistake," Karen said.

"Really? And why is that?"

"You'd be better served if you simply told me—and everyone else— the truth. Consolidated is well known to everyone in the genetic engineering field. Scientists throughout the world have already guessed what's going on. It's just a matter of time before they prove it. When that happens, you'll all look pretty stupid. But if you tell the world what you're up to, maybe you can make it sound logical." She shrugged. "For all I know, it *is* logical."

Gordon fought back a smile.

"We'll manage without your advice," Gardner said. "You told Mr. Talmadge that if he confirmed the fact that Consolidated is a government operation, you'd walk away from this. You also agreed to tell us everything you know. Are you prepared to stand by those statements?"

"I was. Now, I'm not so sure."

"Why not?"

"I don't like being pushed around. That's what you're doing, and I resent it. I came to Gordon with my arms open. I told him I didn't want to step on toes, and I meant it. But when you jerk me around like you're doing, you get me upset. When I'm upset, I'm reluctant to cooperate."

Gardner shook his head, almost in awe. "You're a real piece of work, Counselor."

"Not really. I just know how you operate, and I don't like it. I've told you everything I'm willing to share. I have a client to defend, and I'm not going to desert him to suit your agenda."

Gardner thought for a moment. "Okay, everyone out. I'll talk to Ms. Perry-Mondori alone."

Gordon and the secretary left the room. Gardner loosened his tie and sighed. "Well, you were right about one thing. They've been very sloppy down there at CRE. Here, too. God! At this rate we'll be a third world country before long. We just can't get it through people's heads that this country is still at risk. Why is that, do you think?"

Karen didn't answer. She simply waited.

Finally, after a full minute of silence, Gardner tried another weak smile. "I don't have any desire to make things tough for you. We just have to nip this leak in the bud. There are rumors floating around already. I have it on pretty good authority that the project is on the verge of being declassified very soon. Maybe that's why the people there are so blasé about it. In any case, my job is to keep the lid on until advised otherwise. I need your help."

Karen stared at him. "If you can provide me with a reasonable explanation for what happened to Gerald Brock, one that will clear my client, I'll drop any further investigation into CRE. That's all I can do."

"Fair enough. Give us a day, and we'll have a medical report ready. Just make sure that Travis Weller and Gulf Coast Pharmaceuticals back off as well."

Accustomed to courtroom surprises, Karen kept her expression calm at Gardner's revelation. He'd known all along who she'd been in contact with. His agents had been busy since Talmadge had spilled the beans this morning.

"If they don't back off," Gardner continued, "you—and whoever's been doing the digging for you—will be held responsible. And that's a promise."

At least they hadn't identified Bill Castor as the FBI impersonator, Karen thought with a suppressed shiver, but she'd underestimated Gardner, a terrible mistake.

She didn't like to make mistakes.

FOURTEEN

A few hours later, Karen and Gordon Talmadge sat by the swimming pool in the balmy Virginia summer night beneath a sky awash with stars and a full moon glowing with neon intensity. Carl hadn't been happy when she'd called to report she wouldn't be home until the next day, but she'd had no choice. She had to wait for Fred Gardner to release the information that would clear Herman Gaylord of Gerald Brock's murder.

"You have no idea." Gordon's voice was almost wistful. "I am too damn close to the slippery slope to screw things up with the company now. You keep insisting you understand what I'm saying, but I don't think you really do."

Karen sighed. "The man doth protest too much, methinks. What else can I say?"

Gordon looked away. "It'll happen to you. There comes a day you stare death right in the eye and you realize the only thing you give a damn about is staying alive. It all happens so *fast*. You wake up one day and you realize it's all behind you, everything you thought was important. All gone. You become consumed with living just one more day without screwing up."

"Who are you trying to convince? Me or you?" Karen

164

asked. "You seem to have forgotten I've stared death in the face. Hired killers burst into my home a few years ago, bent on killing me and my family. Unlike those who get an adrenaline rush from living on the edge, I don't enjoy it one bit. Nor do I let it destroy my life."

"It hasn't destroyed my life," Gordon said gruffly, unable to meet Karen's gaze.

"If all you care about is living one day at a time, I'd say it has."

"I'm trying to help you," Gordon said.

"How?"

"I'm trying to convince you to let this investigation go."

"You don't have to convince me," Karen insisted. "I told you from the first, all I want is to clear my client. I have no intention of making this a problem for anyone."

Gordon waved a hand. "Don't bullshit me, Karen. I know you too well. You come here and give me this dreck about how you're not interested in making waves, as if you actually expect me to buy that. You insult my intelligence. I might be hanging by a thread, but I haven't lost my smarts. You're just itching to make a big stink about Consolidated."

Karen shook her head. "If I were really interested in creating a stink, I never would have come to you in the first place. I fully expected you to do what you did, because Robert told me you always follow established procedures. You did what you had to do, so you can suspend the apologies. They aren't necessary."

"I'm not apologizing. I'm trying to get it through your thick, pretty head that this is serious stuff. They won't let you mess with them. Believe me."

Karen sipped her after-dinner liqueur, held it in her mouth for a moment, then let it slide smoothly down her throat. "Relax, Gordon. I'll fly home in the morning, give the police the report Fred Gardner's prepared for me, and that will be that. You'll see."

"But—"

"I'm sure your people will be on me like flies, and that's fine. They'll get bored after a few weeks. However, I really do appreciate your concern."

Gordon shook his head in exasperation, then settled back in the vinyl-covered chair. "They're not my people."

"Whatever."

Suddenly Gordon slammed down his glass and jumped to his feet. "I've done what I can, Karen. For God's sake, be careful. They'll know your every move, your every word. Don't risk your life for this."

Touched, Karen rose and lifted her hand to Gordon's weathered cheek. "Thanks for the warning. I'll be careful."

The following morning, after receiving Fred Gardner's report, Karen took a morning flight into Tampa International Airport. Recalling Gardner's insistence on her mollifying Travis Weller and Dr. Griffin at Gulf Coast Pharmaceuticals, she stopped at a pay phone and placed a call to Travis Weller.

"I just returned from Washington," she said.

"What did you find out?"

"It's a rather long report. I'll type it up and mail it to you. Then we can discuss it if you like."

"Can you give me some indication now?" He sounded upset.

"Sure, but it'll have to be the short version."

"Go ahead."

Karen recalled Fred Gardner's instructions. "Basically, here's what happened. Your father was taken to a

St. Petersburg hospital complaining of abdominal pain six months before he died. While there, he was asked if he would like to participate in a volunteer program involving alcoholics, run by a private company, Consolidated Research Enterprises. He agreed."

"He volunteered?"

"Right. According to the hospital doctor, he was frightened, afraid he might die. I'd guess the doctor reinforced that view. In any case, your father accepted the transfer to CRE. After six months of treatment, his kidneys, liver, and spleen were in fine shape. As you suspected, they were restored to health through some experimental procedures involving DNA manipulation."

"If he was so healthy, why'd he die?"

"The volunteer program is supposed to last two years, but once your father began to feel better, he wanted out. They tried to persuade him not to leave, but he insisted. After his release, he contracted a bacterial infection that caused a heart attack. I have supporting documentation that I'll include in my letter."

"That's it?" His voice was tinged with bitter disappointment.

"I'm afraid so."

"But . . . this sounds so radical. I mean, if they can do that—"

"As I said, the treatment is still experimental. Nothing is being made public at this time. My full report will explain everything."

"Okay," he said, but the tone of his voice contradicted him.

She placed a second call, this time to Bill Castor. "I've got a problem."

"What's up?"

"I can't shake the company I've been keeping. Any ideas?"

"Meet me." He gave her an address in Oldsmar. "Come straight from the airport. I'll take care of it."

Karen took a shuttle to the long-term parking lot and retrieved her BMW. She headed north from the airport along Dale Mabry, then cut west toward Race Track Road. Along a deserted stretch of roadway, lined with cypress forests and cow pastures, she pulled over, got out of the car, and waited to see if she'd been followed.

She reached into her pocket and extracted the note Gordon had palmed her as she left him. "Be careful," it read. "They're watching you, like ticks on a dog."

After ten minutes, satisfied she hadn't been followed, she drove slowly into the little town of Oldsmar and turned down a side street. Halfway down the block, Bill Castor leaned against the driver's door of his car, parked in front of a small bungalow.

"CIA?" he asked as she approached.

"I think so."

"How did you manage to get them on your tail?"

"It's a long story, one I'd like to make sure no one else is eavesdropping on."

"Then you've come to the right place."

He gestured for her to accompany him, and they walked to the front door. It opened before he could ring the bell. A woman stared at Bill for a moment, then laughed, her eyes lighting up like a Christmas tree.

"Bill Castor?" she screamed with delight.

"Madge Collins, meet Karen Perry-Mondori."

"Come on in. Oh, God. Jimmy will be so glad to see you."

Karen followed Bill inside and watched as he gave Madge a hug. It wasn't easy, for Madge must have weighed close to three hundred pounds. Her flaming red hair was piled on top of her head, held with rubber bands. She wore a loose-fitting flowered smock and smelled of lemon oil.

Madge waved a rubber-glove-clad hand. "I've been cleaning house. Once a year, whether it needs it or not. Jimmy's out in the garage as usual. Can I get you a beer?"

"No, thanks," Karen said, and Bill shook his head.

Madge's small white poodle came rushing forward, let out a few yips, and wrapped its front legs around Bill's calf. Its little body moved back and forth lasciviously.

"Fluffy!" Madge yelled and smacked the poodle on the rump. The poodle gave her a wounded look and wandered off sullenly.

"Horny dog," Madge said with a grin. "Just like Jimmy. You're a sight for sore eyes, Bill. How the hell are ya?"

"I'm fine," Bill said.

"You here on business or pleasure?"

"A little of both."

"Bullshit! It's business. I can tell by the look on your face. Well, you'd better get out there. It's great to see you, anyway. And to meet you, Ms. . . . ."

"Just call me Karen."

Karen followed Bill to the garage. A tall scarecrow of a man was bent over a workbench, his ears covered with padded headphones. Bill tapped him on the shoulder, and he turned around.

"Bill?" He ripped off the headphones and gave Bill a hug. "How the hell are you?"

Bill introduced Karen.

"You can guess Jimmy's specialty," Bill said with a wave that encompassed the assortment of electronic equipment that cluttered what had once been a two-car garage. Now it was a high-tech electronics lab. "Keeping busy, I see, Jimmy."

Jimmy nodded. "Every time the bad guys come up with something new, we have to reinvent the wheel. And this stuff is gettin' expensive. I did a job for a guy a week ago. Equipment alone cost thirty-five thousand, and in a year, it'll be damn near obsolete. Things are moving too fast these days. Hard to keep up. What brings you to Oldsmar?"

"I need a rush job," Bill said with a nod toward Karen. "Karen's my client. She's been bugged by the best."

The frown on Jimmy's face turned into a warm grin that accentuated the deep lines of his face. He was rail thin with small eyes that seemed to sink into his skull. To Karen's eyes, he looked seriously ill, but Bill didn't seem concerned, so she assumed that Jimmy always looked that way.

"Okay," Jimmy said to her, "what do you need?"

"I want you to check my luggage and everything in it for bugs. Also my car—and the clothes I'm wearing. I'm sure I'm bugged, and I've got a pretty good idea it's the latest stuff."

"You'll enjoy getting your hands on that," Bill said.

The smile left Jimmy's face. "The company?"

"Probably," Karen said. "If not, it's FBI."

"Do I get to keep what I find?"

Karen laughed. "I'll be glad to be rid of it."

Castor eyed his friend with concern. "If these bugs are as good as Karen thinks they are, the people who placed them will know we've been here. That could be a problem for you. It'll take time to find them, and longer than a few minutes here will be like taking out an ad in the *Times*. Say the word, and we're gone."

"The word?" Jimmy grinned. "The word is fuck 'em." He waved Karen toward the door. "Go inside and

170

strip off your clothes. Madge'll give you a robe. You hungry?"

Bill looked to Karen, and she shook her head.

"Not really," Bill said.

"Bull. We just ate, but Madge'll be happy to fix you something. Watch out for Fluffy, though."

"We met," Bill said. "He wants to get engaged."

Jimmy laughed. "The hell he does. That dog doesn't know the meaning of monogamy. He'll screw anything, moving or not, dead or alive."

Karen left Bill with Jimmy and went into the house.

"I need to get out of these clothes," she told the woman.

If Madge was surprised, she didn't show it. "First room on the left. There are several robes in the closet, mine and Jimmy's. Take your pick."

Karen entered the small bedroom, slipped out of her clothes and shoes. She removed a terry robe from the closet, belted it tightly around her waist, and rolled up the sleeves. She padded back into the living room. Bill was waiting.

Madge stood in the kitchen doorway. "Anybody hungry?"

Karen shook her head.

"No, thanks," Bill said.

"Bull," Madge said, running her gaze up and down Bill's lanky frame. "You could use some fattening up. I'll make you a sandwich. A BLT okay?"

Bill shook his head. "You guys are starting to talk alike. How long has it been?"

"Twenty-two years," Madge said with a happy grin. "Three kids, two dogs, three cats, and countless funny-looking fish. And I want you to know three of those years were pretty good. You two put your feet up while I go cook."

She disappeared into the kitchen. Karen settled into a worn recliner, and Bill sat on a sofa next to her.

"Jimmy and Madge are as comfortable as a pair of old shoes," he noted, "asking no questions, exuding warmth like a blast furnace."

"Have you known them long?"

He nodded. "Jimmy worked as a technician for the Agency for twenty years, took early retirement, and started his own business. He's the best electronics wizard in Central Florida and is making a fortune. Where he's stashing it, no one knows."

Karen glanced around the room, a mishmash of Kmart and secondhand furniture. "They live—frugally."

"Always have. This may look like the home of two slobs, but there's more unfeigned devotion and caring per square foot here than in any other home I've ever entered—with the single exception of my own when I was a kid. Coming here reminds me of that."

"Soup's on." Madge appeared again with a tray of sandwiches and soft drinks. The three watched a ball game on television while Jimmy worked in the garage.

He took three hours. When he finally called Karen and Bill into his work area, his eyes glowed like lasers. The electronics devices were arrayed on the workbench like fine jewels, all resting on a black satin cloth: two buttons, one from Karen's jacket, the other from her skirt; a small, black object about the size of a dime, and two cylindrical objects that looked like green pellets.

"The buttons have the shortest range," Jimmy said. "No more than three hundred yards. The black disc was stuck to the inside of your windshield, down below the sight line where the glass meets the firewall. It beams a weak signal to a satellite, if you can believe that. They know where you are within a hundred feet, anywhere in the world. As for the green ones, one was in the heel of your shoe, the other inside your laptop. They look the same, but they aren't."

He picked up one of the green bugs. "This is the one they put in your laptop. I figure they count on your taking it wherever you go. Has a range of fifty miles. The signal goes to a relay station and then to a satellite. Same deal as the black one. Oh, and by the way, they installed a virus on your hard drive. Would've wiped everything the fourth time you booted it."

"Cute," Bill said with a grimace.

Karen felt as if someone had knocked all the air from her lungs.

"And this"—Jimmy picked up the second green bug—"has a range of ten miles. They buried it in the heel of your shoe."

"Do any of these transmit voices?" Karen asked.

"No. Just a tracking signal."

"What's all this stuff worth?" Bill asked.

"About twenty thousand dollars. They're serious, Ms. Perry-Mondori. You must have pissed them off big-time."

"And they'll know I was here."

Jimmy waved a hand. "Don't worry about that. I've dealt with them before. I pretend not to have found them, and they pretend I'm telling the truth."

Bill laughed. "You like living on the edge, huh?"

"Yeah," Jimmy said with a grin. His expression sobered, and he turned to Karen. "There's one thing you should keep in mind. They may have something I could never find. The odds on that are fifty-fifty at best. Don't leave here thinking you're home free."

"I won't," Karen said. "Can you do a couple more rush jobs?"

"Say the word."

"First, I'll need you to sweep my house, then update

173

my security system. If they bugged my car while it was sitting at the airport, they probably did my house as well."

"Okay. I can do it immediately."

"Then," Karen continued, "I'll need you to check my office in Clearwater. I'll have to arrange this with my partners, but that won't take long."

Jimmy grinned. "For that, I'll have to get paid plenty. I'm stacked up, as you can see."

"Name your price."

"Okay, I'm ready when you are."

"Good. May I get dressed now?"

Karen used Jimmy's fax machine to send a long memorandum to a messenger service in Orlando. The message would be hand-delivered to Travis Weller. She knew he'd be confused, but she counted on the man's intelligence to override his bewilderment. Then, after thanking Madge and Jimmy and advising Bill that she'd be in touch, she headed for home. Jimmy followed.

"I expected you hours ago." Carl met her at the front door, his dark features ruddy with a mixture of anger and concern. He did a quick double take when Jimmy brushed past, tipped a battered Devil Rays cap, and disappeared into the living room. "Who the hell is that?"

"A friend of Bill Castor's. He's checking the house for bugs."

"We have insects?"

Karen shook her head. "Listening devices. The government *is* involved in CRE."

"I knew you should have dropped this—"

Karen felt her shoulders sag with weariness. "Please,

let's not discuss this until Jimmy's done his job. Where's Andrea?"

"At Tiffany's. She'll be home for dinner." He pivoted on his heel and marched toward the den at the end of the hall. With a sinking feeling in the pit of her stomach, Karen followed. She needed his support and advice, but she doubted he was prepared to give it in his present frame of mind.

He strode to the window and gazed out over the back lawn, hands clasped tightly behind his back. "Your mother's been kicked out of Manor Care. She slapped an orderly, among other things."

Karen went to him and slipped her arms around his waist. He stiffened at her touch. "I'm sorry. I should have been here. I'll take care of it."

"I already have."

"You've had her transferred?"

He turned toward her, his stern expression softening into almost a smile. "The old girl is in for a hell of a surprise."

"What have you done?"

"I had her moved to your nephews' house on Cobbs' Landing. They said it's okay. Since they're both away at school, she won't bother them."

"She can't stay there alone."

"Of course not. I engaged Larry Wilson to care for her."

Karen's eyes widened. "The nurse who looks like a young Rosie Grier?"

Carl nodded with satisfaction. "All six-foot-six, three hundred pounds of him. He'll live there with his wife Shanita as housekeeper."

"But they're black. After a few of Mother's insults, they'll both hit the road."

Carl shook his head. "I was there when your mother

175

met Larry. She threw every slur in the book at him—
and made up a few more."

"And he still agreed to stay?"

"Even better, he managed to take the old girl down a
few pegs."

Disbelieving, Karen sank into a chair. "How?"

"Gave as good as he got. Told her that, as a rule, he
didn't like skinny old honky women, but when she
talked dirty like that, made him want to dump Shanita
and run off with her. Especially since he'd heard she
had tons of money."

"Mother must have had apoplexy."

"It's the first time I've seen her speechless. His re-
fusal to be cowed raised Larry in her estimation. I think
they're going to get along fine."

"I hope you're right."

"Deep down, your mother's terrified. Never before
in her life has she had to rely on anyone but herself, so
she hates anyone who witnesses her dependence. Larry
makes a worthy opponent and somehow makes her
feel as if she's still in charge."

"You're a miracle worker."

His stern expression returned. "Drop this case,
Karen. You're in over your head, and I'm worried about
you."

She opened her mouth to protest, then closed it. She
was too tired to argue. She leaned back in her chair,
closed her eyes, and in a few minutes was asleep.

After two hours of work, Jimmy gave up his search.
Surprisingly, her house was clean, free of bugs or taps.
At least none that Jimmy could find.

"I'm not sure, but it could be they wanted you to find
the bugs I found earlier."

Karen shook her head. "I don't think so."

"Why not?"

"They probably figured they had me covered, what with the laptop and the car and my shoes."

Jimmy shook his head. "I wouldn't count on that."

"I won't."

"I'll update your security system. You should know if your line is tapped, but I can't guarantee it. Like I told you, this technology keeps getting better. I'll even provide you a beeper."

"A beeper?"

"No matter where you are, it signals you when the silent alarm goes off. That way, you know the cops are on the way."

"What good does that do?"

His kindly face softened. "Prevents you from walking into a bad deal, for one. Let's say you're out for a walk—or dinner. The beeper goes off. When you get back to your house, you let the cops know who you are right off. Saves you from getting your head shot off."

"I see your point," Karen said with a shudder, glad Carl wasn't hearing this. "Just do what you think is best."

She squared her shoulders and went in search of Carl to report that Jimmy had found the house clear of listening devices.

FIFTEEN

After dinner, Carl returned to the hospital for late rounds, and to throw any surveillance off her trail, Karen took a cab to the Pinellas County Jail to visit Herman Gaylord.

The old man's face lit up when he saw her, but as she related what she'd discovered about Gerald Brock, his treatments at CRE, and the involvement of the U.S. Government, his expression saddened.

"You shouldn't cause yourself so much trouble," he said.

"I won't let them prosecute you to cover their own mistakes," she insisted.

"You have the letter from the FBI, saying the experiments on Gerry precipitated his death. Can't you let it go at that?"

She shook her head. "With the letter and testimony from a witness that Gerry gave you the watch, the charge will be reduced from first-degree to involuntary manslaughter. You'll still do time if convicted."

"But continuing your line of inquiry might put you in serious danger," the man asserted. "I won't have that on my conscience."

"Are you dismissing me?"

His thick white eyebrows shot up in surprise. "No, I—"

"Good, because not only do I intend to set you free, Mr. Gaylord, I intend to stop CRE from performing dangerous 'experiments' on volunteers."

An hour later, almost midnight, Karen stood at the end of the fishing pier on Clearwater Beach. A stiff breeze blew onshore, bringing with it the smell of the gulf. As usual for this time of year, the breeze was cool, and Karen shivered, but it wasn't from the weather.

Earlier, she and Carl had had the worst fight of their marriage. At dinner, he'd demanded again that she abandon her investigation into CRE. She'd refused.

"How would you feel," she asked, glad that Andrea was having supper with Tiffany's family, "if I insisted you refuse to treat a certain patient?"

"This is different." He set his jaw in a stubborn line, and his dark eyes narrowed.

"No, it isn't." She reached out a hand and grasped his arm, but he pulled away. "This is my career. And more than that, if what I think is going on is true, it has to be stopped. I can't turn my back on it."

"You could be jeopardizing your life, our lives. My God, Karen, who knows what these people might do?"

She recognized his fear for her mixed with his anger, but she couldn't give in. She was frightened, too, but she made herself think of the terrified patients involuntarily used as guinea pigs by Consolidated and hardened her heart.

"I'm sorry, Carl. I have to do this."

He had turned his back and stomped off in anger to the hospital.

At the sound of approaching footsteps on the pier, she lifted her head to see Travis Weller and Dr. Griffin making their way toward her. Travis seemed to tower over the shorter man. Both were walking fast, almost running. When they reached her at the end of the pier, Griffin was gasping for air, but he was a game little guy. His eyes glowed with excitement behind his thick glasses.

"I must say, this is most exciting," he said, sucking in air. "When I got Mr. Weller's message, I thought it was a joke, but here your are, just where he said you'd be."

Travis's face, in contrast, was marked by confusion. His blue eyes fixed on Karen's. "We did as you asked, but I don't mind telling you, I'm at a loss to understand any of this."

Karen shook hands with both of them and pointed to a wooden bench about twenty feet away, one that would afford some privacy, since the pier was crowded with the usual glut of fishermen who frequented the place. With the rising tide came tomorrow's dinner for some.

"I'm sorry for all the cloak-and-dagger stuff and for dragging you all the way here," Karen said as they sat on the bench, "but it couldn't be helped. You followed my instructions?"

Travis nodded. "I took a cab to the airport, went through security, then down an elevator. Went to the rest room and changed clothes, then took another cab to Buena Vista, went in and out a few stores, changed clothes again, then drove to a rental agency and booked a car to drive here. Was all this *really* necessary?"

Karen didn't answer. "And you, Doctor?"

"I went through a similar routine."

"That's fine," Karen said. "I think you both did well."

"Why all the subterfuge?" Travis demanded.

"It's simple," Karen explained. "The phone call I made to you earlier was probably monitored. What I said was for their benefit."

"Who's they?" Travis and the doctor asked together.

"Later. Your suspicions, Travis, regarding your father's liver, are right. Its regeneration was the result of genetic therapy all right, except your father did not volunteer for anything."

She turned to the doctor. "As for you, your deduction that Consolidated Research is involved is right on target."

The two looked at each other, then at Karen. They both seemed instantly aware of the pertinence of her words.

"We have a serious problem," Karen said. "Consolidated is not a private company. It's what's known as a black project, which means it's a top-secret operation run by the U.S. Government, probably under the direction of the Pentagon. They don't want me nosing around. They want me to tell you both to forget all about it."

"They talked to you?" Travis asked, wide-eyed.

"They did."

"But how did they know you were investigating Consolidated?"

"I told them."

Travis jerked back as if his face had been slapped. "You what?"

"My late brother had introduced me to his friends in high places."

Travis shook his head in disbelief.

"When you, Travis, told me you believed your father had been the subject of an experiment, then you, Doctor, mentioned Consolidated's penchant for hiring scientists, I remembered my brother talking about black projects, but as I started looking into things, I dismissed the idea. Then, when the evidence started pointing in that direction again, I decided to go directly to the horse's mouth."

"What did you expect to accomplish that way?" Travis asked.

"I hoped I could determine if they were involved. If they weren't, we could let the government do the investigating. On the other hand, if they were running the show, it'd be better to know just who I was dealing with.

"They were very forthcoming. Too much so, in fact, which underscores what I'm about to suggest."

"Which is?" Travis asked.

"My advice is to forget the changes in Mr. Brock's DNA ever happened."

"Forget it?" Travis shouted.

"Exactly."

Dr. Griffin broke his silence. "What kind of advice is that?"

"Honest and logical," Karen said. "While I was in Washington, they hid electronic devices in various items of mine, which means they want to know every move I make. At the moment, they might think I'm still at home, but there's no guarantee of that. They could be watching us this very minute. Your homes and offices might be bugged, too. I realize this sounds paranoid, but it isn't."

"Holy shit," Travis muttered beneath his breath.

"If we call a halt to this now," Karen continued, "I doubt anything serious will happen. But if we don't, they're sure to become aware of an investigation, and they already know both of you are involved."

"You *told* them?" Travis's anger was palpable.

"They told *me* about you both, and it doesn't take a genius to figure out why. For one thing, I made inquiries regarding your father, Travis. The government must have figured who else would have an interest besides his son?"

"But how did they know about me?" Griffin asked breathlessly.

"You mentioned you made inquiries regarding former employees now working for Consolidated. I expect that information was forwarded to the appropriate people. When I became involved, they simply put two and two together."

Karen gazed at the night sky. "It's also possible we've all been monitored for some time, which would mean our previous conversations were overhead."

Travis and Dr. Griffin glanced around, concern clearly visible in their eyes.

"You'll never spot them," Karen said.

Griffin took a deep breath and exhaled. "Well, this is certainly one hell of a situation. One that makes me very angry. By what right has our government . . ." He let his words trail off.

Travis's face glowed with anger. "This is an outrage!"

"Maybe not," Karen said calmly. "As I understand it, the secrets of human genetics are being revealed— rather quickly, in fact. As with any secrets this important, there are those in the government who want to have the information first. If any group of scientists has discovered a new way to heal sick bodies, the ramifications are enormous. I don't think moral or legal considerations are even on the agenda when it comes down to who owns that information."

She looked at Griffin. "Consider this. Is it possible to develop some kind of weapon employing genetic engineering?"

"That's not our area of interest," Griffin said.

"I realize that. I'm asking if it's possible."

The doctor thought for a moment. "Absolutely."

Karen nodded. "You are probably both aware that enough chemical and bacteriological weapons are stored in this country—and others—to wipe out the human race fifteen times over. They're in storage because no one has as yet figured out a way to dispose of them safely. They may never be destroyed."

"I'm aware of that," Griffin acknowledged.

"What we have here," Karen said, "is another, newer, but equally dangerous concept. Obviously, there are those in government circles with the clout to free up billions of dollars to create a secret project that might essentially be a weapons project." She exhaled a deep sigh. "History continues to repeat itself.

"The bottom line is this. If you both drop this issue, you'll probably not suffer any consequences. However, if you decide to press your investigations, I sincerely believe you're placing yourselves in danger. My recommendation is that you forget you ever started looking into this."

Griffin looked shocked. "Do you really believe they would kill us?"

"I don't know," Karen said. "Their experiments have already killed God knows how many, so it *is* a possibility they wouldn't stop at more deaths."

Travis gave her a sour look. "So what you're saying is that you quit."

"That's not what I said at all. I said I recommend that you drop it."

Travis's eyes brightened. "Then you'll continue your investigation?"

"As an officer of the court, I'm provided a certain amount of protection by the law, but the two of you are more vulnerable. I sincerely believe you're placing yourselves in danger if you continue your inquiries. Is that what you want?"

"No," Travis said, "but neither do I want to live in a country bent on creating new and terrible weapons to be used against imagined enemies. This is monstrous!"

"I have no proof that Consolidated is creating weapons," Karen corrected him. "I'm simply speculating. And keep in mind that the enemies might not be imagined. If you examine history, you'll discover that human beings have always managed to create real enemies. It seems to be in our genes, for want of a better word."

"And if we allow some secret project to go unchecked," Griffin added, "our genes might well be changed forever, without our even knowing. We simply can't stand by and let that happen, can we?"

"We don't know what's going on here," Karen said. "The work Consolidated is doing could be totally benign. Just because I have a cynical bent, don't let my attitude influence you. And again, we're talking about power here. We have none and they have plenty. Our chances of success are very, very slim. It's really a risk not worth taking."

"What would you do if you keep investigating?" Travis asked.

"I would try to gather information that will stand up in court. Right now, I have nothing but your father's body, and that isn't nearly enough. We need much more physical evidence and plenty of witnessess."

"Suppose you are able to gather such evidence," Travis pressed, "what then?"

"I'd file a class action law suit," Karen said, "and go to the media. If they're satisfied that the evidence is strong enough, their coverage would force an inquiry, and things would start to come out into the open. That's the only way it can work."

"And how would you get the evidence?"

"I don't know. I'd have to study the problem. If nothing else, I could resort to highway billboards, asking for people with information on suspicious homeless deaths to come forward. That tactic has been used in other cases, but gathering evidence certainly won't be easy, more probably impossible. And as soon as the government realizes what I'm doing, all three of us are in serious trouble. I don't overstate the case, I assure you."

"They'd really do that?" the doctor asked again. "They'd actually kill us?"

Karen stared into his nearsighted eyes. "As I said, it's possible. That's why I want you to give this serious consideration before you make a decision."

"I'll do that," Griffin said.

"And consider this as well," Karen added. "It's also possible that the objective of this project is high-minded and completely ethical. If you or I successfully bring it out into the open, we might be doing something that will be enormously damaging to the country. Do either of you want to be painted with that brush?"

"Do we have to decide now?" Travis asked.

"Take as long as you want. But assume that your phones are tapped and your offices bugged. From this moment forward, imagine every word you utter is being recorded. It probably is."

"How do we contact you again?" Travis asked.

"You don't. And, Travis, one more thing."

"Yes?"

"Find another place to store your father's body. Someplace no one will ever find it."

"I've already moved it once."

"Do it again."

At that moment, the beeper clipped to the waist of her skirt sounded its chattering alarm of an unauthorized entry into her home.

At FBI headquarters in Washington, Fred Gardner sat behind a walnut desk, hung up the telephone, and glared at the man sitting across from him. "That was Orlando. They just finished talking to Jimmy Collins."

Gordon Talmadge leaned forward. "And?"

"He found the bugs. All five of them."

Talmadge looked stricken. "That doesn't mean anything. Karen's a careful and suspicious woman. It would be only natural for her to look for bugs. It doesn't mean she's going to continue her investigation."

"No? Then explain this to me. We can't find Weller or the doctor. The other bugs are still working, and according to tracking data, Ms. Perry-Mondori is still at home. Only she isn't. Her car's there all right, but she's gone. We just sent a man in there, and the woman's nowhere to be found. Our man triggered the security system, woke up the husband and au pair, and had to leave in a hurry, but he was there long enough to determine the lawyer has vanished."

"There must be a reasonable explanation—"

"Putting it all together," Gardner continued, "I'd guess she's meeting with Weller and Griffin, even as we speak."

Talmadge shook his head. "You're jumping to conclusions. You heard the telephone conversation she had with Weller. Exactly as we advised her. The rest means nothing. She has lots of friends, clients. She's probably visiting one of them. You can't jump to the conclusion that she's still investigating Consolidated."

Gardner scowled. "You're really too much, Talmadge. I can see why they put you out to pasture. We know she found the bugs. Why did she hire Collins to install a new security system in her home? Why can't we find Weller and Griffin? Is it conceivable her phone call to Weller was simply a ruse? Is it also possible you've allowed your friendship with Ms. Perry-Mondori to color your thinking?"

"I've never allowed personal considerations to influence my decisions," Talmadge said angrily. "You know that. When she came to me, my first thoughts were to protect the project. They still are. Save the insults. I was the best at this business when you were still in diapers.

"As for Karen, nothing you've said means she's decided to continue her investigation. Why the hell would she? What's her motivation? She doesn't need the money and she certainly doesn't need the aggravation. I think you should calm down. Wait a few days and see what happens."

Gardner pressed a button on his desk, then picked up the phone. "I'm not taking any chances, Talmadge."

"What are you doing?"

The door opened and two men entered the room. Gardner, his voice cold and flat, said, "Take Mr. Talmadge someplace he'll be more comfortable. I want him held incommunicado until I give you the word. I'll clear it with Langley."

The cab let Karen out two blocks from her house. She paid the driver an outrageous amount of money and asked him to wait, then started walking slowly toward her house. It was one of those wonderful, clear nights with the stars shining, the winds calm, and a welcome coolness in the dry air.

She was still three hundred feet from home when she saw the first, then a second car, the occupants hunched down in the seats, waiting. For her?

Probably. Fear started to build. Carl and Andrea were inside. Would these men harm them?

She made a left turn up a driveway, through the side yard of a neighbor's house. In minutes, she'd worked her way to a position immediately behind the first of the cars, a place where she couldn't be seen from the second. She waited.

It was five minutes before she heard a voice from inside the car.

"How long are we supposed to stay?" the voice asked. "I'm about to fall asleep."

"Have some coffee," a second voice said.

"Caffeine does nothing for me. I think I've developed an immunity to the damned stuff. We gonna stay here all night?"

"We stay until she shows. Just remember, do it before she opens the door. The local cops have already been here once when the security system was triggered. We don't want them back. We grab her, then get the hell out fast. So stay awake."

Karen moved away from the car and carefully retraced her steps back to the waiting cab. When the driver saw her approach, his mouth opened in a grin, anticipating another fat fee.

"I thought you was puttin' me on," he said.

"I'm afraid not," Karen said, climbing in.

"The old man's that mad at you, huh?"

"Seems so."

"Sorry to hear it. Where to?"

"Head for Tampa and stop at the first pay phone you see."

The cabbie put the car in gear. "All right, lady. You in a hurry, or what?"

"Yes," Karen said, fighting to hide the fear in her voice. She needed someone to help her, and, even more important, someone to warn Carl.

SIXTEEN

Ben Mulligan, dressed in faded blue cotton pajamas, fluffed up the goose-down pillows, one of the few indulgences he allowed himself, and leaned back against them with a sigh of satisfaction. He used the bedside remote control to turn on the television set. The eleven o'clock news was his sleeping pill. By the time the announcers waded through the truncated, two-minute roundup of world events, the litany of local violence, and finally the weather and sports, he was usually sound asleep.

Ben's wife, Susan, a veteran insomniac, would usually stay awake reading unless a late movie captured her fancy, giving Ben gentle shoves only when his snoring threatened to rip the roof off the house. When she finally approached sleep, she inserted soft earplugs to assure a few hours of blessed rest.

As resident agent in charge of the Tampa FBI office, taking over from Linda Holt, who'd accepted a promotion to the Washington headquarters, Ben Mulligan was considered an executive. As such, he enjoyed the premier perk of his well-earned status: the privilege of sleeping in his own bed almost every night. After over twenty years with the Bureau, it was probably the thing he appreciated most.

On this night, Susan, who had little interest in the news, was reading Scott Turow's latest novel. Reading was her passion, and she preferred the more literary popular writers, like Turow, Wolfe, and Morrison. Ben, after shuffling papers all day, found television more diverting. He was half listening to the news, his eyes already partly hooded by the seduction of sleep.

"FBI agents raided the home of an Oldsmar man this evening and found evidence they say links two people to Miami organized crime figures. While James and Madge Collins were arrested without incident, the FBI has also issued a warrant for the arrest of Karen Perry-Mondori, a Clearwater attorney with a national reputation."

Ben and Susan bolted upright in bed, their attention fixed on the television set.

"According to an FBI spokesman," the news anchor continued, "Perry-Mondori will be charged with racketeering in connection with Colombia's Cali cocaine cartel. She is accused of funneling hush money to defendants, relaying threats from the cartel chiefs, and preparing false affidavits to exonerate the Colombian bosses of the cartel. The Clearwater attorney made national news two years ago with her successful defense of Mafioso Angelo Uccello against cocaine trafficking charges. Now it appears Perry-Mondori has continued working for the cartel. Kind of sad, Toni."

"Yes, it is," the younger anchor with blond hair and old eyes said. "And in Lakeland, a man killed his wife—"

Ben switched off the TV and grabbed the phone. In seconds, he was talking to one of his assistants downtown.

"Hank," he bellowed, "when did that squeal on Karen Perry-Mondori come in?"

The man hesitated before answering. "About three hours ago."

"Why the hell didn't you call me?"

Again there was extended silence. "It's not our squeal. I thought about—"

"Never mind. Read me the goddamn thing."

Hank read the two-page faxed memo from Washington. The only good thing was the cautionary notice that Karen Perry-Mondori was to be arrested without physical violence if at all possible. That, at least, was some relief.

"What's been done about it?" Ben asked.

"We've sent some people out to Palm Harbor. So far, no sign of her. We've also got men at the airport, alerted FHP and the rest—the usual. Nothing so far. She was spotted in Oldsmar this afternoon. Her name came up when they grabbed Collins and his wife earlier this evening."

"They? Who's they? We never had Collins under surveillance."

"Orlando office was staking them out. The orders came from Washington. As far as I can tell, Orlando has been working on this for months. Nailed Collins with a load of U.S. Government electronics equipment. Had the numbers and everything. He said he bought them from Perry-Mondori."

"Bullshit!"

"Ben, take it easy. I'm just telling you what they told me. I know her husband's a friend of yours, and you know the policy on that. The duty order says you're not to be involved in this. They want everything handled by the Orlando office. We report directly to them."

"Is that why you didn't call me?"

"No, it's what's on the cover sheet, Ben."

"Read it."

"Why don't you wait until morning? It'll be on your desk."

"Just read it, Hank."

After some deliberation, Hank intoned in a flat monotone, " 'Attention RAIC Ben Mulligan. Pursuant to section thirty-six, subsection twelve, you are being advised that the outstanding warrant for the arrest of Karen Perry-Mondori is outside the personal purview of the RAIC. All matters regarding Case #38855-BB are to be reported directly to the RAIC Orlando. The RAIC Tampa is not part of the investigation team, nor will he participate in any way. The RAIC Tampa will contact Washington Assistant Director Gardner for further instructions.' "

"This came from Gardner personally?"

"Yes, sir."

Ben slammed down the phone. Susan gripped his arm. "Ben? It can't be true."

"It isn't."

"Then—"

"It's all a smoke screen." He shook his head. "Obviously, Karen is into something she shouldn't be."

"How do you know?"

"Karen came by the office several days ago. She said she had uncovered a matter she needed to discuss with me. I didn't have time to see her. I was up to my ears. Damn! She didn't seem to be in that much of a hurry. She said we'd talk when we all got together this weekend."

"That's right. She and Carl are coming for dinner Saturday night."

He shook his head. "Something must have happened. Gardner, always the consummate idiot, got nervous and hit the panic button. Stupid. If they'd simply turned it over to me—"

"What are you going to do?"

He shrugged. "I have no idea. Talking to Gardner is a waste of time. That asshole can't even draft a coherent memo. I can just see him licking his chops over this. Christ!"

The two went downstairs to the kitchen. All thoughts of sleep had fled. Ben sat at the table, hands tightly gripping a bottle of beer, his face a portrait of concern. Susan, long used to her husband's moods, simply sat with him, her soft hand resting on his, her gaze caressing the man she'd loved for eighteen years.

She knew all about the friendship between Ben and Carl Mondori, Karen's husband. It had started when Ben and Carl were college students, meeting in the center of a football practice field with a thud. Ben came away from the encounter with a broken nose, the evidence still visible today. He and Carl had become fast friends, even though their ways parted between law and med schools, but they had kept in touch over the years. Susan had first met Karen at Carl and Karen's wedding, and the couples had maintained a long-distance friendship for years, until Ben's latest assignment brought him to Tampa within an hour's drive of the Perry-Mondori home.

And now this. Karen Perry-Mondori a criminal? Impossible. Ben had always insisted she was the straightest arrow he'd ever met—especially for a defense attorney. But the Bureau was anything but frivolous. Their pursuit of Karen was real, and only those in Washington would know the *real* reason. And if Ben didn't find out soon what the real reason was, he would burst a blood vessel.

They sat for almost an hour, uttering hardly a word. And then the phone rang. Ben, startled, almost ripped it off the wall. "Mulligan."

"Did I dial the office by mistake?" a familiar female voice asked. "Susan usually answers the home phone."

Susan saw her husband's face almost explode with relief. He held out the phone so she could hear.

"Karen! What the hell's going on?"

"I know it's late, but—"

"Forget that. Just tell me what the hell's going on."

"Excuse me?" From the sound of Karen's voice, she was unaware of the warrant out for her arrest.

"Have you been listening to the news?" Ben asked.

"Why? What's happened?"

"First things first. Why did you call?"

"I need to talk to you. I'm in Hyde Park, at a pay phone. There are people staking out my house. I wondered if they were yours."

Ben's blood pressure soared twenty points. "They're FBI, all right, but not mine. They're from Orlando. This all came down from Washington. What the hell have you done?"

Karen hesitated. "Nothing. What was on the news?"

"Your picture. Also the fact that they're after your head."

"For what?"

"Racketeering, involvement with a Colombian cocaine cartel. Just for starters, I imagine."

There was another pause. "Well, I'll be damned."

"You sure as hell will be. What in God's name have you been doing?"

"It's complicated. Can we meet?"

"Where?"

"Where do you suggest?"

Ben thought for a moment. "Okay. Let's meet across from the place where we all last got together? You understand what I'm saying?"

"Yes."

"Don't drive your car. Every cop in the bay area is looking for you."

"I can't drive my car. It's at the house. Did they mention Jimmy Collins?"

"He was busted. Along with his wife."

He heard her swift intake of breath. "It's a setup, Ben."

He sighed. "I figured that. Remember where we're meeting. Can you make it in an hour?"

"I can make it. Please call Carl and tell him I'm all right and that I'll contact him as soon as I can."

"Will do."

"I'm sorry to drag you into this, Ben, but—"

"Don't sweat it. This is good for me. I've been behind a desk too damn long. I'll see you in an hour."

Ben hung up the phone. Susan was already preparing coffee and pulling the silver Thermos out from one of the cupboards.

Ben grinned at her. "God, you're good."

"I know."

He scratched his head. "You know, our phone might be bugged."

Susan whirled and stared at him. "You can't be serious?"

"Think about it. They know Carl and I are pals, that Karen's our friend, too. It'd be natural for Karen to call me, right? They might have been counting on it." His jaw set, he added, "You feel like taking a drive, dressed like me?"

She nodded. "If you think it will help. But what will you do?"

"I'll go out the back, down three blocks to the mini-market, and call a cab."

"I take it you're meeting across from that restaurant

on the Causeway, so I should head in the opposite direction, right?"

He grinned. "I've trained you well."

She looked at him in surprise. "I think you're actually enjoying this. You look like a little kid who just discovered the secret decoder ring in his Cracker Jacks."

His expression sobered. "I'm no kid, and this is no kid's game. Something's very wrong."

"I'm sorry. You look flushed. I thought it was from the excitement. But it's not, is it? It's rage."

He kissed her on the cheek. "It's rage, all right. And I've about had my fill of bullshit. After this crap with Karen is over—"

He left the sentence unfinished. There was no need to complete it. She knew what he meant. He'd often talked about giving up his job, taking early retirement, and moving to the mountains of Colorado. During the last two years, it was the thing he talked about most. He was still a young man, but in some ways, like many who'd seen too much, he was old beyond his years. They both knew that time was running out. The battle was being lost. It was time to bail out.

Ben met Karen in the parking lot of the boat ramp on the Courtney Campbell Causeway. He was sure he hadn't been followed. Karen was equally confident. Both arrived in cabs, and as the drivers waited patiently, Ben and Karen walked to a point where the seawall overlooked the dark waters of Old Tampa Bay.

"Tell me what's going on," Karen asked anxiously.

Ben told her everything he knew. "So tell me, what have you done to bring this down on yourself?"

Grim-faced, Karen gave him a quick synopsis of her activities over the past few days. When she finished, she added, "You haven't asked, but in case you have a mind to, the charges against me are all unfounded."

"I can see that. You told them you wouldn't get involved. What made them decide you changed your mind?"

Karen looked away. "When I talked to Weller and Griffin on the pier, I figured they'd think I was tucked in for the night. Obviously, they knew I wasn't there, which means they knew I'd found the bugs, which means they've assumed I'm doing exactly what I said I wouldn't do."

"Why didn't you keep the bugs with you?"

"I was concerned for Weller and Griffin. The feds already know who they are. I've been trying to convince Weller and the doctor to leave things alone. I would've been smarter to have them come to my house. That way, the conversation would have been monitored." She cast him a bleak smile in the pale light. "I'm not very good at this cloak-and-dagger business. My plan obviously backfired."

"What will you do now?"

"I don't know. The CIA and FBI apparently won't listen to reason. If they've gone this far, they're committed. That leaves me with only one option. I'll have to break this story wide open to save myself." She looked grim. "And that won't be easy."

"There's a better way," Ben said.

"What?"

"Let me intercede. I'll talk to them, tell them I've met with you and that you really want to let this drop."

Karen shook her head. "You do that, and you'll be in as much trouble as I am. The moment you tell them you've talked to me, your career is ashes."

"Maybe I can accept that," Ben said.

Karen looked at him. "Not this way, you can't. If you

leave the Bureau, you have to leave with a clean slate. Carl would never forgive me, otherwise. No, the best thing you can do is play by their rules."

"And just let you twist in the wind?"

"If you really want to help me, you can figure out a way to do it without sacrificing your career. For now, it's best that you keep your distance."

Ben jammed his hands in his pockets. "I don't think I can do that."

"You have to."

"No, I don't. My frustration with the Bureau has been building these past few months. I'm tired of living with policies I find difficult to support—especially when they jeopardize the wife of my best friend. This might be the best way to leave, with a scream instead of a whimper."

Karen shook her head. "Do you really believe you'll accomplish anything that way?"

Ben didn't answer.

"Exactly," Karen said softly. "If you really want to help, just be there for me in case of an emergency."

They both stared at the lights across the bay in silence.

"You really intend to bust this scheme with Consolidated wide open?" Ben finally asked.

"It's my only hope now of clearing myself. Otherwise, I could rot in a federal prison for the rest of my life."

"How do you intend to avoid arrest while you accomplish your exposé?"

She shook her head sadly. "Avoiding arrest is not the advice I usually give my clients. I don't even know how to begin."

Ben reached for her hand and smiled. "I have a plan."

SEVENTEEN

Karen slept restlessly for a few hours in a cheap motel in East Tampa. As the sun rose above Interstate 4, a knock sounded on her door. She opened it to Susan Mulligan.

"I don't think I was followed." Susan slipped inside, closed the door quickly, and placed a medium-sized carryall on a chair by the door. "I borrowed my neighbor's car."

Karen hugged her. "I'm so sorry to involve you in this—"

"Don't be ridiculous. What are friends for?" She delved into the carryall and pulled out a small, leather-bound folder. "Here's my passport. It should get you out of the country—"

"I can't do this."

"But you told Ben—"

"It's against the law to use someone else's passport, and I'm an officer of the court."

Susan grabbed her shoulders and stared into her eyes. "What they're doing to *you* isn't legal. The only way to protect yourself is to flee until you can reveal what's going on."

"The end justifies the means?" Karen asked with a tight smile.

"You're damn right." Susan gave her a small shake and released her. "If the government gets away with what they're trying to do to you, they make *all* our laws a joke. Somebody's got to stop them."

Karen sank onto the edge of the bed. "You're right. But doing this"—she waved the passport—"goes against my grain."

Susan reached into the bag and extracted a dark bottle. "We're close enough in height, weight, and eye color, but your brown hair will send up a red flag. You'll have to bleach it." She thrust the bottle of peroxide into Karen's hands.

Karen stared at it as if it might bite her.

"There's a change of clothes in the bag, some toilet items, and five thousand dollars in cash."

"How—?"

"Ben keeps an emergency stash at the house, in case of hurricanes."

"This is an *unnatural* disaster," Karen said with a grimace. "Did you talk to Carl?"

Susan's cheerful expression clouded. "I called him at the hospital from the neighbor's phone. We're afraid our line is tapped."

"What did he say?"

Susan squirmed and avoided meeting her gaze. "He's worried about you."

"He's angry." Karen's heart sank. Carl had begged her not to visit Gordon Talmadge, to drop the entire case, but she'd ignored his pleas. Now she was a fugitive from her own government, and only God knew when—or if—she'd see her husband and daughter again.

"He'll get over it," Susan said soothingly, "as soon as

you're home safe again. Here are the keys to my neighbor's car. Leave it in long-term parking at the Miami airport. "I've already made your flight reservations in my name."

"Can you trust your neighbors not to turn me in?"

"They're in Ontario now. Ben and I watch their house when they're away, so we have keys to everything. Don't worry. It's all taken care of." She reached for the phone directory. "I'll take a cab home."

A lump formed in Karen's throat. "How can I ever thank you?"

Susan shook her head. "You and Carl were there for us all through Ben Junior's illness. We'd never have made it through that time without you. If we can pull this off"—she smiled through her tears—"maybe we'll be even."

Karen settled in the tourist-class seat and fastened her seat belt. She'd almost lost her nerve at the boarding gate, but the attendant hadn't given her a second glance. She settled back in the seat and closed her eyes. Anger gave her the strength to go on. All her life, she'd played by the book, following the law to the letter, believing in its sanctity. Now the illegal actions of her own government had forced her to violate the very principles she lived by. She couldn't think of Carl and Andrea, of her clients and the practice, or she'd crumble. She had to concentrate on how she could expose the dubious activities of Consolidated Research Enterprises, not only to take the heat off herself, but to clear Herman Gaylord and save the lives of future "volunteers." By the time the plane touched down lightly on the tarmac at St. Thomas in the American Virgin Islands, she had the beginnings of her plan.

As she made her way down the jetway and into the

relatively new airport building, a portly man with a walrus mustache adorning his rather bug-eyed face held a sign that read "Mrs. Johnson."

She took a deep breath and turned toward Wally Bentworth, the contact Ben Mulligan had arranged.

"Mrs. Johnson," Bentworth boomed, "how good to see you again."

"And you, Mr. Bentworth." Karen forced a smile and shook the man's hand.

"You have a bag?"

"Just my carry-on."

"Splendid. My car's in the lot. Pity it's dark. You'll not be able to see the island as we make our way to my flat, but there'll be time for that, I'm sure."

As they walked through the airport and across the parking lot, Karen reviewed what Ben had told her of Wally, a British citizen. A former operative for MI5, he and Ben had represented their respective countries' interests on several cases, but Wally was now retired. Six months ago, he had decided to immigrate to the U.S., but the thought of total immersion in fast-paced American culture petrified him. He was a man used to living on islands. Moving to the American Virgin Islands seemed an ideal way to develop a relaxed acquaintanceship with semi-American society while still living on an island with a distinct culture of its own. As well, he was but a ferry ride from the British Virgin Islands of Tortola and Virgin Gorda, should he become homesick for Bermuda, his base of operations for most of his years with British Intelligence. While the two islands weren't nearly the same thing, they *were* British. It was enough.

"So," Karen said to make conversation, "I understand you're running into red tape with Immigration."

"It's amazing. I thought the British and the Russians

had the patent on bureaucratic nonsense, but you Yanks have learned your lessons bloody well. The latest word is that I might get a green card in about a year, provided my employers put in a good word."

"Ben said you're working as a consultant?"

"Precisely. I'm not allowed a license as an investigator, so I sit at the office and draw up bloody great reports on an ancient typewriter. My employers seem happy enough, thank God. I might make it to America at that, should I manage to live that long."

"And then?" She wasn't really interested, but conversation of any kind was better than dwelling on her worries about Carl and Andrea and what might happen to all of them if her plan didn't work as she hoped.

"After I get the green card, I have to wait five years before I can become a citizen. You do make it tough on us. Of course, if I were a film star or had the price, I'd be in in a snap. A million dollars gets their attention rather quickly."

"You're sure you want to become an American citizen?"

"Not precisely." Wally grinned. "But by the time I get through the red tape, I'll know. And speaking of nonsense, what's all this about your being involved in the cocaine business?"

They had reached the car. Wally started the short drive on narrow roads to his rented house on Raphune Hill Road, and Karen filled him in. By the time they reached his modest house, a concrete block affair with a tin roof, Karen had covered the matter completely.

They went inside. The house was small and spare, with little furniture and few amenities except a phone and a large TV set connected to a satellite dish.

"It's what made me take it," Wally explained. "Takes a year to get a phone here, but this house came with one. And that bloody great dish lets me pick up all the major television stations."

He placed Karen's carryall on a cot. "That's it, I'm afraid"—his kind eyes twinkled with mischief—"unless you want to share the bed with me. But I warn you, I snore."

"I'll pass," Karen said. "The cot will be fine."

"You look exhausted. Want to call it a night?"

"Sounds wonderful. We'll talk more in the morning."

After Wally went into the other room and closed the door, Karen removed the clothes she'd worn for the past two days, crawled between the soapy-smelling sheets, and fell asleep in seconds.

In the morning, Karen discovered the house had no shower, so she had to make do with a bath, then donned the fresh clothes Susan had provided in the carryall. Wally, a widower for many years, prepared a highly edible plate of crisp bacon, scrambled eggs, and grilled tomatoes. It wasn't what Karen would have preferred, but being the guest, she simply ate and enjoyed it.

Over coffee, Wally said, "I hope there's some way I can be of help. I know you came here to lay low, as they say, but from what you've told me, you'll be up and after these 'researchers' before too bloody long. I'd like to be a part of that. Too little excitement in my life since I retired, and I miss it."

He was basically a gentle man, but filled with purpose and a skilled investigator to boot. She needed help, and she didn't dare contact Bill Castor. They'd be watching him.

"Only if you get paid," Karen said.

"I can live with that."

Karen's expression sobered. "You have to realize this could be a very dangerous undertaking."

"Look around the place. It's not as though I'm risking much."

Karen's eyes narrowed. "That's a very negative attitude."

Wally waved a hand. "I don't mean it like that. I have no death wish, if that's what you're thinking. Far from it. At the same time, I feel myself atrophying as I bash away at that bloody typewriter day after day. A little excitement would serve as a tonic, I expect."

Karen's eyes softened. "To be candid, I don't know what to do at this point. I need time to think it through. But when I decide to make a move, I'd consider it a distinct honor if you'd work with me."

The man blushed with pleasure. "I'll get the car."

Wally dropped Karen off in town, then drove on to work. They planned to meet for lunch. Karen wandered through Charlotte Amalie's colorful but narrow streets and lanes, called gades, purchased a few more items of clothing, fought off the advances of a hundred barkers trying to drag her into various stores, and finally took a respite in the open-air Palm Restaurant, located in a lane called Palm Passage, where she was to meet Wally for lunch. She sipped coffee while she considered her options.

She'd been filled with anger and bravado when she'd told Ben she'd have to break Consolidated's scheme open. That had been the knee-jerk reaction of frustration, and she knew it. Ben probably did, too. But if not an attempt at exposing Consolidated, what could she do to clear herself of the FBI's phony charges?

Turning herself in would accomplish little. If the CIA had gone so far as to drag the FBI into a search for her, they were playing serious hardball. They'd probably back up the trumped-up charges with phony evidence,

Catherine Arnold

and despite her representation by some of the best lawyers in the business, Karen would languish in a federal jail until Consolidated's project was declassified. That could be soon. It could also be never.

What was left? Hiding out, separated from her family, abandoning her practice for years? She didn't like the thought. Enjoying solitude was one thing. Being driven to it quite another.

She was still mulling things over when she noticed a lovely woman doing slow, balletlike turns at the next table. She was obviously a model, showing off some fashions from a local boutique to a young, wide-eyed couple. Karen smiled inwardly. Once they saw the prices, their enthusiasm would quickly dim. Liquor, some jewelry, most perfumes, and cigarettes were lower priced in this duty-free port. Designer clothes were another matter.

The woman finished with the young couple, left them a business card, and moved to Karen's table just as Wally joined her. A pleasant smile on her face, the model did another slow turn.

"This is a pure silk dress by Escada," she said in almost perfect English, but the traces of a French accent were still distinguishable. "It's available at George's, just down the lane. We also handle Moschino and Sonia Rykiel. A fine selection. I hope you'll drop in while you're here in St. Thomas."

Wally leaned toward the model, who had focused her attention on Karen. "Michelle?"

"Wally Bentworth! *Mon Dieu!* What are you doing here?"

"Retired. But I haven't lost my touch. If you're a model, I'm Prince Charles."

Michelle flashed a smile at Karen and continued to

turn and twirl as if answering questions about the dress she modeled. "I'm on a job for *la Piscine*."

Karen watched in amazement as Michelle scribbled something on the back of a business card, dropped it beside Wally's coffee cup, then moved on.

Wally read the card, then shoved it across the table for Karen to see. "I think we may have found an ally."

"Call me tonight. 555-3774," the card said.

Wally and Karen took a cab that night at nine. Michelle's apartment was one of four in a converted house about two miles from the center of the city. Unlike his place, hers had a terrific view of the town now shimmering some three hundred feet below her picture window.

Michelle looked radiant. Her blond hair caressed her cheeks on its way to her shoulders, and her long-lashed blue eyes glowed with an odd combination of intensity and warmth. Even in blue jeans and an oversized sweatshirt, she drew Wally's attention.

"Small world," Wally said as he and Karen took seats on the sofa.

Michelle curled in a large wingbacked chair that faced them. "You can't imagine how astonished I was to see you, old friend," she said to Wally. Then she turned to Karen. "And you. Just last night I was reading the *New York Times* and there you were. A fugitive from justice. Except the hair color is different. Is what they're saying about you true?"

"It isn't," Karen said grimly.

"What, then? And how did Wally get involved in this?"

Wally shrugged. "You know how the Agency operates. Karen here has been nosing around in something she shouldn't. They'd like her to stop."

"And will you?" Michelle asked her.

"It's a little too late for that now."

The blonde leaned forward, an intense look on her face. "I don't get it. Why would they go to such ridiculous lengths?"

"It's a new age," Wally said with a sigh. "The old ways are gone forever. Now they waste no time on subtleties such as due process. They simply create scenarios to fit a particular need, then flex their muscles. The next step is anarchy, and it's not long in coming. This is just an unfortunate accident. Unfortunately, it's one Karen will have some trouble correcting."

Michelle clucked her tongue. "You sound depressed. That's not good, not like you at all. And you, Karen, look like you could use a drink."

Michelle got up slowly, uncoiled gracefully, padded off to the small kitchen, and returned with three glasses. Two held Scotch, the other, sparkling water. She served Wally the water.

"You remembered," he said with a grateful smile.

Karen took the proffered Scotch and Michelle resumed her seat. "You've probably guessed by now, if Wally hasn't told you, that he and I are in the same business. I've been here for three weeks now on the trail of a French businessman suspected of selling secrets to the Libyans. I think he's on the island, but that's all I know."

"What makes you think he's here?" Wally asked.

"We had a tip he was seen on a flight here from San Juan. Usually reliable source, as we like to say. We figure he'll show his face sometime. He's not the kind of man to stay cooped up for long. He likes women and he treats them well. Often, he'll take them on a shopping spree. That's why I'm working at George's. It carries the most expensive women's clothing in town. We know it's a long shot, but we're hoping he'll come to us, eventually."

"We?" Wally asked.

Michelle made a face. "I'm here with another agent. You wouldn't know him. He's new. It wouldn't do to have a woman working alone. You know the French."

Karen glanced around.

"He's staying at the hotel," Michelle said, grinning. "I give my all for France, but there are some limits. Besides, it looks better this way."

Wally laughed. "It may be a new era, but it's nice to see you haven't changed at all."

Karen made an effort to sit still while Wally and Michelle engaged in small talk. She was here to ask favors, so she'd wait her turn.

"I'd have thought you'd be married and settled down by now," Wally was saying.

Michelle shook her head. "I'm married to my work. I'm addicted to that, I'm afraid. Like you."

Wally shook his head. "I was never addicted. I walked away."

They sat silently for a moment, Wally grim-faced, Michelle with a wisp of a smile, and Karen, holding her breath, waiting for Wally to get to the point.

He finally did. "Perhaps we can help each other, Michelle. There are some people in Paris Karen would like checked out. In return, Karen and I'll give you a hand finding your man. It'll help her keep her mind off things while she's here."

"I'd appreciate the help," Michelle said sincerely. "My associate has the brains of a Spanish cow, and I have to give it up in another week. I hate to fail."

"I know," Wally said.

Michelle turned her smile on Karen. "As you Americans say, we have a deal."

She strode across the room to a small desk and extracted a paper that she handed to Wally. "Here's the man we seek."

"Ugly bloke," Wally said, looking at a photograph of the Frenchman.

Michelle nodded. "And very rich and very clever. Have you developed some contacts on the island that might help us find him?"

Wally grinned. "I've been lashed to a desk most of the time, but I've managed a few. He shouldn't be too hard to find. For one thing, he's white, and if he's rich, he's probably staying in one of the better homes. They all have servants, and servants do like to talk, as even the queen has found, to her royal displeasure."

"Can you keep your people out of it?" Karen asked Wally. "This isn't your normal investigation. I need the people connected to CRE in Paris checked out. Michelle needs a good reason to give her superiors for going after the information. That's where you come in."

"Okay," Wally said. "I'll call in tomorrow morning, tell them I'm ill, and get on it."

Wally and Karen stood to leave, and Michelle walked them to Wally's car. Before they drove away, the Frenchwoman leaned in the window and brushed a kiss on Wally's cheek. "Take care, old friend. And stay on that wagon. It's done you good."

Wally put the car in gear and pulled away. "I suppose you're wondering what that was all about."

"None of my business," Karen said.

"But you're curious?"

Karen shrugged. "I assume you used to drink."

Wally laughed loudly. "Drink? Hardly the word I'd use. British are the masters at understatement, but I don't think there's a word that accurately describes what I was doing."

Her host apparently wanted to talk, so Karen forced a question. "How long did it last, the heavy drinking?"

Wally shook his head. "Four years, sad to say."

"Did you ever have a medical examination?"

"Why do you ask?"

"I was wondering if you suffered any permanent damage to your liver, kidneys, that kind of thing."

Wally stared at the road, then nodded. "I was told I'm suffering from something they called a precursor to cirrhosis of the liver. They said it would correct itself over time if I stopped drinking. A year later, I did."

"Would you still show the symptoms?"

"I don't know."

Karen shook her head. "Forget it, bad idea, anyway. Too risky."

Wally grinned. "I'll see a doctor here. Maybe there are some tests they can do."

"No," Karen said quickly. "As I said, it was a bad idea."

"Not at all," Wally insisted. "It's a very practical idea. You'll need someone on the inside of Consolidated. Any fool can see that. What concerns you? The possibility that I'll have to drink to make it credible?"

"Not exactly, though that *is* a concern."

"What then?"

Karen hesitated. "As I explained earlier, they do experiments in there. They interfere with your DNA, and the information I have at the moment points to some serious problems. If you let them work on you, you'd probably be dead in six months. You'd have to find a way to get out before they started their procedures on you, and that place is a fortress."

"A formidable challenge," Wally said, smoothing his mustache with one hand while he maneuvered a curve with the other. "But the idea is not without merit. As for

213

the drinking, I don't think mine was caused by any genetic factor, as some have claimed. Mine was a case of force-feeding."

"It doesn't matter."

"I beg to differ."

Karen gave him a sharp look. "Right now, Wally, at this moment, would you like a drink?"

Wally flicked his gaze toward her, then returned his attention to the road. "I would, indeed. But it wouldn't be for long, would it?"

She'd developed an attachment to her amiable host. "Thirty seconds is too long."

"Well"—Wally turned into the drive of his rented house—"while you wrestle with your conscience, tomorrow morning I'll see if I can't find Mr. Ugly for our lovely French spy."

The following day, while Wally searched for Michelle's quarry, Karen, homesick for her husband and daughter, sat at Wally's small desk and alternated between working on her laptop and trying to figure out a way to extricate herself from what seemed a hopeless situation.

In truth, she was now a fugitive. Those presently looking for her were powerful, well equipped, and dedicated. It was her own stupid fault for revealing her hand to Gordon Talmadge, and while she was not one to wallow in self-pity, her spirits were dimmed by the realization that her position was tenuous. As well, if she was to extricate herself from this morass, she'd need help, and to bring others into this disaster would place them in harm's way.

She needed to clear her head. She donned the sandals she'd bought in town the day before and, head covered with a broad hat and eyes concealed by dark glasses, she walked the narrow lanes of the island. As her feet pounded the unpaved roads, the plan she'd formulated on the flight to St. Thomas began to re-form in her mind. It was risky at best, and it demanded the involvement of others.

By the time she'd returned to the house, she'd made her decision. She would ask for help, and she'd tell everyone about the dangers. They had the right to turn away. They also had the right to determine the course of their own lives. A woman who refused an offer of help, even when that help was needed was a fool. She'd been a fool too long.

Now, fueled by a building anger and a wrenching desire for Carl and Andrea, she prepared a draft of her plan. As she worked with pencil and paper, she saw a glimmer of hope. She picked up the phone.

Cynthia Green was now a senior staff reporter for the *Washington Globe*. Years ago, while still just another unheralded reporter, she had worked on the story involving Karen when she had represented Angelo Uccello and the resulting Senate hearings. Karen had found her to be an excellent reporter, careful with the facts, very bright, and very motivated. Cynthia was also discreet. But Karen hadn't talked with her in the intervening years and wondered if the years had changed her.

When she finally reached Cynthia's desk after several attempts, the reporter seemed annoyed—and rightly so.

"All right, Mrs. Crutchfield," Cynthia snapped, "my editor says you refuse to discuss this 'story' with anyone else. I haven't got all day, so let's hear it."

Karen's heart pounded. She was taking a terrible risk. "Cynthia, before I—"

"Ms. Green, if you don't mind."

Karen grinned. "Okay, Ms. Green. Before I tell my story, I'd like your word that you're not taping this conversation and that no one else is listening in."

Cynthia snorted. "I don't work that way."

"I have your word?"

"Yes, now get on with it."

"This is Karen Perry-Mondori."

There was silence for a full three seconds. "Karen," she said, the hard edge of her voice now gone, "is it really you?"

"The same, but let's keep this our secret for the moment."

"My God! What the hell is all this about you and the mob and cocaine? I couldn't believe it when it came over the wire."

"You shouldn't. It isn't true. Not a word of it."

Karen thought she detected a sigh of relief. "This sounds like the kind of crazy bullshit story the FBI would come up with."

"They had some help."

"Who?"

"CIA."

"You're really messing with the big boys."

"I've stumbled onto something the feds would rather I forget. It might be the biggest story of your life, but it might also be the most dangerous. I need your help, Cynthia, but I want you to know that getting involved could be fatal. And I don't overstate the danger."

Cynthia's voice dropped. "Fatal? I don't like the sound of that."

"I'm serious."

Cynthia hesitated a moment. "Where are you?"

"St. Thomas."

"Virgin Islands?"

"Right."

"Can I come see you?"

"I was hoping you would, but before you do, I need you to check on something."

"What?"

I want you to check the public records in several Florida counties, most of them in Central Florida. You're looking for the death certificates of homeless men who've died from pneumococcal endocarditis the last two or three years. It would be even better if you could check the entire state, but unless there's some database you can hack into, we haven't got the time."

"What's this got to do with the present problem?" Cynthia asked.

"Everything."

"Okay. This may take a couple of days. Where can I find you in St. Thomas?"

Karen trusted her, so she gave Wally's phone number. "You understand, if you reveal my whereabouts, I'm cooked."

"I understand. I'd kill for a good story right now. Must be getting old. The kids in this business are beating me to the punch."

"If this works out," Karen said softly, "you'll leave them in the dust."

After dinner with a dejected Wally, who was getting nowhere in his quest for information, Karen dialed the number of Ben Mulligan's neighbor. Ben picked it up on the second ring. "Yes?"

"Ben? Is this line still safe?"

"So far. How's Wally?"

"A blessing. Thanks for putting me in his care."

"Carl sends his love. This is tearing him apart."

Karen closed her eyes in pain. "Andrea?"

"She doesn't know about the warrant. She thinks you're away on business."

"Thank God. What's happening? I've been watching the news here and there hasn't been a word."

"There's been a total news blackout. After the first announcement, they put a lid on. And that's the good news."

"The bad?"

"They brought in DEA. They've filed papers with the court swearing they found three kilos of cocaine in your office safe."

Karen shook her head. "They didn't learn anything from the Uccello fiasco, did they?"

"It gets worse. They say they had probable cause, something about your Oldsmar pal engaged in illegal activities at your place. Bullshit, I know, but it worked. Then, using county jurisdictional statutes, they invoked seizure under the forfeiture rule. They've taken everything—your house, your car, and your bank account."

Karen sat before her knees buckled. "Carl and Andrea—?"

"They've moved into your nephews' house on the lake until all this is sorted out."

Karen suppressed a moan. Carl and Andrea forced to live in the same house as her mother? Carl would never forgive her.

"Brander," Ben continued, "and your other partners are throwing everything they can at the problem."

"But why is the government doing this to me?"

"They want to shut you down totally."

Rage glowed in Karen like a blast furnace. It was all she could do to keep from screaming. "Can they make this stick? The Supreme Court rulings, especially after *U.S.* v. *Bajakajian* where they set aside a forfeiture for

218

the first time as unconstitutional, were supposed to stop all this stuff."

"By and large they did, according to your partner Brander, but there's a small loophole called—"

"I know. 'Special Circumstances Involving National Security.' I qualify. They don't have to hold a hearing in my case. At least they can't dispose of what they've confiscated for a few months, but if I don't clear this up, everything's gone forever and there's not much I can do about it."

"I'm sorry, Karen. They're playing hardball. What can I say?"

It was a terrible blow, but worst was knowing that Carl must blame her for losing everything they'd worked so hard to build together.

"They came to me," Ben continued, "and asked if we'd talked. Naturally, I said no. They said that if you do contact me, they want me to talk some sense into you. Maybe they're right."

"No," Karen yelled.

"Listen for a minute. Let me be an intermediary. Let me talk to them. I get the feeling all they want is to talk with you and straighten this out."

"Really?" Her voice dripped with sarcasm. "You actually believe that?"

"I have to. They've sunk as low as they can. I can't believe they'll sink any lower. What, do you think they're gonna kill everyone who ever talked to you? That's crazy."

"Now you're starting to get the idea, Ben."

"I don't believe it. Besides, what the hell else can you do? You can't take on the entire U.S. Government, for Christ's sake. You'll have to stay in hiding the rest of your life."

"I can't take the chance on coming in. Do they know we met?"

"I don't know for sure, but I don't think so. I know my house wasn't bugged that night. No one has called me on the carpet. As for the present, I have no idea."

"Did you talk to Travis Weller?"

"He said he and the doctor are gathering the information you wanted. He said he's working on the rest of it as well, whatever the hell that means."

"It's best you don't know."

"Jesus, Karen, if you refuse to play it smart, at least let me help you. Why don't you call again in two days instead of waiting a week?"

"I will."

"What the hell *are* you going to do?"

"I'm working on a plan. There's no way I can do this alone. I'll need plenty of help. That means you, Ben. But if you become a part of this, I can almost guarantee that your career will be over. And that's at best."

Ben didn't hesitate. "I already told you to count me in."

"Just like that? Knowing what they've done to me?"

"Just like that, especially because of what they've done to you," Ben said firmly. "I'm up to here with it."

"Thanks," she said softly. "And Ben?"

"Yeah?"

"Tell Carl I'm sorry."

At noon the next day, Wally arrived back at the house, his face flushed with excitement. "I've found the ugly French bastard. He's staying at a private house less than a mile from here. One of my contacts is the sister of a friend of one of the maids. She's sure of it. What now?"

"We'll go to town," Karen said, "and tell Michelle, and let her take it from there."

They found Michelle in Palm Passage, where an enthusiastic Wally told her the good news. "I'll have to take you there," he said.

"Let me make a phone call first," Michelle said. "I want my associate to be the first one through the door. If there's to be bloodshed, let it be his, the macho pig."

Wally grinned. "You really haven't changed much."

EIGHTEEN

"I'm booked on a noon flight," Michelle said, putting down her cup. "Pretty good coffee for a Brit."

Wally smiled. "Karen made it. She gets up early and tramps over hill and dale before the light of day, well before I've given up my dreams for the night."

Michelle looked at Karen and asked in mock horror, "You *like* to exercise?"

They were both teasing, the relaxed banter a result of an ease in pressure, a job well done, the bad guy in jail awaiting extradition, the good guys basking in the afterglow.

"You have to go back to France right away?" Wally's obvious enchantment with this creature appeared to grow by the minute. "Don't you have to wait until extradition proceedings are completed?"

Michelle made a face. "My associate sees to that. He also gets to hold the press conference when he returns to France with the prisoner. He wants me home and out of the way to insure the glory falls on his shoulders alone."

"I know the type," Wally said.

Michelle executed a Gallic shrug. "It suits me fine. It's best I keep my face out of the public eye. My glory-seeking friend will find that out someday, to his absolute surprise. By then, he will have learned too late. He'll be lying bleeding to death, stupidly wondering how it was that he was recognized."

She stood up, leaned over Wally, and kissed him on the forehead. "I owe you a great deal, my old friend. Without your help, we would have failed. Thank you."

Blushing like a teenager, Wally muttered, "It was nothing. I just showed the photograph around, that's all."

"It wasn't nothing," she protested. "It's never nothing. Look at Karen. Here she sits quietly while all around her people are rushing in all directions trying to extricate her from the terrible fix she's in. Why? Because she helped them all at some time or another. That's what it's all about. What goes around comes around, as the Americans like to say. It's usually pure *merde*, but there are times when it's true. Like now. Though I'm not at all sure we'll be able to repair this situation."

"It'll work out," Karen assured her softly.

"I hope so," Michelle said, her eyes pinched with concern. "I'll get you the information on those two in Paris as soon as I return. Do you have a fax here?"

"No," Wally said, "but there's one at the office."

Michelle looked at Karen.

"That'll be fine," she said. "I appreciate it, Michelle. I really do."

She leaned back in her chair. "It really is nothing. You're sure there's nothing else I can do?"

"Not at the moment."

"You'll let me know—"

"I'll let you know." At the woman's friendly offer, a twinge of homesickness for all the friends she'd left behind tweaked Karen.

223

Wally drove Michelle to the airport and waited an hour for another flight to arrive. A fair exchange, one spy for one reporter. He marveled at it all. And when the plane landed and the passengers disembarked, he stood there like a chauffeur, a large piece of cardboard in his hand with Cynthia Green's name on it.

When she saw her name and headed toward him, he thanked his lucky stars. Between Karen Perry-Mondori and Michelle, he'd been blessed with the company of beautiful women the past week. And now this. She was almost as pretty as Michelle, with long blond hair and flashing green eyes, a spring in her step and a staccato rhythm in her speech.

"You must be Wally," she said with a smile.

"Yes."

She took his hand and gripped it tightly. "How is she?"

"She's fine, actually. Seems to be enjoying the sun. Just another tourist, but mostly staying out of sight."

"As well she might. But she's not relaxing. I can hear the wheels turning from here."

"Yes, I'm sure she's doing some heavy thinking. Do you have a bag?"

"Just this one. Where's your car?"

When she arrived at Wally's, Karen was waiting in the driveway. Cynthia greeted her with a hug. "You look terrible."

"Thanks."

"Of course, under the circumstances, I can understand it."

"It was kind of you to come," Karen said.

"Think nothing of it. It's nothing personal. I'd go to Antarctica for a good story. You know that."

They went inside, then gathered around the table in the small kitchen.

"Wally is more than a good host," Karen said. "He's retired from MI5."

"I know," Cynthia said. "I did some reading before I left Washington. But let's can the small talk. I've got the information you wanted."

She opened her bag, removed a file folder, and handed it to Karen. As Karen glanced over the material, Cynthia gave her the highlights. "Close to a hundred indigents have been found dead in Florida during the last three years. So far, I've been able to determine that forty-two died of bacterial heart disease. They were found all over the state, and since the counties don't compare notes, no one thinks anything's amiss. What the hell, they're homeless drunks, right?"

"Did you tell anyone about this?" Karen asked.

"Of course not. If my research is on the mark, this represents a hell of an increase, but because the bodies are spread out all over the state, no one is suspicious. An anomaly, they'd call it. Now, are you going to tell me what this is all about?"

Cynthia's hair was different, and her contact lenses were of a different color, but the past few years had been kind to her, Karen thought. Perhaps her youthfulness came from her sense of purpose, the drive, the need to right wrongs. Whatever the reason, Cynthia was filled with a zest that colored every breath.

"I'm in deep trouble," Karen admitted.

"I *know* that. What the hell happened?"

"Can we keep this off the record for the moment?"

"Okay, but—"

"Never fear," Karen said sharply. "Do you think I'd cross you after you've come all this way for me?" She took a moment to gather her thoughts, then told the reporter her story.

Cynthia listened intently, made no notes, and asked

few questions. When Karen was done, she said simply, "How can I help?"

"You already have."

"This isn't enough. You'll need some serious investigative work done. I want to be a part of this."

"It's very risky."

"So's sex, but I haven't given that up, either."

Her comment brought a blush to Wally's cheeks. If he lived to be a thousand, he'd never understand Americans.

Two days later, Karen sat quietly on a small, secluded beach a few miles from Cruz Bay on the island of St. John. Behind her, trees heavy with coconuts swayed gently in the breeze coming off the Caribbean. Gentle puffs of clouds floated over an azure sea. A panorama of tranquility to the unobserving eye, but it belied the intensity of the woman sitting, eyes closed, head tipped slightly backward, her tan skin glistening in the midday heat.

She'd been trying to relax for nearly half an hour, yet the rage roiled within her. Her inability to reach an attitude of calm meant her discipline was failing, and the fact troubled her. It signaled danger, a case of emotion winning over intellect, a situation fraught with the stink of failure. Anger could be a powerful ally when controlled. Ungoverned, it was a treacherous enemy that altered the mind's ability to accept reality. And *that* was more dangerous.

In this case, it could be fatal.

She stood and ran to the water, swimming strongly against the incoming tide until her arms started to tire. Then she floated, letting the tide sweep her back to the beach. She stretched out in her chair, drew in slow, deep breaths, and willed her tired muscles to relax. Gradually her anger receded, then disappeared. When she opened her eyes, she knew her rage was now, at last, under control.

She sensed rather than heard the approach of another person, and that pleased her, for it meant she was utterly in tune. And when she stared at the approaching stranger in the dark suit, she broke into a smile of welcome.

Ben Mulligan sat beside her, removed his sunglasses, and wiped his sweating face with a handkerchief.

"What did you tell the Bureau?" Karen asked.

"They think I'm home sick."

"Nothing serious, I hope."

"A nasty case of flu," he said with a grin. "And the sooner you fill me in, the sooner I can get back to business."

"You're sure you should be doing this, Ben? It could be very—"

"Enough of the warnings, okay? I'm in, and that's that. Let's get with the program."

Karen nodded, dug beneath a towel, and withdrew a previously hidden attaché case. She opened it and handed Ben some papers. "It's nice to have friends."

"What's this?"

"The credit report on Consolidated Research. Notice the name Schatt and Gollems."

"I see them."

"Schatt was killed in a car wreck eight years ago, and Gollems died of a heart attack about the same time. The two men now living in Paris using their names are CIA agents."

"How do you know?"

"A nice turn of fate, you might say. Or serendipity. A French friend of Wally's faxed the photos of these two. Wally recognized one of them. He's a French national named Lacombe. He's been a CIA operative for over twenty years. Wally worked with him in France nine years ago."

"He's sure?"

"Positive. These two are simply taking up residence and sitting tight. The office is a front and has been for years. The French are now aware, and they're not pleased. They're willing to give us some time, but they're itching to make a move. Wally says they love to rub CIA noses in the dirt when it's a noncooperative venture. Especially this deal. The smell of competition is in the air."

"They agreed to give you time? How so?"

"Because Wally's friend explained how we can blow this open. If we do, the French will have a clear shot. They see it worth taking a chance."

Ben sighed. "So now we're helping a foreign government. Why do I get the feeling I'm sinking in quicksand?"

"Because you are," Karen said simply. "You can still opt out."

Ben smiled, then shook his head. The enmity between the CIA and its French counterpart, nicknamed *la Piscine*, the swimming pool, but officially the *Direction Générale de la Sécurité Extérieure*, or DGSE, was steeped in tradition dating back to their World War II predecessors. Then, the CIA was the OSS.

Like many professional resentments, this one would never end. But this particular animosity, as Karen had said, was more focused. Ben's limited research had revealed a race for knowledge between the French and the Americans involving DNA research. Both were hoping to catch up and pass the British. The stakes were very high, and for the first time in Ben's experience, the French had seized the moral high ground.

They were the good guys. They wanted to give the knowledge away.

"You trust them to keep their word?" Ben asked.

"For a while."

"Okay, what's next?"

Karen extracted more papers and gave them to Ben. "These are the death certificates of eleven men, all drunks, all homeless, and all without next of kin. There are more, and though we haven't procured the death certificates yet, we will soon enough."

"We?"

Karen smiled. "I've been calling in the troops."

"Anyone I know?"

Karen grinned. "Yes. As you can see, the dead men remain unidentified. And all eleven died of the same thing that killed Travis Weller's father. It's not rare, but it sure isn't prevalent. The bodies have been buried in various potter's fields in Florida. There's not much we can do about that, for it's unlikely we'd ever be able to have the bodies exhumed and examined by Griffin's people in Orlando."

"Why would you want to?"

"I'm sure at least some of them have altered DNA," Karen said. "If we dig them up, we can prove it."

"Okay. What else?"

Karen handed Ben more papers. "Here are some dead folks who've yet to be buried. Nine of them, all dead from pneumococcal endocarditis. These we have a chance of examining, but we'll have to play games."

Ben shook his head in awe. "Where'd you get all this stuff?"

"Don't ask."

"Anything else?"

"Lots. It turns out that there are twenty-four medical examiner districts in Florida. I've been advised that there's been an increase in the number of indigent deaths during the last three years in eight of those districts. An increase of three hundred percent, actually. Too high to be a fluke."

Ben's mouth gaped. "Why the hell would they dump the bodies like that? Don't they think anyone will notice?"

"No one *did* notice until we started checking. The MEs don't compare notes on indigents, and those wonderful folks at Consolidated probably know that. To take a chance and dispose of the bodies on site is much riskier."

"That it?" Ben asked.

"No, but I know you're just itching to tell me something, so fire away."

Ben pulled a sheaf of papers from his jacket pocket. "Travis got the profiles you wanted. The shrink examined the data, such as it is. He figures your best bet is a scientist named Martin Bradford."

"Why?"

"He's the newest CRE recruit, for one thing. The shrink figures they must have some sort of indoctrination program at Consolidated. It's one of two things that would explain why the scientists who go to work there never leave."

"What's the other?"

Ben grinned. "I'll get to it. If you're right about Consolidated, there are obviously some pretty weird things going on in that place, things that would turn a lot of scientists off. It figures that the man with the least exposure to the brainwashing would be the most receptive to being turned. But with this guy, we've got another edge, the other thing I mentioned."

"What's that?"

"Travis talked to Bradford's former employers, including Stanford. They mentioned he's been to an attorney. Travis knows the lawyer. He went ballistic when Travis spoke to him."

"Travis told him the story?" Karen said, suddenly upset.

"Relax. Your Mr. Weller is one sharp cookie. Before he talked to the attorney about this, he made him an associate lawyer on the case. His lips are sealed."

Karen expelled the breath she'd been holding. "Good move. So what did the attorney say?"

"He says Martin Bradford signed a contract that binds Bradford up tight. Obviously, the contract is the other reason all these scientists stay at Consolidated. They're in really deep shit if they try to leave. In any case, this attorney has a reputation for ethics as strong as yours. He wants a crack at these people. I like his style."

"Me, too."

"Anyway, you got a real break. When Travis told Bradford's lawyer what this was about, the attorney said Bradford had just called him, looking for a way out. He says Bradford is a very dedicated, serious guy. His lawyer says there's nothing we can do legally, but he figures Bradford's already close to going out of his mind. That really makes him your best bet, and his lawyer will help us any way he can."

"Where do things stand with Bradford now?"

"This is the curious part. Bradford called his lawyer from a pay phone in Tampa. The lawyer told him he'd think it over and get back to him. Bradford said no, that he'd call him back in twenty-four hours. What does that tell you?"

"That Bradford thinks his phone is bugged," Karen said. "And it probably is. Interesting."

"I thought so, too."

"So when did Bradford make the first call?"

"Last night."

Karen thought for a moment. "If Bradford's that messed up, he could be a loose cannon."

"You think he's paranoid?"

"Not necessarily, but he sounds very nervous. Nervous people scare me."

"How else are you going to get inside?" Ben asked.

"By risking the life of a man who's been a true friend. And unless another friend backs me up, this guy is as good as dead."

Ben looked out over the placid water, then nodded. "I'll be there. So will six of *my* friends."

Karen rubbed her eyes. "Six agents?"

"Yeah," Ben said with pride. "Maybe more if we need them. Thoroughly pissed-off guys, like me."

Karen looked at him with an expression of awe. "I could be all wrong about this. Did you ever think of that?"

Ben grinned. "Yeah. But somehow, I don't think so. I think you're right about what's happening, and that scares the livin' hell out of me. There are times you have to follow your gut instincts. I guess this is one of those times. But you have to get moving. We haven't much time. As for Bradford, I think you should bring him in on this. Let him tell you what he knows."

Karen thought for a moment. "Maybe, but this has to be done right. You're sure Bradford's lawyer will help us?"

"Travis guarantees it."

"Good, because if Bradford is approached by someone he doesn't know, he might think somebody's setting him up. It has to be someone he trusts. His attorney fills the bill."

They talked for another hour, going over plans, accepting those they thought would work, discarding those with flaws. At best, their entire strategy was risky, and they both knew it.

"I should have everything in place within a few days," Karen said. "Then we'll make our move. You're something else, you know that?"

Ben shrugged. "I told you. Staying behind a desk bored the hell out of me. It's the only reason I let you con me into being part of this."

"I know the other reason. It's Carl." She tried unsuccessfully to joke past the lump in her throat. "Has he filed for divorce yet?"

"Aw, Karen." Ben gathered her in a hug. "He's going out of his mind with worry over you, but he's putting up a good front for Andrea. He'll be there for you when this is all over."

Karen pulled away. She stared at the sea, at the clouds, and the brilliant sky. They'd taken her house, her money, and the bulk of her possessions, but she'd be damned if she'd let them take what was most precious to her. She had to uncover what was going on at Consolidated, because what they were doing was wrong.

But more than that, she had to clear her name so she could have her family back.

Cynthia Green parked her car on the street and walked briskly toward the iron gate that fronted the opulent Chevy Chase residence of Senator Warren Denning. She pressed a button on the intercom and waited.

"Yes?" a deep male voice said.

"Cynthia Green, *Washington Globe*."

"The senator is expecting you. Please come right up."

The electrically operated gate creaked back a couple feet, then closed behind her as she made her way up the driveway. By the time she reached the front door, a black man dressed in a butler's uniform was waiting. Denning, a respected liberal, still clung to the old ways, the old stereotypes, for reasons Cynthia could never understand. Like many in Washington, he just didn't get it.

The butler escorted her to the library, where the senator, white-haired and dressed in an outrageous red velvet smoking jacket, waited, a cigar in his right hand.

"Cynthia," he said, beaming, his heavy jowls quivering. "This is a distinct pleasure." He motioned to the butler, who withdrew, then waved Cynthia into a well-worn leather chair. He settled into its mate. "It hasn't been that long since you did that most flattering profile of me, my dear. Again, I express my deepest appreciation."

She smiled. "I wrote the truth, Senator. If it was a flattering piece, it was because you deserve to be flattered. I like what you stand for. It took courage to stand up and say what you did about campaign reform, for it might well cost you the next election. I admire that, even if your colleagues don't."

He chuckled. "I've become persona non grata even in the lunchroom. Most treat me like a leper. My staff thinks I've gone senile. Perhaps I have."

"I don't think so. And fortunately, you remain as chairman of one of the most powerful committees in the Senate. That gives you a bully pulpit."

"At least for a while," he said wistfully. "Already, I see them gathering, like the ancients in Rome, trying to figure a way to stab me in the back. Eventually they'll succeed, of course. Cunning is the prime requisite for political survival, and I seem to have displayed an inordinate lack of it recently."

"Do you regret what you did?"

"Not for one minute. It was the right thing to say at the right time. While my colleagues may wail like wounded animals, my words did play pretty well back home. Too bad my constituents don't read your newspaper. It would help."

"Now who's flattering whom?"

He tapped a long ash into an ashtray and nodded. "In truth, you're good at what you do. I've always found you fair. That's why you're much respected in this town. While others in your profession spend most of their time looking under rocks, you keep your reports within certain . . . boundaries."

"That's because I deal with the issues, though personalities sometimes play a part in those issues. It's one reason I'm here tonight."

The senator's thick, white eyebrows rose. "Another issue?"

"Yes." She smiled sweetly. "But first I want your word that until we agree otherwise, everything I discuss with you this day is off the record and confidential."

The senator frowned. "This sounds serious."

"This is a possible career-ender for a lot of powerful people. I'll need your help to make it happen."

"That *is* serious."

"It's more than serious. If I've guessed wrong about you, my very life may be in danger."

"Guessed wrong? You're not one to be guessing, Cynthia."

"I am tonight," she said softly.

He shook his head. "And cryptic as well."

"Do I have your word?"

He leaned forward, reflected for a moment, pursed

his lips, sucked on his cigar, then smiled. "Of course. What's on your mind?"

Cynthia told the senator exactly why she'd asked for this meeting.

NINETEEN

When Aaron Rich first listened to the anxiety-ridden voice of his friend and client, Martin sounded like a man coming apart at the seams. Later the next day, when Aaron discussed Consolidated Research with Travis Weller, the picture became clearer. Aaron was infuriated, not just for what Consolidated was doing to his client, but for what they were *doing*, period. He pledged his complete support to the handsome young lawyer from Orlando.

When Martin called a second time, Aaron was ready. "What's happening to you is important to me. So important that I'm flying to Tampa tonight. I'll meet you in the morning. What's the name of the hotel closest to the airport?"

"There's a Marriott right at the airport."

"Good. I'll make a reservation. You meet me there first thing in the morning. Say eight?"

"Do you really think you can help me?" Martin sounded shocked.

"We'll talk about it when I arrive," Aaron said crisply.

* * *

The white-haired attorney from Palo Alto took the red-eye from San Francisco and arrived in Tampa at six in the morning on a Saturday.

When Martin arrived, Aaron was astonished by the young scientist's appearance. Once full of hope and adventure, his face seemed to have aged ten years, with lifeless eyes expressing a sense of dread. Even the man's body language announced his terrible depression, his once ramrod stature now hunched, his shoulders slightly sloped, even his head tilted forward, as if hanging in shame.

"It's good to see you," the lawyer said, smiling broadly to cover his dismay as he ushered Martin to a chair. He indicated the table. "As you can see, I took the liberty of ordering breakfast for the two of us. I hope you don't mind."

"I'm not hungry." Martin slumped into a chair. "But I'm grateful you came, even if it's a useless trip."

"I don't make useless trips."

Martin waved a limp hand. "You did this time, I'm afraid. I'll pay for it, though. All of it."

"Don't worry about that," Aaron said, peering into Martin's eyes. "Just tell me what the hell's going on."

Martin took a deep breath and exhaled before speaking. "Our house is bugged, our phone calls monitored—they even read our mail. They control everything from the post office to the supermarket. Grace is so uptight, I'm afraid she'll get sick again. I can hardly function at work, and Tony keeps telling me that if I try to leave, they'll destroy me."

Aaron held up a hand to stop him. "Do they know you're meeting with me?"

"I called you from the pay phone here in Tampa. It's the only way I could be sure they weren't listening."

"How do you know you weren't followed here?"

"I drove to a hotel downtown, went out the back, and took a cab. I'm sure no one saw me."

Aaron nodded. "Excellent. Please continue."

"They try to brainwash you. I talked to a shrink for hours, and she had me thinking this was all just great. But after I talked to Grace again, I realized they're twisting things around, trying to make something terrible seem acceptable. I'm trapped, Aaron."

"I can understand why you feel that way. But tell me, what exactly do they do at Consolidated? What is it that has you so upset in the first place?"

For a moment, Martin didn't respond. When he finally did, his voice was a low monotone, as if the telling was easier by keeping it unemotional. "They experiment on indigent drunks, for one thing."

"Experiment?"

"They take DNA samples, modify them, reinsert them, and six months later, the poor bastards die because their immune systems are shot. They keep trying and trying, but they still haven't perfected it."

"Perfected what?" Aaron asked. He already knew the answer, but he wanted to hear Martin say it. Sometimes it helped just to get it off one's chest.

"A way to program DNA so that damaged human cells are repaired from within. They've made some progress, to be sure. I've seen people healed, people who were terribly ill, and suddenly they're in the best of health—on the surface. But I know that in a few months, they'll all die. It's horrible, and that's just for starters."

Aaron pointed to the table laden with fruit and sweet rolls. "Try to eat something."

Martin shook his head.

Aaron poured two cups of coffee and took his place at the table. Martin stared vacantly at the wall.

"You were saying these experiments are just for starters."

The young man sighed deeply, then sipped some coffee. "There's more. I never would have imagined this could happen in America." He raised his head and looked directly at Aaron. "They'll get me for this, you know? They'll destroy me. I was a fool for taking this job. Now, I'm an even bigger fool, and you can't help me."

"Let me be the judge of that," Aaron said firmly. "Once you've told me everything, we'll discuss what *can* be done. And speaking of discussions, have you mentioned our meeting to Grace or the children?"

"I told Grace you would get back to me. I didn't tell her you were coming here. I didn't want her to get her hopes up for nothing."

"If your house is bugged, they would have heard that conversation, would they not?"

Martin flashed a weak smile. "When Grace and I need to talk, we go for a walk."

Aaron smiled back. "Good thinking. Now, tell me the rest."

Martin took almost a half hour to relate everything that had happened. When he finished, his breakfast was untouched, as cold as his once bright hopes.

Aaron, who'd listened silently for most of it, eating and taking notes, then interjecting a question or two, now placed his napkin on the table and rolled the table into the hall. He returned to the room and sat across from Martin again and scanned his notes. "What's going on there is unconscionable. That's a given. The part about destroying you, they've actually said that?"

"Not in those words, but I know what they're really saying. The fact remains that no one has successfully challenged them."

Aaron grunted. "I've checked the legal records. They've never been sued."

"See?"

"Okay, so simply quitting is unacceptable to them. You're in fear of your life? And that of your family?"

"I know it sounds paranoid, but it's the truth. They're the crazy ones!"

Aaron shook his head. "I don't think it sounds paranoid at all. I think it's the absolute truth. And I might have a solution for you."

Hope flickered in Martin's tortured eyes. "A solution?"

"It'll take courage and trust on your part. And some faith in the government of this country."

Martin shook his head fiercely. "No way. I told you, this project was set up by our goddamn government. You expect me to trust *them*?"

"Correction," Aaron said gently. "This project was set up by some people *within* our government. It's possible very few people are involved, and those who are have taken extraordinary measures to insure that everything is kept secret. The answer lies in exposing the truth to everyone. Remember what happened to Nixon? The president himself was forced to resign from the most powerful office in the world. That should tell you the system works."

"They've learned a lot since then," Martin said cynically. "The last guy who tried to buck Consolidated is now a prisoner in a mental hospital."

Aaron was insistent. "The fact remains, this cannot continue. And you won't be expected to do this on your own. There are others involved, people who want to see this come to an end. With your help, we can thrust Consolidated Research into the harsh light of full disclosure.

241

And when that happens, they won't stand up to the scrutiny. Nor will the contract you signed."

Martin's eyes widened. His anxiety increased another notch. "You talked to people about me?"

"As it happens, some people have come to me. They're looking for help."

"What people?"

"I can't say. But they *can* be trusted."

"How do you know?"

Aaron sighed. This was going to be every bit as difficult as he'd imagined. "That's where the trust comes in. You have to trust me first. Can you do that?"

"Of course I trust you, but—you know the deal. I'm not supposed to talk to anyone. If you've told strangers—"

"I haven't betrayed your confidence," Aaron insisted. "Try to understand. We can't do this alone!"

Martin stared at him.

"You'll have to bring Grace in on this. Where is she?"

"At home."

"Where does she think you are?"

"I told her I was going to Tampa to look at new cars."

"And she didn't want to come?"

"She's been depressed. She left the car shopping up to me."

Aaron rubbed his hands together. "All right. Here's what I want you to do. Go back to Osolo. Tell Grace you've found the car you want, but you refuse to buy it without her okay. Then bring her and the children back to this room. Bring nothing with you."

"Then what?"

"Then," Aaron said quietly, "you're going to disappear—all of you."

Martin's jaw fell open. "What?"

Aaron's voice increased in intensity. "Listen to me,

Martin. Unless you do exactly what I say, you *will* be destroyed, either by conscience or a foolish, misguided act. This is your one chance at getting out from under them."

"You're talking about running away. That's no answer."

"You're not running away. You're going into hiding for a while. When the time is right, you'll resurface. If all works well, you'll testify in front of a Senate investigating committee in Washington. You'll be well protected in the meantime, and when this is over, you'll be able to walk away without fear."

Martin jumped to his feet. "An investigating committee? I don't understand."

Aaron waved him back into his chair. "You asked me to help you. I'm trying to do that."

"But if I cross them, they'll take everything I have."

"Forget about *things*, Martin. We're talking about your very life! You took this job to insure a future for your children, or so you said. Was that the truth or just a bunch of noble-sounding words?"

Martin fell back in the chair. "You know it was the truth."

"Then if you really give a damn about your children's future, you'll stop feeling sorry for yourself and start using that magnificent brain God blessed you with."

"I'm listening."

"You're not expected back at work until Monday morning. I expect this entire story to break within a few days. When that happens, Consolidated will have much more to worry about than the tardiness of one scientist."

Martin thrust his fingers through his hair. "This is all

so . . . vague. Just who *are* these people you keep talking about?"

"I can't tell you right now. Just place yourself in my hands. Do you really have another choice?"

Martin considered him for a moment, then shook his head.

They found him lying in the alley, right where the telephone caller had said he'd be. He was holding his stomach and moaning. His tattered suit was covered with vomit, and his face was lacerated and bruised.

One of the paramedics leaned over him. "You okay, buddy?"

The man, his eyes unfocused, just moaned.

"Where does it hurt?"

"Stomach," the man gasped, his words slurred. "Bastards beat me. Took my wine. Kicked me in the stomach."

The other paramedic attached a blood pressure cuff to the man's arm and contacted the hospital via radio. "Ready to copy?"

"Go ahead, Three."

"Ten-four. We have a male Caucasian, intoxicated, regurgitating, complaining of stomach pain. Permission to transport?"

The man vomited again.

"Ten-four."

A paramedic brought a gurney from the ambulance and the two men lifted Wally Bentworth onto the stretcher, strapped him down, raised the gurney on its legs, and pushed it into the ambulance.

"Just try to relax," the first paramedic said, "and we'll have you in the hands of a doctor in no time."

Wally simply moaned.

They took him to County Hospital, where a doctor examined him, ordered some tests, then left. A nurse attended Wally for a few minutes, then left him on his own, stuck in a corner of the emergency room, his bed surrounded by drawn curtains.

In the distance, he could hear the sounds of other emergency patients being treated. He could smell the disinfectant in the room, feel the softness of the sheet that covered his shaking body. Most of all, he could taste the terrible bite of gin and vomit that even the nurse's careful wiping of his face couldn't remove.

The experience was worse than he'd feared. The room was spinning, and his stomach ached from the pill he'd taken. But the terrible craving for booze was the worst. Like an old and evil companion, the hunger for alcohol was most familiar, uppermost in his mind, blocking his rational thoughts, blunting his purpose, dimming his concentration. He wanted a *drink*, dammit, and Karen Perry-Mondori and the rest could go to hell!

What did it matter about some mysterious U.S. Government facility engaged in sinister research on living strangers? Who the hell cared? What did it matter to him? He needed a drink, and as soon as he could, he'd walk out of this place and find one.

He struggled to sit up. After two tries, he made it. They'd taken his clothes. He wore a flimsy smock that barely covered his naked body. The hell with it. He was getting out now.

He took two steps and fell.

"Mr. Taylor!"

The nurse was back. With the help of a burly orderly, she returned him to his bed.

"I need a drink, blast it," he screamed. "Get me a bloody drink!"

"Of course you want a drink," the nurse said soothingly. "That's why you're here, isn't it? The doctor will

245

give you something shortly. Now you stay in bed, or we'll have to strap you down. You don't want that, do you?"

"I want a *drink*," he wailed.

Strong arms held his feet. He closed his eyes, hoping the room would stop whirling. He told them to go to hell. He wanted out.

"Mr. Taylor?"

A different voice. He opened his eyes and looked into those of a young doctor. "Leave me alone," he groaned.

"You're ill, Mr. Taylor. Right now the nurse is going to ask you some questions. I want you to answer them and behave yourself. The sooner you cooperate, the sooner you'll feel well again. You want to feel well, don't you?"

Wally didn't answer, but in the dark recesses of his clouded mind, he knew this was critical, the reason for his being here, the end product of hours of preparation. His friends Ben Mulligan and Karen were counting on him, for he was the key.

Damn Ben Mulligan! Every time the man entered Wally's life it had been a damn frightening experience. His life was now on the line again. It was Ben who'd talked him into getting drunk again, knowing full well how dangerous it was. Bloody hell! What did Ben care? He was enjoying this, romping free around the bloody countryside, being the hero again, playing the role of a reincarnated Errol bloody goddamn Flynn.

No. That wasn't true. Karen and Ben had warned him what could happen. They had told Wally how dangerous this was, told him he needn't get involved. The bastards had seized everything Karen owned, ousted her family from their home, and branded her an outlaw. A bloody drug trafficker at that, and her such a classy bird. Such damn bloody rot.

"Mr. Taylor?"

Wally groaned.

"Can you answer some questions for me?"

"What questions?" he mumbled.

"I'd like the name of your next of kin."

"Why? Am I about to expire?"

"You'll be fine. We need this information before we can treat you. Please."

"Ahhh . . . I . . . live alone."

"Alone? You have an address?"

He turned his head away. "No. I have no home. No relatives, either."

"Are you sure?"

"I'm sure." Tears formed suddenly in his eyes. They were tears of intense concentration, because lovely little Karen was counting on him.

In Fort Lauderdale, an anxious-looking man in his thirties appeared at the police station clutching a copy of the *Sun-Sentinel* in his hand. He approached the desk sergeant. "I need to talk to someone about this ad."

"What ad?"

The man held the paper aloft. "The ad about the unidentified body you found."

"You'll need to talk to Homicide about that."

The man looked surprised. "He was murdered?"

"No, it's just that the homicide detectives are handling the case."

In minutes, the man was directed to an office on the second floor. A detective greeted him, offered him a chair, and took a seat behind his desk. "What makes you think this John Doe is your father?"

"I'm not sure he is. My father's been missing for a couple of weeks now. I've checked with the sheriff's departments in Dade and Broward Counties, and now

I'm working the local police departments. All I know is that my father was in this area and I haven't had a card for weeks. He wrote me every other day, like clockwork, even drunk as he was."

The cop's eyebrows rose. "He sent you cards every other day?"

"He was a little crazy. It was an obsession with him." The man removed a packet of tattered postcards from his pocket and placed them on the desk. "These are just the few I brought with me."

The cop turned to his computer terminal. "What's your name?"

FBI agent Jack Swift, his vacation time given over to Ben Mulligan, the man he once worked for, said, "Donald Webster."

The cop typed. "Address?"

"536 Lavelle Avenue, Orlando."

"Occupation?"

Swift leaned forward. "May I make a suggestion? Why don't I have a look at the body before we do all this? It's a waste of time if it's not him, don't you think?"

The cop sighed. "Procedure, Mr. Webster. First, we do the report, then you look. That's how we do it here."

Swift leaned back. After answering a score of questions, he was finally taken to the morgue, where the body of a John Doe, now frozen solid, was presented on a video display. At the sight of the body, Swift burst into tears.

"Is that your father?" the cop asked.

"Yes." Swift wiped his eyes with his handkerchief.

The cop clasped his shoulder. "Sorry. You didn't happen to bring any dental charts with you?"

Swift looked at him vacantly. "What?"

The cop shrugged. "Never mind. There are some things we'll have to do. Come with me."

They returned to the police station, where Swift presented identification, signed three documents, and waited. After an hour, another police officer approached the desk and dropped a file folder on it.

"Prints are all smudged. Not even a partial."

Swift, looking confused, stared at the cop.

"We had to check those postcards to see if there were prints on them belonging to the dead man. We have to have some way of verifying your identification. Just routine."

"Oh."

"Do you know where we might find your father's dental charts?"

Swift shook his head. "I haven't a clue. He moved around a lot. If he ever went to a dentist, it could have been anywhere. I have no way of knowing."

"You his only kin?"

"Yes. My mother died years ago. Father's been like this for twenty years."

"But he mailed you a postcard every other day. Weird. I thought I'd seen everything."

Swift waited.

"What would you like us to do with the body?" the cop asked.

"I want to bury him at home, of course. I'll arrange for a local funeral home to do the shipping."

"You have them get in touch with us, give us a copy of the release form I'm giving you, and that will be that. Sorry about your father's death."

Swift thanked him, shook hands, and left the building. Once in his car, he opened an attaché case, removed another set of postcards, then put the car in gear. His next stop would be at a local funeral home.

Then he'd be off to Daytona Beach, where another John Doe awaited. He had three days to get eight bodies released and shipped to Orlando. He had little time to waste.

"Mr. Taylor?"

Wally Bentworth opened his eyes again and saw the doctor.

"How are you feeling?"

"I'd like a drink," Wally said honestly.

"I'm sure. Look, you have some medical problems aside from your intoxication. I won't lie to you. At the moment, this being Saturday, I'm having trouble finding the specialists I need to treat you. I've checked with another facility, and they have some people on staff who can better take care of you. So, if it's okay with you, I'll transport you there."

"What medical problems?" Wally asked.

The doctor sighed. "You're really not in any condition to discuss it. Leave the medicine to me, all right?"

"Not bloody likely. And I'm not interested in being transported anywhere. What's the bloody problem with fixing me up here? I don't need a specialist. All I need is a few pills. Surely you have pills in this hellhole?"

The doctor removed a small bottle from his coat and leaned forward. "This is filled with Gordon's best. You help me out, and I'll help you out. You get in the ambulance like a good boy, and I'll give you the bottle to keep you company. That sound like a good deal?"

Wally's eyes widened, and he licked his lips. "That sounds bloody bang-on!"

The doctor smiled and motioned to the orderly. "Get him ready."

"You'll call Osolo?" the orderly said.

"I will. By the time you get him there, they'll be ready and waiting. Make it snappy."

Wally closed his eyes. "Doctor?"

"Yes?"

"I never got your name. Would you be kind enough to give it to me?"

The doctor laughed and left the room.

Hours later, Wally lay in his hospital bed and stared at the flat-painted ceiling. He was alone in the room, more like a cell, actually, small and white-walled, without so much as a window. They'd taken his watch, so he hadn't a clue as to the time, but he was sure it was night. It *felt* like night. As least the room had stopped spinning, even if his mind was awhirl with odd visions and strange memories.

He remembered being attended by two nurses at first, fussing about, clucking incessantly as they took blood and urine samples, doing the usual workup. They'd injected him with something that might have been pure heroin, such was its impact. He'd been immediately transported on the wings of angels to an island of pristine bliss, tension gone, fears abated, the fires banked.

Then the doctor had come, looking into Wally's bleary eyes and ringing ears, poking at his stomach and chest, then listening to the sounds of his heart and lungs. Wally remembered giggling like a schoolgirl. The doctor, a taciturn type, had been less than friendly, saying nothing.

Now Wally was alone, trying to come out of the fog, fighting the drugs. He remembered the trip to Osolo. He'd employed all his ability to concentrate, managing to spill most of the gin they'd given him, but enough of the evil potion had already entered his system to destroy in seconds what he'd attained through years of dedicated abstinence. Now the craving for alcohol raged anew as he struggled to recollect what it was he was supposed to do. He felt weak and tired, his brain screaming at him to simply close his eyes and fall asleep. For a moment, he did just that. Something jarred him awake.

God's teeth! He had to move.

With great effort, he sat up in bed and looked about the room. No furniture, closets, phones, or televisions. Not even a button with which to summon a nurse. The bed was the only item in the room, save for the metal bedpan beneath it.

He struggled to free his feet from the tightly tucked sheets and let them slip to the cold tiled floor. The room spun for an instant, then steadied. He took a step, then another, until his hand was on the chrome doorknob.

Damn and blast! The bloody door was locked. What was he supposed to do now?

TWENTY

Less than five miles away, Karen Perry-Mondori, drenched in perspiration, her body cloaked by the humidity of the thick Florida summer night, looked at her watch for the sixth time in less than ten minutes. Then she stared at the silent pay phone a few feet away against the wall of the shuttered service station. She shook her head and turned to Ben Mulligan, sitting quietly beside her in the black rental car.

"I was afraid of this," she said softly.

Ben shrugged. "You didn't really think they'd be that sloppy, did you?"

"Let's say I was hoping. Sorry, Ben, but it looks as if you'll have to pull him out of there."

Ben smiled weakly. "I never doubted it for a second. That's why we developed Plan B. They've probably got him locked up and doped up, but we're ready. We'll get him. Don't worry so much."

"Ben, I—"

"Stop it!" Ben snapped. "We've been through all this. I *want* to do this. You haven't talked me into anything. I'm a big boy now, so save your regrets."

"I'll come with you."

"The hell you will. We stick to the plan. You stay

253

here. If we're not back in one hour, you'll know we blew it. Then you'll be on your own, missy. Not even a set of wheels." He grinned. "But you can handle it. You're good at improvisation."

"I hope it won't come to that," Karen said.

"So do I."

Ben signaled to a car behind him. Immediately, with a screeching of rubber, the car departed, heading into Osolo. Karen climbed out, and Ben waited two minutes, during which time he avoided looking at her, then jerked his car into gear. It, too, departed in a cloud of blue tire smoke.

Karen stood in the heat and darkness, alone, worried, wondering, and cursing the fates.

There were six of them all together, two in the first car, four in the second, all of them FBI agents, all working off the clock on a private case that could end their careers—or worse. They had come from Denver and Chicago and Kansas City, one as far as Honolulu. But they had two things in common besides their current status as FBI special agents. At one time in their varying careers, they'd worked for Ben Mulligan and had grown to admire and respect him as a leader and as a man.

They shared Ben's mounting frustration and dissatisfaction with the Bureau. They saw this adventure as a chance to make some kind of statement, even if that statement might never be heard, might cost them their jobs, might even end their lives. They were willing to take the risk, for this mini-revolution, should it be ultimately successful, would send a strong message to those icons isolated in their Washington ivory towers. It was time the bullshit stopped. It was time the Bureau was cut loose from petty politics and allowed to carry out its responsibilities with integrity and a sense of purpose.

The first team was to drive to the residence of Dr. Philip Stiles. They were to locate and neutralize the phone lines and alarm systems, then enter the house and do the same with Stiles. There was to be no bloodshed, no noise, no discussion. After a half hour, they would leave. As simple as that—and as difficult. No radios, no means of communication, just a routine break and enter of a residence probably bristling with security devices. But they were professionals. They were confident.

The second team had the more difficult task. By whatever means, they were to get Wally Bentworth out of the Consolidated Research Building.

Ben covered the five miles in less than four minutes and pulled up to the main gate of the Consolidated complex in a cloud of sandy dust. He flashed a set of credentials at the security guard on duty. "Frank Jasper, FBI. Who's the head security man on duty?"

"What's the problem?" the guard asked.

"None of your business," Ben snapped. "Just answer the goddamn question."

The guard hesitated briefly. "Ahhh . . . that would be Captain Deland."

"You tell the captain to get his ass over here, right now!"

"I'm not supposed to—"

"This is an emergency, asshole." Ben got out of the car and stood face-to-face with the guard. "Get Deland over here, or I'll use the phone myself."

Reluctantly the guard picked up a phone and made the call. After a muffled conversation, he handed the phone to Ben.

"This is Captain Deland," a voice said. "Who the hell are you?"

"Frank Jasper, FBI. Didn't Stiles call you?"

"About what?"

"We've got an emergency. Stiles was supposed to call you. You'd better get your ass down here pronto."

"What emergency?"

"Not on the phone, you idiot." Ben slammed the receiver into its cradle.

Minutes later, Deland arrived in a Jeep, accompanied by another uniformed security guard. A big man, Deland lumbered over to Ben, stood by his car, and peered inside, then turned back to Ben. "What's this all about?"

Ben, hands on hips, glared at the man. "You telling me Stiles never called you?"

"No. Why would he?"

Ben spat on the ground. "You guys are really something. How you've managed to make it this far is a mystery. You're just a bunch of fuckups if you ask me."

Deland was getting angry. "State your business or get off the property."

Ben glared at him. "The St. Pete hospital shipped you a ringer today. We're here to pick him up and clean up your mess before it gets us all fired."

"Ringer? What the hell are you talking about?"

Ben scowled. "The man who arrived from County Hospital today isn't a homeless drunk. He's a goddamn reporter from some New York newspaper. We're damn lucky to have gotten a tip. My orders are to pick him up and take him back to Washington. So let's get with it."

Deland gave him a curious look. "What orders? From whom?"

Ben threw his hands in the air in exasperation. "From

Stiles, you idiot. Though it isn't in his hands anymore. That's why he was supposed to call you."

"Why did Stiles bring you in? We could have handled this ourselves."

"You're wasting my time," Ben said. "Stiles is on his way to Washington. He was given the information in flight. He was also told Washington would handle this, and he was supposed to advise you of that. Washington called us and told us to do it now. We're here, and we're in a hurry."

Red-faced, Deland strode to the security shack and picked up the telephone. Ben held his breath as Deland dialed a number. They waited. When there was no answer, Deland hung up, looking puzzled, and returned to Ben.

"Like I said," Ben insisted, "Stiles is on his way to Washington."

"With his wife?"

"With his wife."

"Funny, he never told us he was going. He always gives us his itinerary when he leaves."

Ben sneered. "Not when his ass is about to be put in a sling."

"What for? What's going on?"

"That's not your concern. Your immediate priority is to find us a guy named Cecil Taylor and hand his ass over to us. You keep screwing around, and you'll be in the same tub of shit Stiles is."

"What the hell for? What did he do?"

"All I know," Ben said, "is that he's out, and you'll have a new boss by tomorrow. Your ass may be on the line as well. Now unless you help us get this asshole out of here—"

"Okay." Deland was finally convinced. "I get the picture. Get in your car and follow me."

Ben climbed into the car, put it in gear, and followed the Jeep fifteen hundred yards to a spot immediately in front of a small steel door, then stopped. As Deland pushed the keypad of the electronic door lock, the four agents exited the car. Deland, standing by the now open door, looked at them and smiled. "It's gonna take all four of you? Jesus, he's only one guy."

"We just do as we're told," Ben said.

They followed Deland to a set of stairs that led to the third floor, then through a series of locked doors leading to what appeared to be a hospital ward. Deland, the chief security officer for the night, was never questioned as he led the agents to the room where Wally was held.

Deland stopped at the door, noted the tag, unlocked the door, and stepped aside. "Cecil Taylor, alive and well."

Ben and the others stepped inside. A man lay on the bed, dressed only in a stained hospital gown. He stared bug-eyed at Ben and his companions, then screamed, "Stay away from me, you bloody sods."

Ben wasted no time. He slapped handcuffs on Wally's wrists and, together with another agent, dragged him into the hallway.

"Where's his stuff?" he asked Deland.

"We threw it out. Not worth saving."

"Who are you bloody bastards," Wally screamed. "Leave me alone!" Then his eyes opened wide in recognition. "Wait, I know you! You're Ben—"

"Fucking whacko." Mulligan's heart stopped beating. "What've you got him on?"

Deland shrugged.

Ben turned and raised a fist to Wally. "You keep your mouth shut, asshole. One more peep, and I'll ram an arm down your throat. Fucking reporter! Jesus!"

In Wally's confused mind, a small light began to shine. *Reporter,* Ben had said. That was the code word. These were *Karen's* people. God's teeth! They were here to take him away, and he'd almost blown it.

He stared at Deland. The man seemed not to have responded to Wally's mistake. Bloody marvelous! Relief washed over him in a tidal wave, and he went limp and closed his eyes.

Two men half dragged, half carried him down the stairs and out into the oppressive heat of the night. Then he was crowded into the backseat of a car that seemed to be traveling a hundred miles an hour. Utterly exhausted, he opened his eyes and strained to speak. "I'm sorry, Ben. I almost—"

"It's okay, Wally. Just relax. We're almost in the clear."

"Righto."

In less than ten minutes, the car carrying the four agents and Wally was out of the complex, racing down an unlit country road at high speed. Wally, his face now wreathed in a big smile, turned to the man beside him. "Did any of you chaps think to bring along some gin?"

"Sorry, Wally. No can do. Are you okay?" Ben asked.

Wally sighed. "No gin? I thought not."

"Well?" Ben insisted.

Wally groaned. "I'm not sure, really. They stuck enough needles in me to sink a battleship, so I don't rightly know. I don't even know how long I was in there. A few days, I expect."

"Less than seven hours," Ben said. "According to the doctor in Orlando, it would take them longer than that to clone your DNA. I'm sure we got you out in time."

"Well, that's a bloody relief." Wally's eyelids began to close. "Say, can we stop somewhere and get a drink?

259

I've been a good boy. I went through with the bloody thing. Don't I get a reward for all this effort?"

Ben cursed under his breath. "We're going to take you to a real hospital. But first we have to pick up Karen. And do me a favor, will you?"

"What?"

"Lay off the 'I need a drink' crap. The poor lady feels guilty enough as it is."

"And so she should," Wally said. "Things were just starting to level out, and then *she* shows up in St. Thomas. This tiny blonde with green eyes steps off a plane and turns my life at sixes and sevens. But it's worth it. What a lady!"

Ben shook his head in frustration and spoke to the others in the car. "Change in plans. Obviously our English friend has a snootful of drugs. I don't want Karen to see him like this. I'll stop a hundred feet short of the service station and get out. You guys take Wally and carry on. I'll wait with Karen until you get back from the airport."

The others mumbled their assent.

Cynthia Green knocked on the hotel-room door and waited. She felt like a hooker. It was three o'clock on a Sunday morning, and here she was in Atlanta, slipping past the security people in the lobby and using the stairs to reach the fifth floor.

The door was opened by a white-haired man who left the chain on. "Who are you?"

"Cynthia Green." She showed him her press pass. "Mr. Rich?"

"I need to ask you a question."

Cynthia smiled. He was being very careful. "Ask away."

"This woman we both know. The first time you met her. Do you remember where?"

"At the Senate office of her brother, Robert Jameson."

Aaron Rich nodded and opened the door. He was fully dressed, right down to the shirt and tie, looking remarkably fresh. The room was large, the bed unused. Papers covered a small desk near the window.

"Where are the Bradfords?" she said.

"Upstairs in another room. They've had a harrowing day, so I suggested they get some sleep until you arrived. I had a doctor administer a sedative to Mrs. Bradford. She's suffering some anxiety, but I'm sure she'll be fine shortly. She was weak with relief when she arrived."

"And Bradford's willing to talk?"

"He'll tell you everything he knows. It isn't much, I'm afraid. He wasn't there very long. But it's enough to establish probable cause. Of that I'm sure."

She sat on the bed. "How did it go with Wally?"

"Mr. Bentworth is now in a South Carolina treatment center. He's in for some intensive therapy, but he'll be fine. If he kicked it once, he can do it again. And he's got the information you needed. I have a fax of his sworn statement on my desk."

"That's not all," she said, peering at the cluttered desk.

"You're quite right. I have the forensics reports on the bodies shipped to Orlando. All have altered DNA. Taken together with Wally's statement, it's enough."

"And Karen?"

"She's fine. My co-counsel is hiding out until the storm breaks."

Cynthia stood. "If we're going to make it rain, we better get going. *Tempus fugit*, as they say."

"Indeed," Aaron said. "And good luck."

* * *

In Washington, CIA Assistant Deputy Director Fred Gardner was awakened from a deep sleep by the insistent ringing of his bedside telephone. He fumbled for the receiver and held it to his ear. "What?"

"This is Jack. Just had a call from Stiles in Florida. He says he was kidnapped and held prisoner in his home for half an hour or so, then let go. When he called security, the asshole gave him some crazy story about the FBI coming in and grabbing some patient."

Gardner, his mind fogged by sleep, rubbed his eyes. "Slow down. Stiles said what?"

"Two guys came—"

"What two guys?"

"He doesn't know. They never talked, just held a gun to his head while they tied him and his wife up. Nobody said a goddamn word. Then they left. Stiles finally worked himself free, called security—"

"They didn't say *anything*?"

"Not a word."

"Go on."

"When Stiles reached security, they told him that four FBI agents had stormed into the main building, yakking about some reporter—"

"Reporter!"

"Yeah. Stiles says the FBI guys claimed they were to grab this guy and bring him to Washington, but when Stiles talked to Washington, they knew nothing about it. Stiles thinks it's a setup."

"Jesus Christ!" Gardner screamed. "I'll be there as soon as I can. Get Stiles and the Consolidated security man on a conference call and keep them there until I arrive."

Gardner jumped out of bed and started dressing.

Then he stopped and picked up the phone again. In a moment, he had the man he wanted.

"There's been a screwup. I want to see you in my office in fifteen minutes. And bring Talmadge with you."

TWENTY-ONE

Cynthia Green slumped in the soft leather chair, her face etched with exhaustion. In a single forty-eight-hour span, she'd traversed the entire nation, interviewed people in five cities, made voluminous notes, and grabbed snatches of sleep sitting up in crowded airplane seats.

Now, showered and dressed in fresh clothes but dreadfully tired, she watched Harwood Carver, her editor and assistant publisher of the *Globe,* as he read the first five thousand words of the feature she was writing. Judging by his expression, he was more than a little shocked.

Outside Harwood's glass-walled office, a few die-hard workaholics bent over keyboards. At this hour, two in the morning, the day's edition had been put to bed. Four stories below, giant presses were already whirling and clanking, spewing out three hundred thousand copies.

Carver, a handsome man in his mid-thirties, was the son of the newspaper's publisher. Though he'd been born into wealth and given his position on the paper at an early age, he'd earned the respect of those he managed, for he was a sure-handed editor with an innate

knack for determining the focus of news stories, sepa-
rating the wheat from the chaff. His critiques, and they
were frequent, were given in a calm, rational manner
and bore the implied imprimaturs of his father, a man
much loved and revered, though it had been many
years since the seriously ill senior Carver had set foot
within the old brick walls of the publishing house.

A cautious man, aware of the prestige of the ven-
erable newspaper, the son was more than a little enam-
ored of those who held the reins of power in this
pulsing city. His view of politics was slightly less
cynical than his father's. Carver was a realist. As such,
he created waves with circumspection, wary of making
too many enemies. He chose his battles with care, and
by doing so, he was allowed access to many arenas held
off-limits to other newspaper editors.

Tonight, he wore a tuxedo, having just returned from
another of the endless charity affairs that gave Washington its reputation as party capital of the world. Harwood Carver loved parties almost as much as he loved
the newspaper business.

He put the copy of Cynthia's story down and
stared at her for a moment. "This is the first of five
installments?"

"I'm just laying the groundwork in the first article."
Cynthia's tired voice was barely above a whisper. "If
we run the installments for a week, we should build a
real fire under somebody by the time the last piece
runs."

Carver rubbed his square jaw. "I'm somewhat
concerned."

She sat up straight, ready to defend her work. "Concerned about what?"

He tapped a long finger on one of her pages. "All of
it, frankly."

She grew even more alert. "What seems to be the problem?"

"It's a very fragmented story. You have bits and pieces here, but I don't see the thread that holds everything together. This isn't like you at all."

Cynthia was stunned.

"I see something else," he added quietly. "I see a high level of subjectivity creeping into this piece. That's never been your style. Do you have some personal ax to grind, or is your friendship with Karen Perry-Mondori clouding your judgement?"

She was immediately furious. "You're totally off base, Harwood. The facts are there."

He raised an imperious eyebrow. "Really? And what facts are those?" He slapped the document, and the paper crackled. "You have a sworn statement by a confessed alcoholic that he was kidnapped and subjected to multiple medical tests at some research facility in Florida."

"Consolidated Research, to be specific."

"Exactly. Clever of you to name *them*, but you've offered no corroborating evidence to support this man's claim that he was kidnapped. Where are the statements from witnesses? You say he was rescued by a mysterious band of merry men, but you neglected to mention who they are or what connection they have to this affair, other than to say they are also friends of the equally mythical Ms. Perry-Mondori."

"That's not fair," she croaked. "You know who they are. To name them would be to place them in—"

"So you've told me. Nevertheless, I'm left with the unsubstantiated statement of a drunk with very little credibility. Consolidated will probably produce a document signed by this man stating that he volunteered for treatment. Or they may provide documentation proving he's just some kook. Isn't that what happened the last time this facility was investigated?"

"Yes," Cynthia said quickly, "but that reporter was an amateur. He didn't have nearly the stuff I've managed to put together. You can't simply write Bentworth off as some buffoon. He never touched a drop of booze until he had to for this story, and then only to make this work. You can't view his statement out of context. You have to consider the whole."

"I *am* considering the whole," Carver said, not unkindly. "Let's move on. You have another sworn statement given by a scientist who's worked for Consolidated exactly three weeks. He claims he saw people being used as guinea pigs, people who were subjected to certain experiments. Sounds suitably ominous, but again, there's no corroboration, and his statement is so full of caveats that I wonder if it was prepared by an attorney. Was it?"

A surge of adrenaline infused Cynthia with additional energy. "I don't know. But how do you explain the bodies? How do you explain the forensics reports of one of the most respected labs in Florida. Those bodies clearly show evidence of genetic engineering, and the people who made statements have sworn under oath. Their names *are* on the record."

Carver smiled. "But you have no evidence that any of the deceased were so much as touched by anyone at Consolidated."

Cynthia bounded to her feet, placed her hands on the desk, and leaned forward toward him, her eyes flashing with anger. "That's the very reason Wally Bentworth risked his life with this excruciating charade. To prove that the chain exists. First County, then Consolidated—"

"Don't get excited. Please sit down."

Reluctantly, Cynthia took her seat.

"The point I'm trying to make is simple. You've managed to relate a series of incidents that would lead one to believe Consolidated Research is everything you say it is. And that's the problem. You're leading the reader. You don't have solid evidence and what little information you have or are prepared to reveal at this time lacks confirmation." He threw her copy onto his desk. "The *Globe* isn't a tabloid. We don't deal in conjecture or innuendo."

"You needn't tell me that," she said heatedly. "I was doing this when your daddy was still in charge."

His eyes narrowed. "And if he were sitting in this chair tonight, my father would tell you exactly what I'm telling you."

Cynthia's face reddened. "I'm not asking you to take this on faith. Karen Perry-Mondori's statement is the capper. Look what happened to her as soon as she started investigating. She was framed, her possessions seized, her family displaced, her life all but ruined in an attempt to cover this up. You must admit she's a credible witness. What reason would she have to lie?"

Carver shook his head. "How can you ask such a question?"

"Come on! You can't possibly think that a woman of her integrity and reputation suddenly starts conspiring with drug traffickers?"

"Why not? Reputations are a sometime thing. You've been in this city long enough to know that. Her statement doesn't *prove* a damn thing. She has no evidence Gerald Brock was ever inside Consolidated. None of this would stand up in court."

"We're a newspaper, not a court."

"We may claim to be objective, but in reality, we make judgments every hour. We decide what we'll print and where it will be displayed. We decide on the attention we'll give a story, and we determine when that story is no longer of public interest. So we are a court, and we have to abide by the same ethics. Ms. Perry-Mondori's story doesn't stand up in *this* court."

"I disagree."

"If we print this story, Consolidated will react, and swiftly. I can see a flurry of lawsuits choking the financial life out of us. And if Consolidated is, as you suggest, part of some secret governmental project, the possible repercussions are magnified tenfold."

"It's our *job* to take risks," she persisted.

He shook his head. "Not those kinds of risks, and not on what little you have. The statement from Perry-Mondori is practically useless. And Dr. Griffin from Orlando works for a company that competes with Consolidated. Is it possible he has his own agenda?"

Cynthia jumped to her feet again. "You actually believe that?"

Carver shook his head. "You still don't see it."

"What I see," she said coldly, "is a man who's lost his courage, a man who's forgotten what this paper is about."

Harwood's eyes filled with sudden sadness. "You're quite wrong, but I expect you're too tired and emotionally involved to think clearly. Personally, I think Ms. Perry-Mondori's telling the truth. In fact, I think they all are. The problem is proving it. Without proof, we risk exposure, and I simply can't take that chance."

Her face flushed with anger. "You're going to kill this story?"

"I want a statement from Consolidated. I want statements from the CIA and FBI. I want everyone, named and unnamed, to have the opportunity to respond *before* we print this. I want balanced reporting, and I want more facts. Rewrite this as a question mark and refrain from tying anything together through conjecture alone. Present the statements you've gathered as statements. You mustn't conclude that Consolidated Research is doing anything illegal or is in any way connected to the government."

"If I write it that way, I might as well not write it at all."

"That's up to you," he said calmly. "Or you can hold off until you have the solid evidence we need to make this stick."

She chewed her upper lip for an instant. "There's something you should know. Something not in the piece."

"What's that?"

"I've talked with Senator Denning about this. He's agreed to call for a complete investigation once the first article appears. We both know he has the clout to make it happen, and once that committee starts calling witnesses, the facts will come out. If you kill this story, you do this country a disservice."

Carver pursed his lips, then smiled. "How did you manage to drag Denning into this?"

"I've developed some contacts over the years."

"You realize that Denning, as powerful as he is, is viewed as less than objective when it comes to the administration. He has his own agenda, and the facts be damned."

"Catch-22," Cynthia said. "Unless we run the feature, there'll be no investigation. Without it, the facts remain buried. And you're saying I must have the facts before we run the piece. That isn't fair."

"I didn't say we wouldn't run it."

"You implied it. Consolidated is carrying out a *secret* operation. Getting as much as I did is close to a miracle. If you kiss this off, we'll never know the facts."

"I'm asking you to rewrite, that's all."

"And if I do rewrite, you'll run it?"

"I'll make that judgment when I see the rewrite and after you've talked to some of the people I mentioned. You might add Jack Smylie to your list."

Cynthia's jaw dropped. It was bad enough Carver was balking on running the piece, but to give the White House chief of staff a chance to shoot it down before it appeared . . .

"Jack Smylie is not mentioned in this story," she said. "Nor is the president. Why should I run it by the White House?"

"Because you're implying this is being done with the administration's full knowledge. I think they should be allowed to respond."

"But—"

"Have the rewrite on my desk by noon." Carver stood, drew himself to his full height, and peered down at her. "Go home, get some sleep. We'll talk about this at noon."

She stared after him silently as he left the office.

Karen Perry-Mondori, her bleached hair covered by a baseball cap, her eyes by oversized sunglasses, finished her morning walk and returned to her motel, a small place just off Interstate 75 near the Florida-Georgia border.

She showered and dressed, then hooked her laptop to the telephone line. In a matter of seconds, she was connected to her Juno account, set up in Susan Mulligan's name. She entered her ID code and downloaded three new messages.

The first was from Ben Mulligan, reporting that he and his cohorts were now back at work, that nothing was amiss, the Bureau having bought his story of a bad case of influenza. He wished Karen luck.

Karen breathed a sigh of relief, then sent Ben a message that she would call him tonight at his neighbor's.

The second message was from Travis Weller. He reported that the bodies were still safe, that no inquiries had been made, and that he was eager to see if Karen's plan would work.

She frowned at the third message. It was from Cynthia Green.

"Editor stalling," the message read. "I'm not giving up. I'll have a rewrite to my editor today at noon and report back to you as soon as I know anything."

Karen switched off her computer and leaned back in her chair. She'd been counting on Cynthia to get the report published. If she failed to do so, what was the next step? A press conference? That would probably solve nothing. Without the witnesses, now hidden all over the country, the press conference would have no draw. To bring the witnesses in exposed them to the same danger Karen was facing.

It had to begin with Cynthia and continue with Senator Denning. The combined weight of an alert media and a reactive Congress was the only force powerful enough to bring Consolidated out from the shadows. There were other reporters, but if Cynthia failed, it would be a dramatic failure, one messy enough to intimidate other potential allies.

Cynthia's message had been sent at 3:05 A.M. It was now seven. Karen had at least five hours to wait. Fighting to ward off negative thoughts, she recalled that today was Brander's regularly scheduled early morning tee-off at Countryside Country Club. She contacted information and placed a call to the golf pro's office, a line she was certain neither the FBI nor CIA would have tapped.

Within minutes, Brander was on the phone. "Karen, how are you?"

"Mad as hell and not going to take it anymore. Has Ben Mulligan filled you in on what's happening?"

"We met for several hours yesterday at a restaurant on the Causeway. I needed as much information as he could give me before I file a motion to dismiss the federal charges against you."

"Forget about me for the moment," Karen insisted. "I'm planning a class action suit under Rule 1.220 of the Florida Rules of Civil Procedure. Since it allows a person who has a claim in common with others to represent the group, I'm naming Travis Weller as the plaintiff."

"Have you located any other family members of these homeless victims to name in the suit?"

"Not yet. And we're having a hard time doing so, since CRE had been so selective in choosing their 'volunteers,' but as long as I have Weller, the suit can go forward for now."

"Won't you be tipping your hand to the government in the evidentiary hearing?"

"Case law's on our side in this one. At the class certification stage, the court will only be concerned with whether the requirements of Rule 1.220 are met. They won't consider the merits of the claims—or the defenses."

"Well"—Brander paused as if thinking—"the adequacy of representation requirement is definitely a given. So are commonality and typicality. All those poor bums suffered the same fate. But you might have a problem on numerosity. I understand from Mulligan you have only eight bodies, nine counting Gerald Brock, but not so numerous that separate rejoinder of each member is impracticable."

"If what the scientist who worked for CRE tells us is true, that number could jump to the hundreds."

"But can you link their deaths directly to Consolidated Research?"

She sighed. Brander always cut straight to the heart of a matter. "Ben and his friends are working on establishing a chain of evidence. With what Bill Castor's already uncovered, I hope it will be sufficient by trial time."

"I've put our entire staff to work on your case. You draft your suit and have it ready. If you need to stay undercover when the time comes, I'll file it for you."

"I'm sorry you and the firm have been dragged into this mess."

"Don't be sorry, Karen. Protecting the innocent is what our practice is all about. Sometimes we lose sight of that fact among all those billable hours."

Karen smiled. "Thanks for everything. I'll be in touch."

She hung up, drew pencil and paper from the motel desk, and began drafting her fallback position—a class action suit against Consolidated and the Government of the United States, brought on behalf of the survivors of Gerald Brock et al.

At noon, depressed as she could ever remember, Cynthia was putting the finishing touches on her revised copy. Calls to the FBI, CIA, and Dr. Stiles had brought nothing. No one would discuss the story. And Jack Smylie had refused even to return her call.

Her phone rang.

"This is Harwood. Had lunch yet?"

"No."

"Good. Take a cab to the Hyatt in Bethesda. I'll meet you there. And bring the hard copy."

"It's not finished."

"Bring what you have, and do it now."

The line went dead. She printed out the last of the revised copy and headed for the door.

A half hour later, she arrived at the Hyatt. A grim-faced Harwood waited near the entrance to the dining room. When she approached, he pointed to the elevators. "We're meeting some people for lunch. Privately."

"Who?"

"You'll see."

They remained silent as the elevator took them to the sixth floor. Harwood guided her down the hallway and rapped his knuckles lightly on one of the doors. It opened immediately.

Inside the suite were two men, both dressed in business suits. Neither was familiar to Cynthia. One was tall, about forty, square-jawed and lean, his thinning hair combed across his head. The other was stout, older, with eyes as sad as a beagle's.

The taller man made the introductions. "I'm Tom Ferris. This is my partner, Frank Christano. We both thank you for coming."

Cynthia glanced at the table, laden with food, then at her boss. "What am I doing here?"

"There's nothing to be concerned about," Ferris said. "Mr. Carver and I thought this might be handled over lunch, quietly, reasonably, with some mutually beneficial understanding and consideration."

Cynthia glared at Harwood. "You still want to kill the story, right?"

"Please," Harwood said, "sit and let Mr. Ferris explain."

"Who are you?" Cynthia demanded of Ferris.

"We're with the National Institutes of Health."

"What's the NIH have to do with this? Is Consolidated Research one of your operations?"

Ferris smiled. "Hardly. Our budget is an open book. Consolidated has a three-billion-dollar budget. It would be pretty tough for us to hide that, don't you think?"

"Anything is possible," Cynthia said. "If Consolidated has nothing to do with you, what's your interest?"

"Please," Ferris said, "let's eat."

He motioned toward the table. Cynthia reluctantly took a seat and the men gathered around the table, but nobody touched the food.

"I'm not comfortable with this," she said to Harwood. He patted her hand as he might a child's, infuriating her.

"Correct me if I'm wrong," Ferris began, "but the story you've written originated with an attorney named Karen Perry-Mondori, did it not?"

"What do you mean, 'originated'?"

"Until you were contacted by her, you had no intention of doing a story on Consolidated Research, isn't that true?"

Cynthia looked to Harwood. "How much have you told them?"

"Not much," he said. "I let them read your first draft. They figured things out on their own."

He seemed bemused by it all, and that made her even more angry. "You had no right to show that story to anyone. You may own the newspaper, but you can't trample my rights as a reporter."

She stood. "I quit, Harwood. Take your paper and

shove it. If you won't print this story, I'll find another publisher, one with guts."

"Ms. Green!" Ferris said.

Cynthia glared at him and grabbed her attaché case.

"Please," he said, "hear us out before you leave. That's all we ask."

"You introduced Mr. Christano as your partner. That's not NIH talk, mister. That's cop talk. Just who the hell are you anyway?"

Ferris smiled. "You watch too many movies. Will you please listen?"

She glared at the two strangers. "It's irrelevant that I would not have been involved in this story except for Karen Perry-Mondori. Suffice it to say, I have the story and it will be printed. Somewhere."

Ferris seemed unperturbed. "If we were to produce evidence that the story you've written is absolutely untrue, would you be willing to drop it?"

Cynthia didn't hesitate. "That can't happen. I know the story *is* true."

"You're sure."

"Positive."

"And the fact that Karen Perry-Mondori has been twisting in the wind for two weeks has nothing to do with this?"

"No, I'm saying the story is true. Period."

"So," Ferris mused, "no matter what evidence we presented, you'd reject it?"

"Absolutely."

"Why?"

"Because I'd immediately assume you manufactured the evidence."

His eyebrows rose. "Why?"

"Because I don't trust government agencies. I've been lied to too many times. For this story, I've listened carefully to all the people I've interviewed. They were telling the truth. I've seen the bodies and the forensic evidence with my own eyes. I know exactly what happened."

"And that was?"

"You've read my story. There may be a hundred more cases of such homeless drunks that Consolidated killed with their experiments. Given the time, I'll prove it. But right now, I'm leaving."

"Hold on," Harwood said.

"For what?"

"An explanation," Ferris said. "I'd like to talk with Ms. Perry-Mondori. She's the key here. She influenced you, and I can understand that. She stumbled onto something she perceives as evil and persuaded you to help extricate her. Perfectly natural, since she was, as you surmised, framed."

Cynthia's eyes flashed. "How would you know that? You're not from NIH at all. Just another goddamn lie."

Ferris's expression turned cold. "We need to talk to Ms. Perry-Mondori. What she perceives as a conspiracy can be explained fully. If she comes in and talks to us, she'll not be harmed, arrested, or otherwise inconvenienced. You have my guarantee."

Cynthia snorted. "You can't guarantee any such thing."

Ferris shrugged. "Maybe not, but the director of the FBI can."

"I don't trust any of you," she said.

"Whom *do* you trust?"

She thought for a moment. "Right now, the only person I trust is Karen Perry-Mondori."

"Isn't there anyone within the government you trust who can explain why this story must never be printed?"

Cynthia shook her head.

Ferris sighed and pulled a letter from his coat pocket. "This is not for publication."

Cynthia unfolded the letter and read:

My dear Cynthia, since last we talked, I've had the opportunity to discuss your concerns with those responsible for the project. They have agreed to meet with us at my Virginia cabin later this evening, at which time they will provide you with an explanation for such a project's existence. I urge you to meet with us.

The letter gave the address and time of the meeting. It was signed by Senator Warren Denning.

TWENTY-TWO

The first hint that something was terribly wrong came when Karen checked her E-mail later in the afternoon and read another note from Cynthia. The reporter was meeting with some unnamed people later that night at the request of Senator Denning. According to Cynthia, she would be given an explanation as to why she shouldn't print the story—something in the national interest, something she had to explore.

Karen felt the hairs on the back of her neck standing at attention. She smelled a setup. Risking a fix on her location, she drove to a nearby restaurant and used a pay phone to call Cynthia at work. The reporter was out, they said. Karen left an urgent message that she contact Ms. Crutchfield at exactly six via computer bulletin board. She placed a call to Cynthia's home and left the same message on her machine. Then she checked out of the motel and into another twenty miles closer to Atlanta.

When Cynthia hadn't contacted her by six-thirty, Karen's sense of urgency increased tenfold. She used a pay phone to place a call to Ben Mulligan's home. No answer. A call to Ben's office was out of the question.

She then called Aaron Rich. "There's a problem. I think they're on to us. It looks as if Cynthia has been picked up. After what happened to me, anything is possible. I suggest you gather your client and his family and move to another location. Use assumed names. Pay cash at some cheap motel and there'll be no questions. Once you're located, I'll come to you."

The usually self-assured Rich sounded very tentative. "How will I get in touch with you?"

Karen told him, then placed a call to Travis Weller. No luck. No one in his office knew where he was. A call to Dr. Griffin brought the same response. It was as if they'd dropped off the face of the earth.

Karen climbed into her rental car and headed for Greenville, South Carolina.

The clinic was located in a suburb of the city. Karen approached the night nurse. "You have a patient named Brickstone in residence. I'm his attorney. He wants to be released."

The nurse gave her a searching look. "The FBI brought him here."

"Mr. Brickstone is not under arrest. I intend to take him with me."

"I can't release him without his doctor's okay."

"I'm afraid I don't have time for that."

"But the doctor—"

"Doesn't want to be charged with kidnapping, I'm sure." Karen smiled with a flash of steely purpose. "Where is Mr. Brickstone?"

The nurse noted the determined expression on Karen's face. "I'll take you up."

Wally was in a room on the third floor. When Karen entered, he started to smile, but stopped as soon as he saw the warning expression on her face. The Englishman looked like death itself, white-faced, droopy-eyed, his right hand trembling.

"Get dressed," Karen said. "You're getting out of here."

"I'll have to call the doctor," the nurse said.

"Not until we've left," Karen snapped. "I don't want trouble with doctors." She glared at the nurse. "And you don't want trouble with me, understand?"

The nurse nodded.

A few minutes later, Wally was sitting in Karen's car as she drove away from the clinic.

"How are you?" Karen asked.

Wally let out a breath. "How am I? That's your bloody question? You come storming into the hospital alone, drag me off without a word of explanation, and you want to know how I am?"

"Yes. How are you? Really."

He sniffed indignantly. "All right, I guess. They gave me some vile-tasting potion to settle me down. I don't think it's done much good. I feel about fifty percent. More important, what's gone bloody wrong?"

"Everything," Karen said, "and don't ask for specifics because I don't have the answers. I'll know more when we get settled. I'm sorry to drag you out of there, but I had no choice. I think they're making a sweep, picking up everyone involved in our little adventure. It was only a matter of time until they found out where you were."

Wally leaned back in the seat and sighed. "I take it we're on the run."

"Big time," Karen said solemnly.

"I can't say you didn't warn me. Have you been able to contact anyone else?"

"No. It doesn't look too good, my friend."

"We shall prevail," Wally said with conviction.

Karen gave him a long look. Obviously, the man was still loaded, divorced from reality.

Karen and Wally checked into a motel just off Interstate 85 on the outskirts of Atlanta. She connected her computer and checked for E-mail messages. There was only one, from Aaron Rich via the Internet in the form of an announcement that the monthly meeting of the Friends of Stone Mountain would take place at the Decatur Shores Motel on the following Wednesday, 7:00 P.M. sharp. It was signed by a Mr. Tapscott. Karen looked up the number of the Decatur Shores and called Aaron.

"Are you all okay?" she asked him.

"I think so. Can you tell me what the hell is going on?"

"I'd like to. Just as soon as I've figured it out, I will. In the meantime, stay in your rooms. I'll come by as soon as we have a plan put together. It may take a day or two, so be patient. If you need me, I'm at the Buford Inn on I-85, Room 23."

Karen gave him the telephone number and wished him good night.

Wally was splayed on one of two double beds, looking sick and exhausted. "You didn't happen to bring my medicine along, did you?"

"Sorry. I was in a bit of a rush. If it's really bad, I can take you to a hospital."

Wally shook his head. "I'll manage. I've had enough of hospitals, thank you very much. So, what's the plan? We must be to Plan D or E by now."

Karen reattached the modem of her laptop to the telephone outlet. "Unless there's E-mail for me pretty soon, we may be down to Plan Z."

"Sounds properly ominous," Wally said.

Karen murmured agreement, then accessed the Juno network.

She had a single message, from Cynthia.

The contents of that message almost knocked her off her chair.

TWENTY-THREE

Once before, Karen had been in this hallowed room—the Oval Office. Carl and her brother Robert had been there with her when the president had congratulated her personally for her part in uncovering corruption within the FBI during the Uccello investigation and subsequent hearings. What wouldn't she give for Carl and Robert's stanch and comforting presence now. But Carl was a thousand miles away, and Robert was dead. This time, she was on her own.

Now she found herself in the historic office under far different circumstances, and in the presence of a different president. Despite its size, the room seemed crowded with people. The president, casual, tieless, sat on a long sofa rather than behind his desk. For effect, Karen assumed. Also present were the White House chief of staff and Philip Stiles, CEO of Consolidated Research. And there was Fred Gardner, his beady eyes and round face an advertisement for the bankrupt mind that lay behind the ugly mask.

They all stared openly at Karen and Cynthia, as if the women were deformed creatures who'd just emerged from some slimy, primordial soup. Raw hostility hung in the air like smoke.

Cynthia's bone-deep exhaustion etched the skin of her pretty face and reddened the whites of her eyes. Karen, having gone without sleep for two days, looked even worse. As she sat silently, she wondered just what the president of the United States wanted to say to her. Damned if she was going to ask.

"Thank you for coming," the president said.

Karen simply nodded.

He scrutinized her a moment before speaking again. "Ms. Perry-Mondori, you and Ms. Green have stumbled onto something rather important. At this point, there's little to be gained by not being frank with you. I've ordered Dr. Stiles to explain what this is all about and to hold nothing back."

He turned his attention to Cynthia. "Ms. Green, after you've heard Dr. Stiles's explanation, if you still want to break the story you have to this point, no steps will be taken to interfere in that decision. But I must ask, for reasons that will soon be self-evident, that you not reveal anything that will be discussed in this room tonight. Are we agreed?"

Cynthia looked at Karen.

"It's your call," Karen said. "I'm here as an observer, that's all."

"You're here because you've put us all in a difficult position," the president said quickly.

Karen looked directly at the president with cold eyes. "It was only after I was falsely charged with conspiring with drug traffickers and God knows what else that I decided definitely to act.

"But you did act," the president said, "and now we're faced with a problem of monumental proportions."

"I'm not here to argue with you, sir. However, I would like to know what's happened to Gordon Talmadge and a few other people."

The president looked to Gardner.

"Mr. Talmadge is at home now," Gardner said. "The same is true of Mr. and Mrs. Mulligan, Jimmy and Madge Collins, Mr. Weller, and Dr. Griffin. All were detained for a few hours, as was Ms. Green. An unfortunate precaution, given the circumstances."

He sounded disappointed as he added, "All have been released on the orders of the president. As for you, Ms. Perry-Mondori, your property is in the process of being returned to you. We've given the wire services a story that you have been exonerated, as have the Coopers, after being falsely accused by a demented former CIA official with a long simmering grudge, a man who has committed suicide rather than face capture. You can check it out if you like."

Karen sighed. "I'm sitting in the Oval Office. If you're lying to me here, this country is in serious trouble. What about Dr. Bradford?"

"We'll deal with Dr. Bradford later," Gardner said. "Right now we have far more important considerations."

"Back to the question of confidentiality," the president said. "Are we agreed that nothing discussed here tonight is to leave this room?"

Cynthia looked to Karen, then back to the president. "I agree."

The president looked at Karen. "Ms. Perry-Mondori?"

"Provided there is no action of any kind taken against the people already mentioned, plus Mr. Bentworth, Mr. Rich, Ms. Green, and me."

"You're in no position to make deals," Gardner bellowed.

"That's true," Karen said calmly. "But the fact is, you're not going to be able to stonewall what's going on at Consolidated. Too many people know too much. It's only a matter of time before someone else talks."

The president fixed his clear gaze on Gardner. "Clearly, mistakes have been made. Ms. Perry-Mondori has a right to be upset. She should not have been treated in the manner she was, nor should the CIA and FBI have been so heavy-handed in their approach to others involved in this affair. An apology is not nearly enough, but it's all I have available at this time."

Neither Karen nor Cynthia responded.

"I can assure you," the president continued, "that I knew nothing of these matters until today, and I've taken steps to insure that such things never occur in the future."

With some difficulty, Karen suppressed a smile.

"You have a deal," the president said to Karen.

"Thank you."

"As you will shortly learn," he continued, "there are compelling reasons for maintaining a high level of confidentiality relating to the work of Consolidated Research. I hope, after you've heard from Dr. Stiles, you will agree that most of the steps taken have been absolutely necessary."

Karen just looked at him.

"Ms. Green," he said, "if you insist on printing your story, you should be aware that everything possible will be done to discredit it. This issue is too important to be derailed by the ambitions and attitudes of a newspaper reporter, however well intended."

"That's interesting," Cynthia said sharply. "You've just righted some wrongs, now you're prepared to commit more?"

"I said steps would be taken to discredit the *story*. Nothing will be done to discredit you personally, but the story itself cannot be allowed to stand. I'm being as candid as I know how."

"Thank you for that," she said coldly.

The president, clearly angry now, waved at Stiles. "Doctor, you have the floor."

Stiles walked to an easel covered with a green cloth. He glared at Cynthia. "While you are correct in your assumption that we are close to developing a process that allows much of the human body to repair itself, the rest of your assertions are quite wrong.

"The possibility exists that we will soon have the technology to repair damaged organs through genetic engineering. Aside from the tremendous advantages afforded the afflicted patient, the technology will save billions of health care dollars.

"But that's not what Consolidated is about. We have one key target, which I'll get to in a minute. But, as is often the case with medical research, when you are looking for the answer to one question, you often find answers to others. The organ renewal process is but a welcome supplement to our main focus. Simply put, the human body is instructed to repair itself. As yet, we have not perfected the process, but we will.

"Whether it's cancer or any other disease, the key to both prevention and treatment is the body's immune system. We now know that the immune system can be successfully altered, beefed up if you will, through the use of genetically altered DNA. Once we've completed our research and the procedures have been determined safe, the information will be released.

"But, as exciting as these breakthroughs are, they are *not* the reason Consolidated was established. It is not a case, as Ms. Green has inaccurately and maliciously implied in her story, of the United States trying to compete with French scientists or corner the world market on human genetic engineering technology. Nothing could be further from the truth."

He pulled back the cloth covering the easel and revealed a large photograph, a picture of something Karen couldn't recognize.

"This," Stiles said sternly, "is a greatly magnified photograph of an HIV virus. You'll note its unique shape, one of the features that makes this virus so hard to destroy once it's within the human body."

Karen and Cynthia stared at the photo. Suddenly, the entire tenor of the meeting had changed.

"There is not one HIV virus," Stiles said, "but many. We've managed to classify types A through F so far. And within each type are subtypes. Possibly as many as two or three hundred different types exist, and all must be identified before an effective vaccine can be developed."

With a flourish, he removed the first picture to uncover another beneath it. "This is another virus, one we call GH366. On the surface, a very simple virus, one of hundreds that cause symptoms related to the common cold. In point of fact, there *is* no common cold, but that's another matter. And despite the incredible medical advances over the years, the common cold remains with us."

He removed that photograph and revealed a third. "This is a virus we call T199. You'll note its similarity to the HIV virus."

Quickly Stiles placed the first two photos back on the easel, covered them, and took his seat. He appeared to be gathering his thoughts. Finally he looked at the president, who nodded.

"Seven years ago," Stiles said, "research in a Swiss facility revealed that, in a clinical environment, and under specific conditions, the HIV-A virus and the

GH366 virus *could* join forces, so to speak, creating a new virus that would make AIDS an airborne disease, one as highly contagious as the so-called common cold. And available in an infinite variety."

He paused to let the weighty fact sink in. "The third photograph, the T199 virus, is the result of just such a union."

Suddenly, Karen found the room very cold. And smaller.

"Four years ago," Stiles went on in a carefully measured tone, "and after extensive research, it became apparent to us that this joining of two viruses—one relatively benign, the other extremely deadly—is about to take place naturally, through extraordinarily accelerated but entirely spontaneous mutation. The road to this inevitable mutation is being traveled as I speak.

"When we started our research, there appeared to be nothing we could do to stop the mutation. Some dramatic changes have already been evidenced in HIV viruses. They are among the fasted mutating viruses known. It's only a matter of time, possibly as few as ten years, before a consolidation such as we witnessed in the Swiss experiment actually takes place. The result, a plague like nothing in history is loosed upon the world.

"Conservatively speaking, as many as four-fifths of the world's population could die. If we look at the worst case scenario, the epidemic could mean the end of human existence."

The room was alarmingly quiet, save for the nasal breathing of the president.

"We have but one hope," Stiles said, "and that is to develop a way to make the human immune system impervious to viral attack. Finding that is the work of Consolidated Research and the reason they are operating as they are. What you've learned here tonight has

291

been and will continue to be kept secret in the interests of national security. If the general public were to learn that AIDS is capable of becoming an airborne disease, we'd have a worldwide panic on our hands.

"Because of the time factor, we have to move quickly, which means abandoning ordinary test procedures. During the initial stages of our research, we used a wide range of the usual volunteers, such as prisoners and terminally ill patients. While these volunteers responded to treatment, we discovered one small group responded especially well. Long-time alcoholics with specific liver damage fit into a narrow category of statistically significant responses. We have now confined our research to this group.

"We called for volunteers, but the number responding was pitifully small. We were forced to use subjects who had not volunteered. We chose carefully, picking only men without families and without hope, who would be least remembered at death.

"This is not a precedent. It's declassified now, so you probably know that during World War II, experiments were done on soldiers of the U.S. army without their permission on the effects of certain drugs, like LSD. And soldiers as well as civilians have been used to determine the long-term effects of exposure to radioactive materials. Other precedents, as yet classified, still exist."

Karen bit back an exclamation of disgust, but Stiles heard and turned to her. "As repugnant as these actions appear on the surface, the results of these experiments have proved beneficial to hundreds of thousands.

"To date, we have experimented on two hundred thirty-five homeless alcoholic men and women. Initially, the experiments resulted in death within a month. Tonight, the life expectancy of our subjects is approximately six months. We have developed a way to rally the immune system, but we have a long way to go. Given the time and the resources, we *will* succeed in developing a genetically engineered treatment that will provide the immune system the means to fight off not only the existing AIDS-causing viruses, but also the projected airborne virus."

His eyes shone with a zealous light. "As a corollary to this research, we will have created a treatment that can be used on an unlimited number of diseases, because the immune system is the body's natural defense. By strengthening that defense, we make it as close to inviolate as possible. The potential is almost beyond comprehension. We might be on the way to developing techniques that can extend the average life span by as much as twenty years."

Stiles surveyed his listeners as if assessing the impact of his claim. "We are damned if we do and damned if we don't. On the one hand, we are facing the possible destruction of the human race by an unstoppable virus. On the other, we may be creating a life span that will only hasten the exhaustion of Earth's natural resources. While some ethicists would cry for an end to this research, we're well aware that similar research is being conducted in other parts of the world. It would be folly for this country to step aside and let others control what happens to the results of this research."

He glared at Cynthia. "If you print your story, you will not only raise real fears and false hopes, but you will also create a situation that demands a full and complete investigation of Consolidated Research. Uninformed and partisan individuals will rush to judgment and demand explanations. Our work will be hindered for a short time, but it will continue. If we must, we'll move the operation to another country.

"We will never admit to what has been revealed here tonight nor will we give credence to your story. Each and every point you make will be successfully refuted. Your story would only serve to temporarily depress and alarm the populace and to delay for a few months the vital work being done. Printing your story would achieve nothing worthwhile, nor would you effectively prevent our research.

"But if this story is printed, it *will* disrupt us for a few months, and therein lies the danger. Those few months might make the entire difference. If we fail to meet our deadline, we face possible annihilation. For that reason, for all humanity, I ask you now to drop the matter."

Again the room fell silent.

"Well?" the president asked Cynthia.

"I'm sorry." Cynthia fixed the president with a level stare. "I'm not sure I believe any of this."

"What?" the president's face reflected his surprise.

"I'm not a scientist," Cynthia said. "I wouldn't know a virus from a bacterium. What Dr. Stiles said may be true. There's no way I could ever know. But even if his story is true, I still want to print my story."

"Why?"

"Because the people have a right to know. It's that simple."

The president's disappointment was evident. "It's *not* simple. Surely you can understand that this research is imperative."

Karen spoke up. "Whether Cynthia prints her story or not may be a moot point."

"What do you mean?" the president asked.

"Copies of her articles and sworn statements from witnesses have already reached my law partners. First thing tomorrow morning they will be filing a class action suit against the government on behalf of the fami-

294

lies of the 'nonvolunteers' who have died in these experiments."

"You're not serious?" Stiles demanded with horror in his voice.

"I'm *very* serious," Karen said. "And as a safeguard, copies of the suit papers have also been sent to a dozen other attorneys around the nation with instructions to file if anything happens to me or my partners."

"You can't do this," Stiles insisted.

"I have no quarrel with the fact that further research is required," Karen said. "But not in secret and not with involuntary subjects. What Consolidated is doing flies in the face of everything this country stands for. You also deny others the opportunity to work on the problem."

"Such arrogance," Stiles bellowed. "Who are *you* to determine how we—"

The president held up a hand to silence him. "Continue, Ms. Perry-Mondori."

"If what Dr. Stiles has said is true, he's saying the means justifies the end. I don't accept that. On the other hand, isn't it possible this AIDS story is simply a smoke screen, that the real purpose behind Consolidated's research *is* to be first, to own knowledge, to squeeze out the French, who said they want to give the information away with no regard to financial rewards?"

The president raised his eyebrows. "You don't believe Dr. Stiles?"

Karen took a moment before she answered. "Maybe he's telling the truth, maybe not. I can't tell. You're not a scientist either, Mr. President. It's possible you're being lied to as well. It wouldn't be the first time someone in government has lied to the president."

The chief executive showed his exasperation. "I can assure you that what Dr. Stiles said is true."

"How can you be sure?" Karen insisted.

"I'm sure," he said angrily, "and I don't appreciate your attitude."

"*My* attitude? You've already declared your intention to discredit Ms. Green's story. You're prepared to lie to the American people for what you perceive as their good. Why would I trust you? Why should I trust Dr. Stiles?"

Her resentment boiled over. "Bodies were unceremoniously dumped all over the State of Florida. I wonder about people who can be that callous. I've talked to a man almost driven mad by his conscience. I'm acutely aware of what was done to me. If Dr. Stiles's story is true, it's sad—and frightening. But no one has the right to keep that information from the people. I'll keep my pledge not to reveal what you've told me tonight, but that suit *will* be filed in federal court first thing tomorrow."

"And I intend to print my story," Cynthia said. "If that leads to an investigation of Consolidated, so be it."

The president's face reddened with anger. "And if it leads to worldwide panic? Will the two of you accept responsibility for that?"

"No," Karen said.

He appeared astonished. "No?"

"No," Karen repeated. "I'm just the messenger. You people—the ones with the power to make the decisions—are the ones playing God. The people have a right to know what you're doing."

Again the room hushed. The president's hot gaze shot quickly from Karen to Cynthia. "I have a suggestion. Your story contains a statement by a scientist, Dr. Martin Bradford. Do you trust his opinion?"

"I'm not sure," Cynthia said.

"What if," the president asked, "Dr. Bradford was allowed complete access to the research being done? If he studied the test results and reported to you that what Dr. Stiles said is true, would that influence your decision to print your story? And yours, Ms. Perry-Mondori, to file suit?"

"No," they both said instantly.

The president shook his head. "I cannot understand your obstinacy."

Karen tried and failed to rein in her world-class temper. "That's how it always is with you people, isolated within the Beltway from the real world. You think you know what's going on, but you really don't, and when you make an occasional foray into the real world, you're surrounded by people who insure your safety and continued isolation. And being isolated clouds your judgment. If Dr. Stiles is telling the truth, the world can stand knowing about it."

"Karen's right," Cynthia said. "There might be a panic, and that would be tragic, but you also might well have thousands of Americans willing and eager to risk their lives voluntarily, as they always do in a crisis. Better yet, you could have the entire world trying to help find a solution to the problem."

Karen nodded. "If you tell the people what's really happening, you won't have to waste time concocting stories to counter the truth. Your energies could be better spent giving people cause for hope."

The president took a deep breath. "All right. You run your story, and you file your suit. Let the chips fall where they may. But I want you to have all the facts before you make your final decision. If I arrange for Dr. Bradford to return to Osolo and have access to the main research, would the two of you interview him?"

"Under what conditions?" Karen asked.

"Under the conditions that the information he provides you is not included in the story or the suit until I
release you from the pledge you made tonight."

Cynthia wrinkled her brow in confusion. "I don't
understand. Why would you want me to write that
story?"

"I don't want the story written at all," he said, "or the
suit filed. You've said I might have been lied to. You've
insulted Dr. Stiles and implied I'm either too uninformed, protected, or dense to know the truth. I'd like
the two of you to return here after you've talked to Dr.
Bradford. I want to sit here and watch you eat your
words."

"We have a deal," Karen said quickly.

A White House limousine returned Karen and Cynthia to the *Globe* building. Neither spoke during the
trip, not until they reached Harwood Carver's office.

Carver, looking unusually chipper, stuck out his
hand. "It's nice to finally meet you, Ms. Perry-Mondori.
I've been reading the wire reports of your vindication. I
expect Cynthia has interviewed you for a feature by
now."

"She hasn't had the time," Karen said. "We've been
busy."

"Indeed you have. How did the meeting with the
president go, Cynthia?"

She grimaced. "In short, he doesn't want us to run
the story."

"I gathered that. And your recommendation?"

"I want to run it."

"I see." He took a seat behind the desk and steepled
his fingers. "Have you given this sufficient thought?"

"I have."

"Suppose you took a day to think things over carefully. Then decide."

"I don't need to do that."

Harwood picked up a sheaf of papers. "Well, your rewrite makes no accusations, draws no conclusions, simply reports the facts as you know them. It contains the statements of several people who've been sworn. If it turns out they lied, I guess that's their problem. Is there anything you want to add from your meeting with the president?"

"No," she said, brightening.

"Off the record, was it?"

"Uh-huh."

"Can you tell me anything?"

"Nothing."

He seemed not to be surprised. "Your story is already slotted. I hope you're ready for the backlash."

"So am I," she said.

It was almost midnight by the time Karen finally checked into a hotel. Settled in her room, she picked up the phone and called home. Carl answered.

"You were on all the late newscasts," he said. "Are you okay? How did you get them to drop those ridiculous charges? When are you coming home?"

"I called the Cobbs' Landing house first and Shanita said you'd gone home. What happened?"

"The authorities contacted us this afternoon and allowed us to move back in."

"Is Andrea all right?"

"Sound asleep now in her own bed. I told her you'll be home tomorrow."

"I can't."

An ominous silence deepened on the other end of the line. "You haven't seen or talked to your daughter—or husband—in weeks. What's so goddamned important that you aren't coming home right away?"

"Please, Carl, don't be angry. I'm exhausted, it's late, and I can't explain now."

"When can you work me into your schedule?"

His sarcasm stung. "Don't be this way. You'll understand when you hear the whole story. I have to fly to Osolo tomorrow at the request of the president."

His voice softened. "I've been through hell worrying about you. Not to mention living the past several days in the same house as your mother."

"I've missed you more than words can ever say, and I promise I'll be home as soon as I possibly can. Kiss Andrea for me."

"I love you, Karen. Be careful."

"I love you, too. See you soon."

She hung up the phone, wiped tears from her eyes, and reached for her small notebook. She had many more phone calls to make before turning in.

TWENTY-FOUR

The first issue of the *Globe* containing the initial installment of Cynthia's story hit the Washington streets at
4:12 A.M. By 5:30, the story was the lead item on the all-
news channels. The major television networks picked it
up at 6:00, and the first White House comment was a
short response given by Press Secretary Helen Simms
at 8:30.

"We really don't have much to say," the harried-
looking woman said to a White House Press Room
crowded with cranky reporters, angry at being scooped.
"We haven't had a chance to digest any of the information contained in the story. You may rest assured that
we'll be checking into it, and as soon as I have something pertinent, you'll be the first to know."

A barrage of questions followed, all answered vaguely.
The army of reporters, like sharks sensing blood in the
water, circled for the coming onslaught.

Hours before, platoons of them had fanned across
the nation in search of people named in the story. Early
flights to Tampa, usually filled with sleepy business-
men, were now crowded with media employees, all
carrying bags filled with electronic or photo gear.

At nine-thirty, Senator Denning, standing stiffly and

bristling with outrage, appeared on the Senate steps and announced his intention to call an emergency meeting of his powerful committee. Hearings into the work of Consolidated Research Enterprises would begin soon, he said, by week's end at the latest. Already, he told the assembly of reporters, his committee investigators were on the job. And yes, witnesses would be subpoenaed, including Karen Perry-Mondori and Cynthia Green.

"Without confirming or denying the unstated but clearly implied allegations contained in the story," he said, "it is my profound desire to get to the bottom of this matter with immediate dispatch. Americans need to know the truth. My committee will insure they do."

At the same moment, Karen and Cynthia were on a flight bound for Atlanta, where they were to meet Martin Bradford and accompany him back to Osolo. The arrangements had been made by the White House through Aaron Rich, who'd insisted on a guarantee of safety for his client signed by the president—and more. To his complete astonishment, he'd received all he'd asked for.

Karen looked past Cynthia at the rising cloud columns reaching up threateningly, cinched her seat belt a little tighter, and stared straight ahead.

"What happens now?" Cynthia asked.

Karen shrugged.

"Care to make a guess?"

Karen thought for a moment, then shook her head. "Your story has grabbed the country's interest, that's for sure. And soon news of our class action suit against Consolidated and the government will add to the furor. But the White House has had time to prepare, thanks to your boss's reticence to move on the story. That extra day gave the people at Consolidated the opportunity to clean things up. I'd be willing to bet that an investigation now will turn up little, if anything. I can almost hear the paper shredders humming as we speak."

"That wasn't the question," Cynthia said.

Karen glanced at her. Cynthia had been up much of the night drafting the second installment in her series. Exhaustion was etched on her face. And worry.

"They won't harm us," Karen said firmly.

"You're sure?"

"They've been embarrassed by the revelations, and they'll try to paint you as hysterical and me as a money-hungry attorney. They'll deny and deny. That's nothing new. The government is expert at hiding the truth. But for them to harm any of us is pointless. What with your article and the legal action, harming any of us would be like waving a red flag at the entire media. The government isn't *that* stupid."

Cynthia leaned back in the narrow seat. "I hope you're right."

"Tell me something," Karen said. "Has your boss ever held up a story like that before?"

"He's always been picky. He's a hands-on guy. Even when he delegates, the associates had better follow his lead or be prepared to clean out their desks. But this was different. At first, I thought he was just being cautious, but when those two uglies showed up at the hotel, I knew Harwood had talked to someone in the White House. To my knowledge, he's never gone behind a reporter's back like that before."

"So delaying this story wasn't his usual behavior?"

"He always demands that we get comments from the subjects we write about, and I hadn't done that because I was in a rush. I can live with that, but when he suggested I run it by Smylie at the White House, I was stunned. The story wasn't about the president. It was about Consolidated."

"And when you made your calls, no one would talk to you, right?"

"Right."

"And that held the story up for a full day?"

"What are you getting at?" Cynthia asked.

"I don't know. He's your boss, not mine. What do *you* think?"

"I don't think it was a deliberate effort to give them time. Harwood is a little obsequious with politicians, that's all. He keeps thinking that by sucking up to them, they'll confide in him. He doesn't realize they eat brown-nosers for breakfast. If he were being devious, he could've killed the story altogether. He didn't do that."

"Your boss seemed quite happy when I met him last night. A little smug, actually, as if he'd pulled something off. I had the strange feeling he had the president's blessing to run the story."

"Can't be," Cynthia said. "You heard the president. He practically begged me to kill the story. Why would he turn around and give Harwood his blessing to print it?"

"I don't know. Something just strikes me as odd, but I can't put my finger on it. Where do Harwood's politics lie?"

Cynthia narrowed her eyes and looked at Karen. "What are you driving at? Do you really think he's in cahoots with the president?"

"I'm not sure."

"Harwood was supportive of the president during the campaign, but that's no big deal. If you ask me, I think he's afraid of a lawsuit against the paper. These days, that's a real concern. He made sure I never mentioned Consolidated other than in the sworn statements."

"True."

Cynthia frowned. "You're beginning to scare me. what's really going on in that legal mind of yours?"

"Take the meeting with the president. We were told to wait in front of the Washington Hilton, were picked up by a White House staff car, and driven to the White House. After the meeting, the White House car drove us to your office. Scores of people saw us. At the meeting, we were asked to take a verbal pledge to keep our mouths shut. No papers, no contracts. That's not the way things are done."

Cynthia's eyes widened with interest. "Maybe there wasn't time. The president was trying to persuade us to kill a story that was only hours away from publication. I still don't understand where you're headed."

"Neither do I. I guess I'm just tired. Maybe we'll know more after we meet with Dr. Bradford."

Karen closed her eyes and was asleep in less than a minute.

Martin Bradford seemed very confused. When Karen and Cynthia arrived at Aaron Rich's hotel suite, Martin shook Karen's hand and mumbled something about being very grateful, a comment he repeated to Cynthia. But he couldn't understand why he was being asked to go back to Osolo.

"What did the president tell you?" Karen asked.

"Just that Dr. Stiles would explain once I got there. He said you two weren't in a position to discuss it. What's this all about?"

"Have you been watching the news?" Karen said.

"I saw the story, but that doesn't explain why the president—"

"All I can tell you now," Karen said, "is that the president wants you to examine the research going on at

305

Consolidated. You were just on the periphery. Now you're going to be told everything having to do with the main research. After you've made your findings, you'll give Cynthia and me a complete report. In turn, we'll give it to the president. Its contents will be held in confidence until such time as the president approves its release. In the meanwhile, you'll be protected. There's nothing to fear."

"Why not have Stiles give the report directly to the president?"

"Because Stiles is suspect. We want your verification," Cynthia said.

Martin ran a hand across his eyes. "This makes no sense at all."

Karen smiled. "All this is crazy, I'll admit, but just bear with us, okay?"

Martin turned to Aaron. "What do you think?"

Aaron seemed equally confused. "I confess, I don't understand any of this either. When the call came from the White House, I was stunned. I wondered why in God's name the president would ask Martin to become involved in this, but I also saw it as an opportunity to get Martin off the hook. I demanded and received an agreement that releases Martin from his present contract and provides him complete protection."

"Under what conditions?" Karen asked.

"A pledge from Martin that he won't reveal to anyone except you or Ms. Green whatever he learns at Consolidated. He didn't explain his reasoning for that request."

Karen nodded. "I have a feeling all your questions will be answered eventually."

Aaron shrugged and turned to Martin. "You made a deal, and you have to keep it."

"This has been the most incredible period of my life,"

Martin said. "The minute I took that job I was immedi-ately plugged into the twilight zone. They bugged my house, tapped my phone, and treated me like a lab animal, and now I get a call from the president asking me to return to the scene of this insanity. Will someone please tell me I'm dreaming, that I'll wake up soon and this will all be over?"

"It will be over soon," Karen said.

"Will it really?"

"We're to meet Dr. Stiles in Tampa. You'll go with him to the research facility. He'll explain exactly what the president wants you to do. It may take a few days, and Cynthia and I will wait in Osolo for the duration. Do you mind if we stay at your house?"

"It may be a bit crowded, what with Grace and the kids—"

"I think it best Grace and the children come back to California with me," Aaron said. "For now, at least. I want to keep them out of the limelight. I'll find a com-fortable place for them that's out of the way."

"That's a good idea," Martin said. "They'll be safe, at least."

"Don't worry about you or your family being harmed," Karen said. "I'm convinced you have nothing to fear. Cynthia and I will be with you all the way. And as your attorney says, you've made a deal. Are you ready?"

Martin sighed and nodded. "Let me say good-bye to my wife and kids. Then we can go."

Stiles met the trio at the Tampa airport, after arriving an hour earlier by private jet. The head of the research project looked grim and offered only curt greetings. The four climbed into one of Consolidated's chauffeur-driven Cadillacs and rode in silence to Osolo.

As they neared the Consolidated Research facility,

Karen noticed a crowd of media vehicles by the entrance—everything from small vans to large tractor-trailers with their giant parabolic antennas aimed at the sky. A small army of uniformed security people held back reporters and photographers.

On some kind of unseen signal, the gate opened as the car approached. The Cadillac flew through the opening. When they arrived at the entrance to the building, Stiles and Martin got out of the car. Stiles instructed the driver to take Karen and Cynthia to Martin's house. Martin handed Karen a key ring. "These are the keys to the house and Grace's car. Make yourselves at home."

"I've instructed security to make sure you're not troubled by the press," Stiles said. "In fact, the entire residential area is blocked off." He glared at them. "I wish you'd been as thoughtful before you allowed that story to be printed and filed your lawsuit. The entire world may pay a terrible price for your selfishness."

"I have just one question." Karen's eyes flashed with anger.

"What?"

"Is the house still bugged?"

Stiles turned away, grabbed Martin by the elbow, and stormed toward the door. In seconds, both men disappeared inside.

When Karen and Cynthia entered the Bradford house, Karen switched on the television set. A CNN announcer was saying, ". . . French authorities accuse both men of being CIA agents. They are charged among other things, with having used the identities of two men who have been dead for some years. No motive was given for the duplicity, but the arrests seem to add fuel to a firestorm of speculation building in Washington concerning a Florida company, Consolidated

Research Enterprises, now believed to be a secret U.S. Government operation. France has officially protested to the U.S. Government. Claude DesChaines, Minister of Health, had this to say . . ."

Facing a forest of microphones, an obviously angry minister spoke in heavily accented English. "We deplore the actions of the United States in this most important matter. Until now, the Human Genome Project has been a triumph of international cooperation. To learn that the perceived American cooperation is but a pretense, a cover designed to allow the United States to be first in unlocking the secrets of the human genome, and worse, to have those secrets patented, is more than disappointing. It represents the ultimate in greed."

The camera cut back to the anchor. "There has been no official U.S. Government response to the French charges, but Senator Warren Denning has announced that hearings will start as early as tomorrow morning, and he will call the president to testify, if needed. At the moment, subpoenas are being issued. A list of those named on the subpoenas is unavailable at this time."

Cynthia turned down the volume. "Because he can't find any of them."

"He will soon enough," Karen said.

Martin had never seen this part of the building. He was in its inner core, the main research room, a vast, high-ceilinged, climate-controlled area that contained more electronic equipment than he'd ever seen in one place. A million small light-emitting diodes blinked on and off, their varying colors accentuated by the stark black steel housing the equipment.

Populated by at least a hundred scientists, the room measured sixty by eighty feet. The heat thrown off by the electronics equipment was removed by an air-conditioning system that seemed to suck the very air from Martin's lungs.

Stiles, his eyes betraying his still-burning anger, introduced Bradford to the head of the project, Dr. Aldo Westfield, a tall, white-haired man of about fifty, who seemed surprisingly affable. Martin knew Westfield by reputation. Until five years ago, he'd been one of the top geneticists in the field. Then, he'd supposedly retired.

"You are to give Dr. Bradford your complete cooperation," Stiles told Westfield in a cold, harsh voice.

"So you said on the telephone."

"I might not like it, but those are my orders. How long will this take?"

Westfield shrugged. "How much in depth do you want it?"

"Simply prove to Dr. Bradford's satisfaction that we know what we're doing, that we're not imagining things or concocting lies, and your job is done. Could be all our jobs are done. Without the subjects, we're months behind."

Martin was baffled. "What's happened?"

Stiles fixed him with a hostile stare. "Thanks to you and your friends, we've been forced to move all our subjects out of the country. Tomorrow I'll be conducting a tour for the goddamned media. I'm being forced to show them much of what goes on here. There are fires that must be extinguished. But we've done it before, and we'll do it again. And keep this in mind, Bradford. You may have been released from your old contract, but that does not apply to what you'll learn here today. You understand?"

"I do."

"Very well, Westfield, he's all yours." Stiles strode out of the room.

Martin gazed around and saw some of the scientists staring at him. "Do they know what I'm doing here?"

"No," Westfield said, "but they know what you've done. By giving your statement to the press, you might have closed this operation down. Time will tell."

"And you think I'm a traitor, right?"

Westfield shook his head. "Actually, I think you did the right thing, and I'd guess half the people in this room support your actions. Unfortunately, the other half don't."

Martin blinked in amazement.

"You shouldn't be surprised," Westfield said. "The question of ethics has been argued often in this room, as it has wherever the subject of genetic engineering comes up." He chuckled. "There've been times when we've been close to actual blows, but we've never been able to resolve the ethics issue among us. You've taken it out of our hands by bringing matters to a head. In any case, it's show-and-tell time. You ready?"

"Yes."

"Let's go to work."

TWENTY-FIVE

While waiting for Martin's return, Karen borrowed Mrs. Bradford's car and drove to St. Petersburg. She wanted to see Carl, but his nurse reported he'd be in surgery for the rest of the day. In the meantime, Karen intended to clear up a question that was troubling her.

The office of Frances Scott, the attorney who checked on Travis Weller's father, was locked up tight. Karen tracked down the leasing agent at a high-rise three miles away.

"Ms. Scott leased that office for a year," the agent told Karen. "Gave me first and last, plus a five-hundred-dollar security deposit. A couple of days ago, she walks in and says she wants to break the lease. At least she had the courtesy to tell me. Most of them just take off. She paid me another five hundred, and I ripped up the papers."

"When did she first lease it?" Karen asked.

"Four weeks ago."

"Did she have references?"

The agent shrugged. "If she did, I never asked for them. To tell the truth, that's a tough place to rent. Can't get rid of the restaurant smells no matter how hard you try."

"Did Ms. Scott leave a forwarding address?"

The agent nodded, looked through some papers on her desk, and found a note. She copied the information and handed it to Karen.

Karen raised her eyebrows. "She moved to Detroit?"

"That's where she came from. At least that's what she told me. Said she was tired of winters and was trying to get established in Florida."

Outside at a pay phone, Karen called her office and asked Liz to look up Frances Scott in the Florida Bar Association listings.

"There are two attorneys named Frances Scott," Liz said. "One in Naples and the other in Jacksonville. Both have been in practice for years."

"Thanks."

"When are you coming in? Brander's biting his nails with worry."

"In a few days at the most." Karen replaced the telephone receiver. Now, at last, the puzzle was starting to make sense.

Karen awoke with a start, shaken from her slumber by strange visions of blood cells as large as elephants rushing toward her, mumbling in some unintelligible dialect and bent on attacking her.

For a moment, she didn't know where she was, but as consciousness reached full rush, she realized she was in Martin Bradford's Osolo home. Her left arm was numb, the circulation hindered by her awkward position on the sofa. She glanced at her watch. She'd been asleep two hours.

"Cynthia?" Her voice echoed in the empty house. She walked to the guest room, found Cynthia asleep, then tiptoed back to the kitchen. She located the coffee and the pot and sat at the kitchen table as she waited for the coffee to drip through.

She switched on the small television set on the counter and punched the channel selector until she located an all-news channel. The Consolidated story was still the lead there.

Their reporter had found Dr. Samuel Eagleton. The emergency-room doctor from County Hospital was trying to get into his car, but the crush of reporters was making it difficult. In the background, several uniformed policemen stood by, making no effort to assist the harried doctor.

"Did Consolidated pay you for those drunks?" one reporter asked.

"How long have you been doing this?" another shouted.

"Did you get paid by the head?"

Finally the grim-faced doctor found sanctuary inside his Lexus, started it, and pulled away from the mob of reporters.

The camera focused on one journalist, microphone in hand. "That was just a few minutes ago outside St. Petersburg County Hospital where, according to a story in the *Washington Globe,* scores of homeless men and women began their fateful journey to eternity. The chief administrator, Dr. Marc Iverson, is not here today, according to a hospital spokesman. Nor is the nurse who is alleged to have helped Dr. Eagleton in his apparently illegal and self-serving emergency-room activities. Neither has been located so far this morning.

"Local and federal law enforcement officials still refuse to comment when asked if charges are pending. All they will tell us is that an investigation is under way. Meanwhile, in federal district court, a class action lawsuit has been filed against Consolidated Research Enterprises and the U.S. Government on behalf of the families of the homeless men allegedly killed in CRE's experiments. Brander Hewitt, senior partner in the law firm of which Karen Perry-Mondori is a member, filed the suit but refused all comment, except that his firm will call a press conference within the next few days. In Washington, things are moving fast. Here's Tom Pickett with an update."

The scene switched to Washington where, in the shadow of the Capitol, another reporter gazed into the camera lens. "Here rumors abound, as they always do when a story this sensational hits town. The most persistent rumor concerns a possible presidential address tonight. The White House has refused to confirm or deny the address, but we have learned that at least one major network has been asked to clear time.

"Meanwhile, in Osolo, Florida, Dr. Philip Stiles, director of Consolidated Research, has surprised everyone by announcing that a small pool of reporters will be allowed access to the research facility tomorrow afternoon. Dr. Stiles will conduct the tour personally."

Karen poured a cup of coffee, sipped it slowly, and felt the caffeine begin to energize her exhausted body. She turned off the television and dialed Bill Castor's number on the kitchen wall phone.

"Don't say anything," she said when he answered. "This line isn't secure. I want you to do an intensive background check on our attorney friend from Orlando. I need the information as quickly as possible."

"Will do. Where do I contact you?"

"You don't. I'll be in touch."

She hung up just as Martin walked in the front door, his face white as chalk. He slid into a kitchen chair across from her.

"You okay?" Karen asked.

"Stunned is all."

"Did they tell you everything?"

He threw her a rueful smile. "Not everything. That would take weeks. But they did tell me the basics."

"And?"

"This house is bugged, remember?"

Karen grimaced. "No wonder you were losing it. Want to take a walk?"

He stood. "Let's do it. I've got plenty to say."

She stood to join him.

"I can say this much. I saw some people with Dr. Stiles as I was leaving the building." Martin smiled. "He was in handcuffs."

The president's speech was short and to the point. He spoke from the Oval Office, the epitome of calm confidence.

"Good evening," he said with a thin smile. "I want to discuss with you, the American people, the results of a preliminary investigation undertaken as the result of a story that appeared first in this morning's edition of the *Washington Globe*.

"Since that story first broke, hundreds of wild stories have been circulating, most of which have been issued by fearmongers less interested in the welfare of the people than in ratings or newspaper circulation. Therefore, I have decided to speak directly with you in order to end this wild conjecture. I will be candid.

"When I entered this office," he continued in his familiar nasal drone, "I was, as are all incoming presidents, given information of a highly sensitive nature. For reasons relating to national security, this information was withheld from the American people. It's even been withheld from incoming presidents until after they've taken the oath of office. I have no quarrel with that. It is essential that this nation remain vigilant and strong, and while we are a democracy, there are very compelling reasons for the procedures now in place.

"At the same time, on occasion, those charged with the responsibility of maintaining our security have exercised poor judgment and overstepped the bounds of their authority. When that happens, the people are entitled to know about it. And so you will tonight.

"We have entered a new millennium, and this millennium promises to be more exciting than any previous period in the history of the world."

Looking more stern, he continued. "Consolidated Research is indeed a secret United States Government operation. And there is a very good reason for its inception. Four years ago, the Pentagon established what was essentially a crash program to find a cure, through the use of genetic engineering, for a potentially deadly virus. I want to stress this virus *does not yet exist.* In fact, it may *never* exist, but there is reason to believe that at some time in the future, the AIDS virus, as it is commonly known, *could* become more contagious than it is now.

"We know that AIDS attacks the human body's immune system. The research being done at Consolidated has shown that genetic engineering can contribute significantly to a treatment that will make the human body completely immune to both the existing AIDS virus and the new virus, should that mutation ever appear.

"There is a strong indication that we may be able to eradicate AIDS entirely within the next few years. Not only will we have a vaccine that will prevent contraction of the disease, but we expect to have an effective treatment that will destroy the virus in those already afflicted.

"Genetic engineering will, within a few short years, virtually eliminate many diseases that have plagued mankind since time began. I'm sure you agree that this vital research must continue unabated.

"Consolidated Research Enterprises was, and is, a scientific endeavor devoted to saving lives. Already, the research being conducted in that facility has produced a staggering number of discoveries that will eventually benefit all of mankind. The entire sum of those discoveries will be published in medical journals within the next few weeks. The information will be made available to the world's medical community.

"Again, I want to stress that we do not yet have the cure we seek. But we're very close, and the decision to keep this research secret was made because we did not want to frighten people with news of a disease that does not exist.

"Still, the scientists at Consolidated feel strongly that a new AIDS virus is a possibility, and not making every effort to find a cure would be a serious dereliction of duty. I agree. The research must continue.

"At the same time, we have discovered that, in their eagerness to find answers, the people in charge of the research at Consolidated employed certain practices that are totally unacceptable. The allegations that certain homeless men were subjected involuntarily to experimental procedures are, unfortunately, true. That must not, and will not, happen again, for while I share the enthusiasm that discovery engenders, the basic rights of all Americans must never be subjugated.

"Those responsible for breaking established rules will be punished, I assure you. At the conclusion of my remarks this evening, the director of the FBI will hold a

318

press conference. He will release the names of those who are to be held accountable for breaking the laws of this land.

"The research facility known as Consolidated is hereby declassified by executive order. As for the homeless men who were experimented upon, every effort will be made to identify their remains and reparations will be made to their families."

After the president concluded his speech, Cynthia Green boarded a plane for Washington. Martin Bradford took another plane bound for San Francisco.

And Karen Perry-Mondori was getting into a cab headed for Palm Harbor and home.

TWENTY-SIX

Three days after the president's address, Karen met Travis Weller for lunch at Clearwater's Key West Grill. It had been an eventful three days. Fourteen people, ranging from a three-star army general named Perkins, to Dr. Stiles, to emergency room Dr. Eagleton, had been arrested, charged, and released on bail. The charges, presented in both state and federal courts, ranged from manslaughter to civil rights violations.

The people hadn't panicked. Instead, a collective sigh of relief echoed throughout the world, an unusual expression of patience, faith, and wide-eyed amazement. Consolidated's story almost pushed everything else from the world's air waves. And Cynthia Green's stunning cap of her series with an interview of Dr. Martin Bradford was expected to cinch her the Pulitzer Prize.

Already, the first of several teams of scientists had arrived in Osolo. Sixteen medical reports had been rushed to publication. The world was astonished to learn that, among other things, genetic engineering procedures were about to eliminate malignant melanomas and some brain tumors, cystic fibrosis, Alzheimer's disease, and even enable a person to grow his own bypass veins and arteries to replace those blocked by disease.

This news was coupled with the announcement that medical science would, within the next two years, be able to prevent many other diseases through an immunization process involving the alteration of DNA. The process would be simple and affordable.

Not all reaction was positive. Some sociologists saw the news as a harbinger of disaster and publicly claimed that people might well live too long, straining the planet's ability to feed its population. They were joined by some religious leaders who maintained that humanity had committed the worst of all possible sins, and that the long-awaited Apocalypse would only be hastened by this blasphemous intrusion into God's rightful province.

The raging debate seemed far away as Karen and Travis sipped white wine and examined the restaurant menu.

"Thank you for taking the time to see me," Travis said. "I wanted to thank you again for all you did."

"You're welcome."

"You must be glad to be back home."

"I missed my family very much," Karen admitted.

"I hope what your efforts uncovered was worth it. Dr. Griffin says the people at Gulf Coast Pharmaceuticals are especially pleased with the results."

"That surprises me," Karen said.

"Why?"

"Because now the data gathered by Consolidated is in the public domain. Anyone can use it. I'm sure Gulf Coast invested in research that is now useless."

Travis smiled. "Sure, some of their specialized research is down the drain, but overall they'll come out just fine. Someone has to manufacture all these new wonder drugs. Not to change the subject, but were you surprised to learn that Martin Bradford has returned to Osolo permanently?"

"Not really. He's a dedicated man. Now that everything is out in the open, he can do the work he always wanted without all the craziness."

"And your friend Wally?" Travis asked.

"He's fine. He'll stay in the clinic a few more weeks just to be sure."

"He seems to have suffered the most, aside from those poor homeless men who died."

Karen nodded. "He'll be okay. He's a tough old bird."

"What are his plans?"

"He wants to go back to Bermuda. It's probably the right idea."

"He was working as a private investigator?"

"Yes, but now he wants to write his memoirs. They've already been sold. Wally will be a rich man."

Travis grinned. "You could be rich, too, if you'd write yours."

"I'm already rich in the things that count," Karen said, thinking of Carl and Andrea and friends like Ben and Susan Mulligan. Even her mother was no longer a worry, since Larry and Shanita Wilson had agreed to accompany her back to Miami to care for her in her own home.

Travis leaned back in his chair. "It's remarkable, don't you think?"

"What?"

"What's happened. It's not at all like I thought it would be. I expected total chaos when people learned the truth. Instead, there seems to be new optimism about the future. People are smiling and laughing and just plain feeling good. It's almost euphoric. The little things don't seem so important anymore. It's as if they've finally discovered the fountain of youth is just around the corner. Don't you feel a bit giddy?"

Karen shook her head. "We all have a tendency to overreact. If you'll remember, AIDS didn't exist thirty years ago. Something else will come along real soon, something that will send them all scrambling back to their test tubes and new experiments."

"True enough."

"And it's too soon for the drug lobbies to react." Karen continued. "Gulf Coast may be okay, but some of the pharmaceutical companies will be pretty upset that they poured money down a rat hole. With the release of the Consolidated research, they stand to lose plenty. We'll be hearing from them soon."

Travis shook his head. "Are you always this cynical?"

"It's not cynicism," Karen said. "It's pragmatism. those research scientists were playing God."

"You disapprove of genetic engineering?"

"I'm ambivalent. It's human nature to be inquisitive, but sometimes we go too far." She removed a photograph Bill Castor had sent her from her purse and placed it on the table.

"What's this?"

"Take a look."

Travis picked up the photo and looked at it. Suddenly the color drained from his face. Very slowly, he put the picture back on the table, then stared out the window.

"This means, of course," Karen said, "that my class action suit against the government will have to be withdrawn. Stiles was thorough in his selection of 'volunteers.' We've been unable to locate a single surviving relative of any of them. Makes it hard to press a suit without a plaintiff."

"How long have you known?" he finally said, his voice barely above a whisper.

"Just a few days."

He sat silently, not moving a muscle. "You must be mad as hell."

"I was at first, but when I really thought about it, I realized it was all for the best." Carl, especially, had been pleased when she'd announced she wouldn't be suing the government. As a result, they were leaving in an hour for a long family vacation in Colorado. "This isn't the first time I've been used. Probably won't be the last, either."

"You were never in any real danger," Travis said earnestly.

"I know that now."

"What else do you know?"

Karen leaned forward. "I don't *know*, but if I were to guess, I'd say that the president was pretty upset when he took office and was initially briefed on Consolidated. But, being a man of wisdom, he realized that throwing his weight around would embarrass and antagonize too many important people. Am I on the right track?"

"Go on," he said.

"A president always needs the support of Congress, and some of the heavy hitters were on the inside before this president came into office. If he really drew their ire, he'd be shut out. So, while he badly wanted the Consolidated thing to come to light, the pressure had to come from the *outside*, not him, to save his political skin. So he confided in you and sought your advice."

Travis sat, grim-faced, saying nothing.

"You were practically a kid," Karen continued, "when

you worked on his last gubernatorial campaign. You were extremely bright and just as highly principled as the president. Being principled can be political suicide, but he managed to hide it pretty well. Because you thought alike, he turned to you often for counsel. But because you were a Washington outsider, he kept this relationship quiet. You, not as ego-driven as most, were smart enough to do the same. He dropped the Consolidated problem in your lap, just as mine was beginning, so you used me."

She raised an eyebrow, inviting a comment, but Travis said nothing. "I had several things going for me. I live and work in the vicinity of Osolo, I have Washington connections—through my late brother—and I'm a tad iconoclastic, which made me a cinch to bite at the bait you dangled. Also, having boned up on my background, you knew I had friends, such as Cynthia Green, in the media.

"So you knew the story would make the papers if I were successful. That meant the president would be forced to react, and the Consolidated situation would be out in the open. The president could rightly claim he was forced to go public, thus avoiding the wrath of both Congress and the CIA. Very neat."

Travis sipped his wine and said nothing.

"Some people," Karen said, "will have their feet to the fire for a while, but eventually all the blame will be tossed at the previous administration. Some of those responsible will serve jail time, but not the people who put the scheme into motion."

She picked up the photo and put it back in her purse. It was a Polaroid shot of a tombstone erected over a grave of one John Weller, Travis's real father, who was buried in a Dallas cemetery three years ago.

"You realize I can't discuss any of this," he said.

325

She shrugged. "That retainer you offered me initially, from Gulf Coast Pharmaceuticals. Was that federal funds?"

His jaw dropped. "Gulf Coast was never a part of this."

"I didn't think so. You conned them like you conned me. Were they already a client, or did you recruit them?"

His face reddened.

"You're really good at this stuff," she said. "I thought Charlie Bond was especially good. When I met him, I thought he looked a little too healthy for a man living on the streets. And when he gave me that story about Gerald Brock's hating his lawyer son, I bought it. Charlie must be asthmatic, which would account for his wheeze. That was very clever."

Travis shifted uncomfortably in his chair.

She laughed. "But the very best was Frances Scott. All I have on her is a phony address in Detroit. Where did you dig her up?"

Travis's face was beet red. "I told you I can't say anything."

She leaned back in her chair. "So you did. But Scott was terrific. She had me fooled all the way. I don't know what she normally does for a living, but she should be in Hollywood. She's one of the best character actors I've ever seen."

Travis said nothing.

"At least," Karen said softly, "you're not trying to lie your way out of this. I respect you for that."

Remorse etched the handsome contours of his face.

"If you're going to make this kind of work part of your repertoire," Karen said, "you'll have to learn to stop feeling guilty about it."

"It's *not* part of my repertoire," he said.

Karen smiled. "Let me tell you something about politicians, even the good ones. Once they start playing games, they begin to like it. It becomes addictive. You'll be called on again."

"I have nothing to feel guilty about," Travis insisted.

"Good. Now, tell me about Frances Scott, and I'll leave you alone."

"I can't."

"Too bad. She had some *very* interesting things to say about you."

"She did? Like what?"

Karen grinned. "Can't tell you."

"That's not fair."

She shrugged. "Maybe we can make a deal."

The look of sadness finally left his face. "Ms. Perry-Mondori, you're a real piece of work." He withdrew a rectangular package from his briefcase and handed it across the table. "This is a small token of appreciation for your, uh, inconvenience."

She slit the wrapping and opened the paper to reveal a thick accordion file. "What's this?"

"Gerald Brock's medical records from Consolidated, including his attending physician's documentation of his time of death, minutes before he was abandoned in that St. Petersburg alley. Too many innocent people have suffered and died for Consolidated's actions. Maybe this will insure that Herman Gaylord doesn't."

Karen gathered the package and stood. "Thanks. Now, if you'll excuse me, my husband and daughter are waiting for me. We have a plane to catch."

She didn't look back as she left the restaurant. She'd been used, all right, but she wasn't bitter. Lives would be saved because of what she'd gone through. She hugged the accordion file to her chest. Particularly the life of one sweet old man called The Professor.

CATHERINE ARNOLD

DUE PROCESS

'Lawyer Catherine Arnold's first novel . . . it's cleverly put together' *Sunday Telegraph*

'A winner. *Due Process* has sharply drawn characters, clever plotting, super suspense and fine writing' Nelson DeMille

Jack Palmer stands accused of raping a popular celebrity and brutally murdering her husband; with no alibi and a powerful motive, it's an open-and-shut case. Until Jack persuades a criminal defence lawyer he's met only once, Karen Perry-Mondori, to defend him.

Shocked by the crime, but even more outraged that one of their neighbours is defending the accused, some residents decide to administer their own brand of rough justice. And as the trial begins and evidence mounts against her client, Karen knows she must find clues which will crack open the case before it destroys them both . . .

HODDER AND STOUGHTON PAPERBACKS

CATHERINE ARNOLD

IMPERFECT JUSTICE

'A fast-paced, slickly told story, with a heroine who manages to stay a step ahead of the opposition inside and outside the court' *The Sunday Times*

'Karen Perry-Mondori is that rare species of lawyer you can love' Nelson DeMille

When alleged Mafia underboss Angelo Uccello singles out Karen Perry-Mondori, partner in Florida's largest law firm, to defend him against charges of cocaine trafficking, something compels her to consider the case. Against the advice of her associates and family, she decides to investigate Uccello's assertions that he has been set up.

As Karen gets to know Uccello – and even reluctantly grows to like him – sinister events begin to take place both in her professional and private life. But maintaining her hold over the case, Karen examines all the evidence and eventually stumbles across far more than she ever bargained for.

Attorney Catherine Arnold's second Perry-Mondori novel is a compelling tale of long-concealed secrets, political ambitions, personal animosities and above all the desire to correct a very imperfect justice.

HODDER AND STOUGHTON PAPERBACKS

CATHERINE ARNOLD

WRONGFUL DEATH

'Nice surprises and shocks in and out of the courtroom' *The Sunday Times*

Is there such a thing as rightful murder, in the case of wrongful death?

Karen Perry-Mondori is a first-rate criminal attorney. But when her brother, a respected US senator, is found dead from a bullet wound to the head, the political becomes shockingly personal.

All signs point to suicide. But a man in her brother's position has many enemies. Karen soon finds herself caught between legal ethics and personal loyalty. And wondering where the truth fits in ...

HODDER AND STOUGHTON PAPERBACKS